AF095302

Space Lords of Strata

-SPACE MASTERS EXPANSION-

BECKETT BLAISE

SHADESILVER PUBLISHING

Space Lords of Strata

Copyright © 2025 by Beckett Blaise

All rights reserved.

No part of this book may be reproduced in any form or by any electronic or mechanical means, including information storage and retrieval systems, without written permission from the author, except for the use of brief quotations in a book review.

This is a work of fiction. Names, characters, businesses, places, events, and incidents are either the product of the author's imagination or are used fictitiously. Any resemblance to actual persons, living or dead, events, or locals is entirely coincidental

Contact info: author.beckettblaise@gmail.com

Front Cover Design by Beckett Blaise

Print Cover Design by Beckett Blaise

Editor: Mark Tyson

FIRST EDITION : MARCH 2025

10 9 8 7 6 5 4 3 2 1

Join in on the fun!

My newsletter has free books, sales on books, exclusive deals, and more. You can also get the latest news on my new releases! Just scan the QR code below.

Space Lords of Strata

-SPACE MASTERS EXPANSION-

A Sci Fi Progression Gamelit Adventure

BECKETT BLAISE

SHADESILVER PUBLISHING

Contents

1. Chapter 1: Expansion — 1
2. Chapter 2: Hungry Like the Swolf — 9
3. Chapter 3: The First Planet — 16
4. Chapter 4: The Evil Gem — 26
5. Chapter 5: Progression — 35
6. Chapter 6: The Professor — 42
7. Chapter 7: Ruins — 51
8. Chapter 8: Mr. Ris Goes to Swashingtown — 60
9. Chapter 9: Carousing — 69
10. Chapter 10: The Archives — 78
11. Chapter 11: Master of Disguise — 87
12. Chapter 12: Galactic Empire Unlocked — 94
13. Chapter 13: Conscription — 105
14. Chapter 14: Mining Planet — 115
15. Chapter 15: Revelations — 126

16.	Chapter 16: Repair, Rebuild, Level Up!	133
17.	Chapter 17: Arsenal	142
18.	Chapter 18: Friday the 13th	153
19.	Chapter 19: The Death Moon	163
20.	Chapter 20: Beyond Current Ability	173
21.	Chapter 21: Just Tenth Level	181
22.	Chapter 22: Regroup, Reassess	193
23.	Chapter 23: Nelius Prime	200
24.	Chapter 24: The Forgotten City	210
25.	Chapter 25: Passing the Trials	221
26.	Chapter 26: Secrets of the Alteri	230
27.	Chapter 27: Confrontation	241
28.	Chapter 28: Antelis VII	254
29.	Chapter 29: Preparations	266
30.	Chapter 30: Memories	278
31.	Chapter 31: Final Showdown	287
About the author		300

Chapter 1: Expansion

Damien pushed himself up from the highly polished floor. His head was throbbing, but he soon forgot about the pain when he focused on his surroundings. Confused, he looked closely at what seemed to be a high-tech control room; just like he saw in a drawing of one in an expansion module for the role playing game Space Lords of Strata. He turned to look behind him. He stumbled backward almost falling over a console jutting out into the middle of the room. Before him was a huge window looking out over the curve of a planet beyond. He appeared to be in outer space. He picked at his clothing and realized he was wearing the high tech brown flight jacket, brown trousers and the cream-colored, projectile proof shirt of his character, Damien Storm. He had a mark V blaster pistol strapped to his side.

Before he could process what he was seeing, the side door made a swish sound as it opened and admitted a man wearing what Damien recognized as a black and white engineering jacket with pockets and tubular spaces for delicate instruments. The man had salt and pepper hair and a goatee. "Who the hell are you?" He snapped.

"I'm Damien," was all Damien could think to say. He had somehow forgotten his real name. He could not recall it at all.

The man smiled and walked to him, circling around him and occasionally picking at Damien's flight suit, "Cool! You're dressed like your pilot." He put his hands on his chest, "It's Dean!"

"Dean? You don't look like yourself at all."

"I know, and neither do you. You look like your character."

"This is what Dean Reyes looks like? I pictured you looking a little differently, though. Where are the others?"

"You're the only one I have run into so far," Damien said. He looked around the console and pressed a few buttons. A feminine voice began to speak.

Tutorial mode engaged...
expansion 1 Space Masters loading...

Welcome Space Lords founders Damien Storm, Ris Harne, Cornelius Jorell, Mic De'gene, Dean Reyes, Dr. Amelia Mann, and Dr. Thomas Bright. This tutorial will explain how to advance.

"What the hell?." Damien leaned in toward the screen, "Computer, where are we?"

You are aboard the space station known as Satellite 2, Orbiting the planet Wolf 359-3.

"Why, how did we get here?" Dean asked.

Satellite 2 is the beginning spawn point and entry point for enhanced humans known as alternate replicants.

"You had better give us the full tutorial," Damien said. "How do you know our characters?"

Voice verification...Damien Storm...Verified.... Space Masters is a new expansion with 10 new levels, a new playable race, and the seven original members of The Space Masters from 1986. You are designated as level 1. To complete the simulation, you will need to reach at least level 50, 60 is preferable, and defeat the final boss before the system will restore your previous memories and return you home. As you advance in skill, personality, and abilities, you will actually become the Space Masters. Once you engage in the simulation you will be Damien Storm. Memories have already been altered but scrubbing of old identities will take a while to complete its process. All the traits and stats from your character sheet have been implemented. To access your character sheet, enter C on your interface bracelet. There are other commands accessible from the interface. Good luck! End tutorial mode...

"Wait a minute!" Reyes said, "Our memories have been altered? How will we get them back?"

Voice verification....Dean Reyes....Verified... memories are stored in a secure location and will be restored upon completion of the simulation. Former memories are not important to the system, only the memories from past gaming sessions are relevant. Your memories will eventually be from this world only.

"I don't like that at all!" Damien said.

"If they can override our memories, they can restore them." Reyes said.

"They? Who is *they?* How can we trust them?"

"Doesn't look like we have much of a choice."

Damien held up his right arm and sure enough, there was something a few sizes bigger than a calculator watch interface device around his wrist. "Wait, what did it say about these things?"

"That's how we will know about levels and new abilities, I guess."

Damien pressed some buttons on the wrist device, and it displayed information like level one and a handful of unremarkable skills like running and climbing.

"Shit! I hope that wasn't the entire tutorial because that sucked. It barely told us anything." Dean said.

"I think that was the point. We are supposed to figure out the rest as we go. Kind of like a gamemaster would give you the basics and you explore the rest and find your way. Computer, are we supposed to explore and figure out what to do on our own?"

Correct Damien Storm, the rest of your party approaches...

"Wait! Can we access you at any time or? Damien let his words trail off as the screen went dark, "I guess not."

The door slid open and the other four role-players stepped in led by a man in grey robes with short cropped blond hair and a plain sword hilt strapped to his side. He was followed by a beautiful brunette woman wearing a skimpy blue and white mini-skirt and carrying a med kit, a tall man with brown hair wearing a tan Kevlar jacket and black pants with a red stripe down the center of the leg, and a hulking alien with brownish skin wearing some kind of dull colored armored suit and carrying a huge, strange-shaped blaster rifle.

They all suddenly turned giddy and began to circle each other chattering about their manner of dress and marveling at the detail. Damien explained what the computer tutorial had just told them.

"I don't like it!" Cornelius said. "As we level up and gain skill we lose more and more of ourselves? Do we really want to become our characters with all the faults and drawbacks we added to them! That's not good."

"It might be fun!" Amelia said. "The game had us make up backgrounds, drawbacks, and faults to make the characters interesting. Real life is boring."

"Your character is a foul-mouthed hypochondriac and a self-medicating, borderline drug addict!" Cornelius pointed out, "Do you want to live that?"

"Sure, why not?"

"Are you crazy?' Cornelius said. "You actually want to get squeamish around blood and start self-medicating."

"Fucking-A, you're already in character acting like an asshole. I say what the fuck. I can't wait."

"Whoa language!" Dr. Bright said. "You don't have to use that language do you?"

"I can't fucking help it. The game is doing it. It's me being in character."

Bright eyed her dubiously.

Dean nodded, "It's okay. Look, our characters are just extensions of ourselves. We won't be losing anything. We will just become fantasy versions of ourselves. The system already told us it is keeping our real life memories stored securely for when we beat the game."

"And you trust them, whoever they are?" Cornelius asked.

"As I told Damien, what choice do we have?"

Cornelius pointed at Damien, "Oh SHIT! I just realized you are our pilot? Our *drunken* pilot! The one who always gets lost and falls off things!"

"I'm also a damn good pilot." Damien corrected. "I think we will have more of our free will than you think. I don't have to drink and fly if I don't want to. I'm sure I can decide what I want to bring to the game."

"I hope you're right," Cornelius said.

"Ris, you had better not play like you normally do either. You always wear the worst equipment until it practically falls off you." Dean said.

"You should talk, assmunch, You are always running head-first, Leeroy Jenkins style, into groups of mobs without even giving us a chance to get ready to fight them."

The screens flashed and garnered everyone's attention. It began to countdown. *Simulation begins in 5...4...3...2...1...begin!*

"I guess we started," Damien said. "I wonder what we are supposed to do now?"

"It's a game, we look around until we see something pointing us in the right direction." Ris said.

Damien cleared his throat and pointed, "What the hell is that above your heads?"

A hologram appeared above each of their heads with their name and level.

Ris began to press buttons on his wrist interface, "I don't like it. There has to be a way to hide it." He pressed a few more buttons and it disappeared from above his head.

"It's gone," Damien said.

"Here let me show you what I did." He showed the others, and they got rid of the hologram.

Damien looked around for clues on what to do next when he noticed Thomas was no longer with them. "Hey, what happened to Bright?"

Concerned, Ris went to the nearest door, and it opened automatically as he got close to it. He saw and recognized the interface on the door and went to it, "This should be the computer interface." He spoke into it clearly, "Computer, Locate Dr. Thomas Bright?"

Failure! There is no one present with that designation, The computer sounded off.

"You mean Dr. Thomas Bright," Damien said. "You asked for him by his real name, Dr. Thomas Bright."

"That's what I said. You realize you just repeated the same name twice. right? Whoa, I don't remember *your* real name!"

"I did? Yeah, I can't even say his real name. The game corrects it.

Cornelius took his blaster in hand, "We will look for him."

"Wait, Damien said, "Computer, locate Dr. Thomas Bright on Satellite 2."

Dr. Thomas Bright is not aboard Satellite 2.

"Computer, can you locate Dr. Thomas Bright outside of Satellite 2?" Ris asked.

Negative, long-range scanners do not detect Dr. Thomas Bright.

"Is Dr. Thomas Bright in game?" Cornelius asked.

Dr. Thomas Bright is in game at his designated starting area.

"Ah, he just started somewhere different. It's all part of the game. We'll probably meet up with him later then. Come on, let's tour the station." Ris said.

Assessing...Character Guide...Alter egos established: Beginning Memories... altered and replaced...complete!... Space Lords of Strata initiated. Cross-over... complete. Undesirable traits erased...

Shall we play?

Chapter 2: Hungry Like the Swolf

"This way." Damien walked into what looked like a laboratory with his blaster pistol pointed straight ahead.

"What is that fucking chittering noise?" Amelia asked. "I'll probably get a damned fucking space disease from some fucking space bug!"

"Or an allergy." Cornelius pointed out.

Amelia sighed, "I get it. You're trying to prove your point. I still like myself despite my fucking flaws."

"What? I don't know what you're talking about? Cornelius said, "See, she is always attacking me again for no apparent reason."

"Can it, you two." Ris said, "You're both being ridiculous."

"WHAT, Amelia say? SPACE BUGS? Mic no like damn bugs! Mic make them die!"

"Easy big guy, I doubt there are many bugs in space. Especially on a space station." Reyes assured the hulking alien.

"Then what that!" Mic pointed to a spider-looking thing with a wolf's head feeding furiously on what was presumably at one point a lab worker.

"Wolf 359-3, crap!" Reyes hit the palm of his hand on his head and then pulled out his blaster. "Wolf 359! Remember the spider wolves? We've been here before."

"Oh yeah," Ris laughed, "I remember. What's that band Dean's always playing on the ship?"

"Duran Duran," Damien said. "I remember the last time we were here. He kept singing hungry like the swolf! Why-i-i-i don't you shoot them, tryeieieiei not to boot them."

"That's enough of that!" Cornelius said.

Ris took the sword hilt from his side and held it out. A disk-shaped piece on top raised in front of a plasma charged telescoping bar. When the disk and rod finished extending it burst into a cold flame. "Sing that again and I'll make sure it's the last time you sing, ever! Don't you sing it either, Dean."

"Oh, that's cool!" Dean Reyes said, "I remember what happened the last time. I won't be singing. As I remember it, these little buggers are hard to kill."

"What you get that energy blade?" Mic fumbled with his English.

"It's called a power sword," Ris said. "And it's where not what."

"E'cuse me damn ass." Mic said.

"Dr. Mann teach you how to talk like that?" Ris asked.

"No need teach, you are ass."

"Guys, I don't mean to interrupt, but I think it saw us," Cornelius said, pointing at the swolf moving toward them. "Don't worry. I got it." He confidently aimed his blaster and fired. It dodged his blast, screamed and charging faster. Cornelius fired again and again but his blasts were going everywhere but not finding their mark.

"You don't have any skill in blaster yet. Here, let me," Damien said. He fired with much the same result. "And neither do I!" Soon a horde of the swolves emerged from other rooms and began skittering across the floor. Ris began wildly swinging his sword and he did manage to hit a few but his swings missed more than they connected.

"What the hell is wrong with us?" Reyes shouted in between blasts.

Damien blasted a few more times, missing each time, "I told you, we don't have any skill in weapons yet."

"We're fucking first level!" Amelia shouted. "We might as well hurl rocks!"

"Then why the hell did they stick us in the middle of a bunch of mobs?" Reyes complained.

"Amelia right. I look at wrist thing. We first level!" Mic said. "Can't hit nothing because no skill." He let his weapon swing on its strap, and he ran full speed at the creatures, "But I can smash! Agggghh, Mic hate damn bugs!" Pieces of spider began to rain down on all of them as Mic De'gene ripped them to shreds with his bare hands. A blue haze appeared around the huge alien and then a bunch of yellow sparkles rained down on him accompanied by the sound of a bell and a computer voice saying:

Ding! Mic De'gene is now level 2

"What! Level 2!" Reyes jumped into the fray and started punching one of the spiders and then he began hitting it in the face with the butt of his pistol. "Why don't you die, stupid swolf?" He finally did it in with a lucky blow.

Ding! Dean Reyes is now level 2

One of the spiders attacked and then started gnawing on Damien. He heard a loud beeping sound coming from his wrist. He knocked the spider away for a moment. The pain of the spider's venom stung as he gazed at the beeping wrist interface. His red life bar was at about a quarter full and flashing. Between looking at the interface and keeping the creature at bay, he managed to find his power dagger and stab the creature in the head.

Amelia kneeled down to Damien and injected him with her hypo-spray. He felt strange like he was the strongest man alive but his heal bar was still beeping. "Crap, I gave you a strength stim! Hold on." She started rummaging through her pack. "I hate fucking first level. I don't know a stim from a glass of water!"

"I hate first level too!" Damien said. "I always have. We have been here before. Why are we starting over?"

"It's the way of life," Reyes said. "We must have pissed off the gods or something and they started us over. It's no big deal. We got this."

"Here," She injected Damien with another hypo-spray and he immediately felt better. "There, that should do it."

Ding! Damien Storm is Level 2.
Ding! Amelia Mann is Level 2.

"Thanks!" Damien said getting back to his feet. The others had finished off the spiders and were covered in their goop and body parts.

Ris manipulated his wrist interface, "Hey, did everyone level up? We have points to put into skills and abilities for level 2. That's the good thing about being low level, the experience to get to level 5 or so is pretty low so it will be quick." His face went grim, "Uh oh. We need to get off this station, now."

"Why, what is it?" Damien asked.

Ris pointed his wrist interface to the wall and pressed a flashing button. It projected his interface onto the blank wall.

"Hey, I didn't know it did that," Reyes said.

"Look! Ris said. The interface showed a bunch of red blinking dots converging on their location. "I just put my new skill point in tech expertise, so now, if I read this right, those are the hundreds of swolves coming this way!"

"I'm going to put my skill point into blaster!" Damien said.

"No wonder they attack! Dog spiders must be hungry. Stuck on space station with no food." Mic cleared his throat, "Mic hate talking like stupid alien!"

"You are a stupid Alien." Cornelius said.

"You ass too."

Dr. Mann gathered her med pack, "As soon as the crew is gone, they will begin to eat each other. Or us, if we can't find a way off this fucking station.

Ris went to the consoles and began to work the buttons and screen slides. He swiped left a few times before he stopped, "Here, we have to go through those doors and down one level to the escape pods."

"Is there a hanger with ships?" Damien asked.

"Sure, there is but who will fly it?" Ris asked.

"I'm a pilot, remember?" Damien said.

Ris cocked his head sardonically, "You're second level and you just put your lone skill point into blaster!"

"Oh yeah, true, but, I bet I could wing it. It's all starting to come back to me now."

"To the fucking escape pods!" Amelia said. She opened the door and carefully peered outside. "It seems safe."

"Out of Mic's way!" The big alien pushed Amelia aside and ran down the hall.

"He really does hate bugs," Reyes said.

"Come on," Ris motioned for Damien to follow the others to the pods, "We have to get out of here before it's too late."

Damien followed Reyes, Mic, Amelia, and Cornelius down the narrow stairway to a big room with several open pods embedded into the walls. Half of them were gone. Ris brought up the rear, flashing his power sword in case there were stragglers stalking behind them.

When they were secure in the room, Ris went to the control console. "The crew members of this station, the ones that survived the attack. They all went down to the planet. The other pods are set to the same coordinates." He rounded the console and entered one of the pods. "Now, how do we get these pods to activate?"

Skittering sounds from the hallway began to be accompanied by a strange barking.

"Ewww, they're fucking barking," Amelia said, "That's so weird!"

"Get us out of here!" Cornelius said.

They all squeezed into the pod.

Ris found the launch button and hit it just as the swolves entered the room. The back door whirred shut and the pod ejected from the station.

Loading the first planet ...

Loading Characters...

Chapter 3: The First Planet

Damien opened his eyes to see Amelia's pleasant face staring back at him. The escape pod was directly behind them. Ris, Cornelius, Mic, and Reyes were all stepping out of it and milling around, almost in a daze. Damien felt his side. His blaster was still there. He looked at the interface device on his wrist. Several lights were blinking wildly. "I remember this thing is important."

"What are you talking about? Your wrist interface?" Amelia asked, "Yeah it's important. We all get them at damn near fucking birth. What's wrong with you? Did you hit your head on the way down or something?"

"Yes, probably. I seem to fall a lot. How does it work again?"

"Sheez, let me see it. Look, see the allocation stim buttons? There are skills, stats, and profession stims. We didn't allocate them all. It looks like you have some available. They become available more and more if you are able to stay alive. The makers gave them to us as kids to help survive the planets out here when we don't have a clue as to our surroundings. They can scan the surrounds and modify accordingly. You really did hit your head." He set his profession point to pilot skill and the stat point to increase his quickness stat bonus. He thought it might be helpful for both his piloting skills and his blaster use. He felt the chip in the wrist interface access the pilot stim and inject it into the skin beneath wrist interface. He suddenly remembered how to manipulate the controls on hundreds of ships. "Ahh, that's better. It's like a fog was just lifted."

"Great, I'm glad our pilot remembers how to fucking fly!"

"What is this place?" Reyes asked after he allocated his points in engineering, planetary science, and blaster. Damien looked up at the facility, actually noticing it for the first time. It resembled a small space port with enormous exterior windows and multiple points of entry. The port couldn't have been very old, but the plant life of the planet had already begun to overtake the buildings in some places. There were also several open areas around the main building that Damien surmised could be used as landing pads for medium-sized spacecraft. A couple of buildings beyond, in the background, could have been hangers for spacecraft, he couldn't be certain until they inspected them up close. The entire place appeared to be abandoned now.

"I just had a terrible thought," Amelia said. "What if the swolves followed them down here?"

"Or what if the swolves followed the people from down here up to the space station?" Ris suggested.

"Great!" Reyes said. "This is fun. I always wanted to be eaten by coniferous, wolf-headed spiders. We'll never even *see* 3rd level!"

"Go inside to find out for sure," Mic said. "Maybe find translator that help me talk normal!" He started off for the main building.

"I think the way you speak is charming, big guy!" Reyes said.

"Shut up or will smash you into goo!"

"Ready your weapons," Ris said.

The door frame of the building was broken from its hinges allowing the party to easily pass through the threshold. As they passed through a foyer-like lobby, Damien noticed a hologram flickering over a holo-base that has been knocked over at some point. Curious, he walked over to the hologram and set it upright so it could play normally. The hologram began to whir, hum, and reboot. The base emitted a scanning beam.

The hologram was of a nondescript humanoid wearing a grey, futuristic jumpsuit and jacket with the initials JC in the upper left corner. There were words playing on the base: *Scanning...Scanning...Confirmed!* "Welcome to the Jaddus Collective's latest and greatest expansion: The Space Masters. You have been brought here to participate in the most innovative expansion of the game. In fact, the entire game has been revamped to include all the books and modules of author Damien Storm. We hope you will enjoy this homage to you; the role-players of old.

Diagnostic mode....The game expansion appears to be already running, all systems normal. How may I help you?"

"What the fuck?" Amelia said. "These people come here to play some kind of game?"

Damien peered behind him at his companions and then back to the hologram, "Are you talking to me?"

"Yes, Damien Storm. I recognize you as one of the founders. How may I help you?"

"Founders?" Damien asked. "What has happened here?"

The hologram glanced around at the damaged foyer.

"Accessing...Accessing...Confirmed! The Jaddus Collective has been attacked. The fail-safe protocol has been damaged or disabled."

"Who attacked you?"

Accessing...Accessing...Confirmed! "We don't know, but we suspect the Alteri Dominion."

"You're a helpful one," Reyes joked. "Who is the Alteri Dominion?"

"Thank you, Dean Reyes." The hologram bowed slightly. "The Alteri Dominion is the designation of an ancient race whose ancestors originally colonized this planet. They are now suspected of working exclusively for House Davosi, one of the five major families of this region of space. Did you find this information equally helpful, Dean Reyes?"

"No, I wasn't...oh, never mind."

Ris stepped up to the hologram, "Was this attack part of the narrative of the game? Were we meant to find you so you could lead us into gameplay?"

Accessing...Accessing...Confirmed! "My only function is to welcome and serve you, the founders, and make your stay pleasant. Your participation is voluntary. *Accessing...* do not understand the word gameplay. Please elaborate."

"Voluntary! Something went wrong then." Cornelius spouted.

"Give us the original parameters of the expansion," Ris said.

Accessing...Accessing...Confirmed! "We do not understand the question."

"Why were we...the founders brought here?" Damien asked.

"The founders were brought here as invited guests to take place in the Space Masters Expansion. If agreed, the founders may participate in the expansion and experience an adventure along with the millions of subscribers in the Jaddus Collective.

"What do you mean by if agreed?" Reyes asked.

"Founders must agree to become their role-playing alter-egos because their consciousness is uploaded into their characters. As time progresses, the founders will become their characters with all the faults and drawbacks programmed. The only way to reverse the process is to level up, gain loot, and complete the expansion. However, the entire process has been compromised. The fail-safe protocol has been damaged or disabled."

"We don't understand." Ris said. "Are we in *real* danger?"

Assessing...Assessing...Confirmed! "Affirmative! You are all in real danger. The failsafe protocols have been damaged or disabled."

Ris gasped, "All right, explain and elaborate, please!"

Assessing...Assessing...Confirmed! "It was necessary to program fail safe protocols so that if the character dies while experiencing an adventure it can be respawned without actually killing the founder in the process. It is strongly encouraged that you bind your spawn point to the closest node. Currently, your spawn points are located on the space station Satellite 2. *Scanning...*You have already been reprogrammed irrevocably." The hologram base began to hum and sputter.

Accessing...Accessing...Confirmed! "Stand by for emergency message."

The hologram flickered and was replaced with a portly man dressed identical to the hologram. He was leaning against the hologram base, and he was wounded. He was obviously working on the controls when he recorded the holographic message.

"Founders, I am sorry I had to do this to you but I had no choice. I am Denec. I am the developer who oversaw the Jaddus Collective expansion project. I am a huge fan of all the Damien Storm space adventure books. I wish I could be there to welcome you and see you in person! I modeled almost all of the storylines from the books. I modeled them after the books, but I did not copy them, so your experiences will be fresh. I have tried to restore that part of your memory so you will remember the plots of all the books, but I think the upload failed. It was our plan to bring you all here for the expansion launch, but the time travel apparatus we used disrupted the wolf-spiders in their natural habitat and they poured out of the ground by the thousands to attack us. We quickly routed them and transported them to Satellite 2 to starve and die. The invitation bot had already been deployed and I completely forgot that the satellite was your starting point. If you are seeing this, you have thankfully escaped the satellite and have arrived on the first planet. I am sorry, but I uploaded your personalities immediately to your characters for your safety. You probably will not understand what I'm telling you. If you do remember your former selves by some miracle, know this was the only way I could insure your survival. Had I left you as you were, you would have been dispatched almost immediately upon arrival. By implementing the protocol. I may have given you a chance.

Due to the emergency, I tried to start you at level 10, but I didn't have time to level up your characters up for you. As a result, you will probably experience random skills popping up on your wrist devices as if they are coming out of the blue, I am sorry. The wolf-spiders started the simulation before it was supposed to run. Now, there is no choice but to play it out. I found out right before I recorded this message that the wolf-spiders were placed here on purpose. You must stop them. Remember, now that the system has been compromised everything you encounter in this game is one hundred percent real to you! I hope you see this before the process is completed, but I fear you will not. You are the Space Masters now. I did manage to allocate you some more stims on your wrist interfaces, and more are here in the facility in the infirmary. Go get them and it will give you enough skill to survive. There is no choice. You must level up and save the collective. I cannot boot you from the expansion without the danger of causing you permanent brain damage. Which reminds me, you may encounter other players from the collective. I didn't have time to boot all of them from the game, but the system should purge them as you go through your adventures.

Once you complete the simulation, if you complete it, the results should be the same, complete restoration of your former memories. As a bonus, you will get to keep the memories of your characters and your experience here. Remember, look for quests to help you. Good Luck! If you happen upon other players, they will be competition for you so you must defeat them. I imagine you would like to level up as quickly as possible and escape this nightmare. Oh, and one other thing, the creators of the wolf-spiders are... No! they have found me! arggghhh."

Amelia turned away from the hologram as swolves ripped Denec apart as if he were made of paper. "Fuck, that's nasty!"

"It's okay Amelia." Damien reassured her, "That was just a hologram. Surely just part of the game. What do you think, Cornelius, is the whole attack really just part of the simulation?"

"Yeah, I think so. I don't buy that they were attacked and it has disrupted the game," Cornelius said. "We're supposed to believe him. What was he talking about. He pinched himself.

Yep, I'm real. "The message, Denec, it's all part of the story line. He is supposed to be an unreliable narrator."

"You sure about that? The attack seems pretty real to me." Amelia said.

"Set up or not, we need to find those stims if they exist!" Ris said. "What do you think Mic?"

The huge alien flexed his muscles, "Mic can't die? Mic can't wait to use new stims!" He slammed his fist into his hand.

"Yes!:" Ris said.

"Wait a minute." Cornelius continued, "We still don't know! Is the "something-gone-wrong with the game" a part of the game or did something actually go wrong? We need to know for sure."

"We don't need to know! Who gives a fuck?" Amelia said. "It's the same 'ol same 'ol, survival is the first directive of the day."

"Yes," Ris said. "Until we find out for sure what has happened here, we should proceed on the assumption that we may die if we are not careful and try to keep ourselves alive. Survival is the directive of the day."

"Stop saying that!" Cornelius said, holding up his hand.

"If we are in some kind of simulation, maybe if one of us dies we can confirm reality." Reyes said.

Mic pointed his rifle at Cornelius, "We confirm now!"

"No, wait!" Cornelius objected.

"All right," Ris said. "That's enough. Let's move on. Look for those stims. We need all the help we can get. I don't buy the simulation thing either, but you know what I do buy? I'm hungry and I want to survive after I get some rest. I say we proceed as if the game protocols are shot, and we are in danger just to be on the safe side. If that's the way they set it up on purpose then that's how we are supposed to play it anyway."

"Agreed," Damien said. the others nodded.

Accessing...Accessing...Confirmed! Shutting down!

"Hey, what's this?" Damien began to flip some switches on a console beside the hologram. a screen with a rotating planet flickered on.

Warning: stand by for scan.....scanning...

Accessing...Accessing...Confirmed! Founders are now bound to the visitor's center.

"Hmm," Damien said. "Whatever that means."

Chapter 4: The Evil Gem

Dr. Thomas Bright woke disoriented in an office complete with desk and furniture. He pulled himself to his feet and glanced around. An enormous glass window to the outside looked down upon a deck with workers scurrying about. He moved closer so he could see what was going on below better. The deck was marked platform D. He turned back to the desk. A placard on the dark, wooden surface read Dr. T Bright. Administrator. On his wrist was some kind of device with a screen. Dr. Thomas Bright shook it but nothing happened. He started pressing buttons and the device flashed all its light and launched into instructions...

Tutorial mode engaged
expansion The Space Masters loading...

Welcome Space Masters Damien Storm, Ris Harne, Cornelius Jorell, Mic De'gene, Dean Reyes, Dr. Amelia Mann, and Dr. Thomas Bright. This tutorial will explain how to advance

Accessing...Accessing...Confirmed! Dr. Thomas Bright...Verified....The Space Masters is a new expansion with 10 new levels, a new playable race, and the seven original members of The Space Masters from 1986. You are designated as level 1. To complete the simulation, you will need to reach at least level 50, 60 is preferable, and defeat the final boss before the system will return you home. As you advance in skill, personality, and abilities, you will actually become the Space Masters. Once you engage in the simulation you will be Dr. Thomas Bright. All the traits and stats from your character sheet will be implemented. To access your character sheet, enter C on your interface bracelet. There are other commands accessible from the interface. Good luck! End tutorial mode...

There came a knock at the door.

"Yes?" Bright said.

A portly, balding man in a black jump suit entered the room, "Forgive me, administrator, but the men have found something...unusual. You asked me to tell you if something like this ever occurred."

"What is it?"

"A glowing gem has been found in the mines."

"Glowing, is it radioactive?"

"Humorous, but no. Radiation scans were negative, sir."

He exhaled loudly, "All right, take me to it."

The portly fellow led him out onto platform D and onto an elevator. The lift moved swiftly down the shaft for what seemed like a half hour. Either they were extremely deep underground or the elevator was slow, he couldn't tell. The temperature had increased considerably. Once they were at the desired level, the man stepped off the elevator and led Dr. Thomas Bright through a few more tunnels until they reached a control room. Just beyond was a mobile drill and several crew members milling about.

"These particular mine shafts are not part of our usual working mines. They were originally dug by the Alteri Dominion long ago. They were looking for some kind of artifact but gave up too soon. If this is their artifact, I can see why they wanted it, the thing already killed two of my crew just for touching it.

Bright went out to the site where the blue-green orb was glowing in the ground. The thing was whispering to him, calling his name. He turned to the portly man, "Your name is?"

"You don't remember my name sir, it's Felder."

"Felder, who found this orb."

"I did." A woman wearing a lab coat stepped up. "I am Dr. Felicity Bliss."

"What is it?"

"The locals call it the Devil's Testicle. It is an artifact left behind from the ancient wars. It was thought to be only a myth."

"Such things are always thought to be myth," Bright said. "How do they even know what the devil is? Do they have access to earth religious documents or something?"

"Sir?" Dr. Bliss asked confused.

Bright chuckled, "Never mind. It's called the Devil's Testicle, you say?"

"Yes," Dr. Bliss took a set of tongs she had retrieved before Bright had come down and clamped the orb. She picked it up, "We need to study it, closely"

In a whim, Bright reached out for it. Dr. Bliss pulled it back, "Don't touch it. It has already killed two of our workers who also tried to pick it up. They just disintegrated into nothingness!"

Bright recalled his conversation with Cornelius about the movie with the mysterious glowing green gem and he laughed to himself. "I'll be damned if it isn't Cornelius' evil gem!"

"Maybe it has side effects," Dr. Bliss said. "You are acting very strange, administrator Bright."

On a whim and in a moment of nostalgia he reached for and seized the orb. He knew it wouldn't hurt him. This was all a game. The evil gem was meant for him.

"Stupid bitch, it's my Loc-nar!" He laughed hysterically. Felder and Dr. Bliss backed away. Dr. Bliss had an offended scowl contorting her normally handsome face. He blinked at the thing in his hand, "What did I just say?" He let the orb fall to the ground. "Something is wrong, I..." He felt an overwhelming urge to retrieve the orb. To his horror, the blue-green glow crept up his pant leg, paralyzing him as it crawled up his body and completely engulfed him. His mind closed on him as the blue-green glow engulfed him. He reached down and took the Orb in hand. He held it above his head triumphantly as he looked down at the startled Dr. Bliss, "Cornelius is going laugh his ass off when he finds out that I actually have the evil gem!"

"Get a medical team down here." Felder commanded one of the workers nearby.

"No" Bright said, "I'm fine. All is as it should be."

"Sir, you're spouting nonsense. You're not well. Let us take you to the infirmary. Dr. Bliss pleaded.

Bright blinked a couple of times. Something in his memory that was just there seemed distant and unrelated to him now. He shook off the feeling. "You say this thing killed two of our men?"

"Yes, sir. It *should* have killed you too."

"Have scientific processes bring up a container and isolate it in field. It's too dangerous to be out in the open. We can study it once it's safely in stasis."

"Yes, sir. I am glad to see you back to making sense, sir." Dr. Bliss said.

Bright stared at her for a moment. He felt he should have been able to recall what she was talking about but her meaning eluded him. "Dr. Bliss. I don't know what you're talking about. I always make sense. Just because you do not understand me or what I am saying doesn't mean anything to anyone." He said sarcastically. "Now, do as I ask and get this thing under lock and key."

Dr. Bliss nodded and left the room for a moment. When she returned she carried with her a small containment unit. Bright surmised she must have already called to have one brought up before he arrived. The device hummed as she activated the stasis field. Bright dropped the orb into the container, watching it float suspended in the blue energy field.

"Take it to the lab," he ordered. "I want a full analysis." She nodded and began to walk away, "Wait, I want you to label it L-a-u-c-n-a-r, Laucnar. That's pronounced lao-knar with the c silent."

"Sir?"

"You heard me. Loc-nar is too on the nose. I want it to *my* evil gem!"

"If you say so, sir. I really strongly suggest you report to the infirmary for an evaluation, sir. The Lu... Laucnar may not have killed you but I think since you touched it, you should be seen. You don't seem yourself."

"I'll take that under advisement." He said.

A tremor rocked the cavern. Dust and small rocks showered down from the ceiling. The miners scattered for cover.

"What was that?" Felder steadied himself against the wall.

Another tremor, stronger this time. The mining equipment rattled. Warning klaxons blared through the tunnels.

"Sir, seismic activity increasing!" A technician called out from the control room. "Multiple epicenters forming throughout the mine complex."

The ground buckled beneath their feet. Bright grabbed the containment unit as it nearly toppled. "Everyone out! Evacuate immediately!"

They rushed toward the elevator shaft. The tremors intensified, bringing down chunks of rock and support beams. Miners streamed past them toward the emergency exits.

"The lift's stuck!" Felder shouted over the chaos. "We'll have to take the emergency stairs!"

Bright clutched the containment unit to his chest as they climbed. His legs burned from the exertion. Behind them, the mining level collapsed with a thunderous roar.

They emerged onto Platform D amid pandemonium. Workers ran in all directions as more tremors wracked the facility. Through the massive windows, Bright saw geysers of dirt and rock erupting from the ground outside.

"What the hell is this?" Bright asked.

"Look!" Dr. Bliss pointed. Dark shapes burst from the newly formed holes - eight-legged creatures with wolf-like heads.

"I know what those are. They are Swolves," Bright whispered. The word just came to him, along with a flash of memory - fighting these same creatures aboard a space station sometime in the distant past.

The beasts swarmed across the platform, pouncing on fleeing workers., their howls and barks mixed with human screams.

"This way!" Felder led them toward the administrative wing. They barricaded themselves in Bright's office.

"What are those things?" Dr. Bliss gasped, trying to catch her breath.

"Wolf-spiders," Bright said. "They're not supposed to be here yet." He blinked, confused by his own words. "We called them swolves when we encountered them. I don't remember the ones we encountered being this big or this strong."

"Who?" Felder asked.

"Friends of mine. We encountered them before."

Scratching sounds came from the other side of the door. The swolves had found them.

Bright's wrist interface suddenly lit up with an alert:

Warning: Hostile entities detected. Emergency protocols engaged...

Character binding activated...

accelerated experience...granted!

He felt a strange sensation wash over him as knowledge flooded his mind - combat training, xenobiology, advanced physics. His confusion about his identity melted away. He was Dr. Thomas Bright, xenobiologist and founding member of the Space Masters.

Ding! Dr. Thomas Bright is now level 4!

"Stand back," he told the others. He drew his mark IV blaster - when had he gotten that? - and aimed at the door.

The first swolf crashed through in a shower of splinters. Bright's shot found it's mark and struck it in the head, dropping it instantly. His interface chimed:

Ding! Dr. Thomas Bright is now level 5!

He looked at the other two but they didn't seem to be phased at all by the chime and level notification from the wrist device.

More creatures poured in. Bright fired methodically, each shot finding its mark with his newly enhanced skills. But there were too many.

"The window!" he shouted. "We need to get to the landing pad!"

Dr. Bliss grabbed a chair and hurled it through the glass. Wind whipped through the office as they climbed out onto the narrow ledge. A shuttle sat on the pad twenty feet below.

"Jump!" Bright commanded.

"it's too far." Dr. Bliss said.

"Well, climb down further until you feel like you can drop down safely."

He watched Felder and Bliss leap down before he followed them all the while clinging to the containment unit. The orb pulsed brighter as they ran for the shuttle.

Chapter 5: Progression

*A*ccessing...Accessing...Confirmed! *"Founders have entered the bind point of the Visitor's Center. Your souls are now bound to the Visitor's Center. Congratulations, the Founders will now receive 25% experience boost on the first planet! Ding! Congratulations, Founders get 2 extra skill points per level on the first planet! Ding! Congratulations, Founders inspire others, therefore aura of the founders is cast: Founders benefit with 2 extra profession stims per level on the first planet.*

"Sweet!" Damien said. "I don't understand everything it's saying but I understand the word stim! I like these interface wrist watches or whatever," He held up his wrist interface device. "I wonder if it does actually tell time? He pushed a few buttons.

"Current world time is 7:807.6 hours daytime."

"...and it does!" Damien said triumphantly.

"Great, Damien, you have discovered a fucking wristwatch," Amelia said.

"So, we are stuck on the newbie planet?" Cornelius lamented.

"It's a good thing," Ris said, "Where would you rather start?"

"It just seems a little boring," Cornelius said. "I've always hated the first ten levels; you can't do anything! Too bad the guy in the hologram failed to level us."

Amelia clutched her medical bag and raced off ahead of the group. The others kind of looked at each other and then followed her. Damien realized as they got close to her that Amelia had spotted a survivor lying on the ground under some debris. She worked feverishly on the woman, who was wearing a dirty white lab coat, until she stabilized her. The piece of debris was deeply embedded into the woman's thigh.

"Mic move debris!"

"No, Mic, leave it. The chunk of debris is the only thing holding her artery. If you remove it she will bleed out before we could get her to the Visitor's Center."

"I can cauterize it with my power sword," Ris said.

"No," the woman said, "You have to get out of here. We were attacked by the Alteri Dominion. They are pawns of house Davosi, genetic engineers bent on conquering the galaxy. Her breath shortened, "My gods, you are the founders! This whole event was set up for you. It was supposed to be a tribute."

"Relax," Damien said. "Yes, we are the founders. We have been brought here and forced to play the game. We need to find out what happened."

"How dare you! Look at my leg, do you think I am playing games? What do you mean forced?"

"Forced, against our consent." Damien said.

"I don't understand." She said. "You are the founders. You can do anything. No one can force you."

"Uh hmm, remember what I said about NPCs?" Ris reminded him. "This is all real."

"Sorry, I didn't mean to offend you," Damien said.

"Founders, you need to get to the archives. They are in a vault within a cavern to the south. The Alteri Dominion has a company of men trying to break in the facility as we speak. They must not be allowed to steal the archives!"

"Why are the archives so important? How will they help us?" Cornelius asked.

"They hold all the research and innovations of my people. There are some valuable papers in there and inventions that can help and benefit all races but the Alteri and House Davosi will mishandle them and turn them into dreadful weapons. If you want clues and answers into what is going on here, that is where you will find them. However, if the Alteri Dominion gets their evil hands on the archives, they will have more than enough knowledge to take over the entire galaxy." The woman began to cough up blood and then quickly expired.

The wrist devices lit up.

"You have been offered a story QUEST: The Archives

Accept Quest Y/N

Note: this is a story quest. If you decline it, you may disrupt your questline progression in the future

Reward: choose one upgraded race/class/profession appropriate weapon

"Accept it," Ris commanded, "If we don't we might not be able to finish the simulation. Damien, you must remember that the NPCs are in a real world. They cannot fathom their surroundings as anything but real life."

"Yeah, I have a real problem with that."

Amelia and the others all accepted the quest.

"I couldn't save her. My skill is just not high enough yet." Amelia said with a tear.

"It doesn't really matter, I think she was a just a quest-giver and meant to expire." Ris said. "What would we do with her if you could save her?" He examined the readout on his wrist, "Does every medical encounter like this give you experience?"

Amelia examined her wristband, "It appears to be so."

"Then you will have the skills you need in no time the way this day has been turning out for us."

"How will we all stay the same level without out-leveling each other?" Damien asked. "If we are gaining experience for different tasks."

Ris shook his head, "We don't. At some point, some of us will gain more than the others and level faster. There is no way we will be able to keep all our experiences exactly the same. Progression will vary for each of us."

"It does no good to keep debating this. As I understand it, the more we progress the more we become our characters. As we add skills and abilities there is only one way this comes out, we will progress." Cornelius said. "This is some advanced stuff. We will always be in control but our characters will eventually become as powerful as we had them on paper. We might as well embrace them and get some levels!"

"Thanks, that helps, actually," Damien said. "And another thing, I am beginning to feel a kind of mind fog, like my memories are fading. Are any of you feeling it too?"

"Not me. It's probably your imagination," Amelia said. "A side effect of us entering the game and playing through it. It has you spooked that you will not be you or something."

"It's doing a good job. I can't remember how we even got here now."

Amelia grabbed Ris by the arm, "Ris, I saw you put your first skill point in tech," She picked up a square box that resembled a small portable radio. "Here is her scanner device. Find the cavern."

"Hey, that looks just like a Tri-cord –"

"Don't say it!" Damien scolded."

Ris grinned, "If a tricorder is ever invented on our world it will most likely be called a tricorder, regardless."

"That's probably true." Cornelius nodded. "I never understood the name. Does the device record three things or something?"

"Who knows, who cares." Damien countered.

"If I read this right, there is a cavern with several life signs due south," Ris said.

"let's go then," Amelia replied.

They walked south following the device as it beeped and hummed. Finally, they reached the mouth of the cavern. Several players rode up to the cavern on speeders. They got off and pushed Damien and the others aside, "Get the hell out of the way, noobs!" one of them said. The brief flash above their heads indicated they were 5th level and above. "We got this."

The group let the players pass.

"The hologram said we needed to defeat players." Cornelius pointed out.

Ris smirked, "We will if need be, right now, they are assuming all the danger and risk by moving up ahead. As long as Dean doesn't go running in there, any mobs will attack them first."

"Hey!" Reyes protested.

The party collected themselves and followed the 5th level characters into the mouth of the cavern. They reached a room with a sunken metal door along the cavern wall. Several men had torches and other equipment and were trying to burrow a hole into the door. A huge alien that looked very much like Mic stood guard. The 5th level group approached the alien, who had a large question mark floating above his head.

"HALT! What is purpose here? What you hope to find?"

"Phat ass loots!" One of the 5th level players responded.

Ding! The alien's eyes lit up and he lurched forward, "There are no PHAT ASS LOOTS here!"

Vault guard hits VALORIAN for 4,993,488 points of damage.

VALORIAN is now dead!

The words floated above the now unconscious player.

"Hey!" One of the dead players' companions rushed the guard. The guard stoically swung his yellow flaming power sword and leveled the rest of the 5th level players with one mighty blow each before returning back to his original stance.

Chapter 6: The Professor

How are we supposed to get past *him*? Damien asked.

Ris studied the alien guard, "Hmm there has to be some kind of trick to it. He is ultra-powerful so we can't fight our way through him."

"That's for sure. Look at us," Cornelius said. "We have basic weapons, no armor or gear, and we are barely level two."

"Mic find out!" The tough alien march confidently up to the guard.

"What is purpose here? What you hope to find?" The guard asked.

"Knowledge," Mic said and then immediately ducked.

"Ah, you must be part of expedition and excavation team, then?"

"Yes!" Mic lied.

"There is much to learn in cavern. I have been there and seen archives myself, but without professor's orders I not allowed to let anyone enter until he returns."

"Where is the professor, we have been separated from him," Ris said, now joining Mic's ruse.

"At camp, I assume."

"What happened to the Alteri?"

"The Alteri?" The guard seemed confused.

"We were told the Alteri was trying to break into the archives," Ris said.

The guard slammed his fist into his hand, "Let them try!"

"Who in cavern now?" Mic asked.

"Just one of professor's survey teams." The guard responded. "Say, you better get to professor in hurry if you want to join expedition. He doesn't wait for anyone who dawdles around."

"Thank you. We will go find him at once." Ris said.

Mic leaned in so the alien could hear his muted tone, "You better check survey team. I don't think they from professor."

The alien studied Mic's face for a long moment and then smiled while he pounded his hand into his fist. "Thanks, brother." He said before turning and hurrying off after the team.

"We go in now?" Mic suggested.

"We don't have to. I think we need to speak with this professor." Ris said. "Besides, if there really are Alteri in there, I think they are about to have their hands full."

Their wrist devices made a soft sound of a bell tinkling. Ris brought his up to eye level. The display was flashing the words

Episode 1: The Professor under the tag labeled quest log, just below the Archives quest. They were both outlined in red. As soon as he and Mic rejoined the others, Ris took out the pocket scanner and began pointing it all around. "If there is a camp nearby, this scanner should spot the lifeforms."

"Good work, Mic," Amelia said patting the alien's enormous back as far up as she could reach.

"Someone had to do it," Mic said.

"Got it. There is a large concentration of red dots about two clicks to the south, it has to be the camp." Ris said. "These quests are red. If they follow normal game progression, I believe that means it's above our levels, or at least they are above mine."

"Well, yeah, we're only 2nd level. Almost any quest will be above our level." Damien pointed out.

"So, we find a away to gain a few levels. We can go find a lower level quest or a bunch of swolves or wild animals to dispatch and get experience from, Besides, you don't know how to read that thing that well. Those red dots may indicate life forms." Cornelius reminded him, that is to say a*ll* life forms. They could be a pack of some kind of 2nd level creature."

"You're not a very optimistic person are you!" Damien said.

Cornelius shrugged, "I am just realistic."

"We'll be careful. If they're mobs, we gain some XP. No harm done. Come on." Ris said, heading in the direction of the life forms.

When they approached the area, it was clear it was a humanoid camp. White smoke from campfires and cook fires rose up through the thin trees, the smell of cooking food, and the chatter of persons made it abundantly clear. They cautiously approached the men standing on the trail near a cluster of canvas tents. The men appeared human. Ris looked at his armband, which registered the outline of the men as blue while the guard they had faced was outlined in purple.

"That's far enough strangers," The closest of the men said, "What can I do for you?"

"We are looking for the professor," Ris said. "We wish to join in the expedition and excavation of the cavern."

"Ah, the recruits. The professor told me to keep a sharp eye out for you. Please come in." He waved them into the camp. "The professor is in the biggest tent near the center. You can't miss it."

"Thanks!" Ris said.

"My pleasure." The guard reciprocated.

A soft bell sounded from their wrist device. Ris looked at the display.

Tutorial mode: Merchants are non-player characters where you may buy and sell goods and repair damaged equipment and weapons. Several merchants have been detected in the immediate area. Quest, seek out a merchant and sample their goods. The quest entered the quest log outlined in blue.

"I think I understand this quest log better now," Reyes said. "Ris was right. I think the quest lines we have been following are too high level. This merchant side quest is blue. I take that to mean it's easier and closer to our level."

"I agree." Damien said. "Time to do a few side quests and gain some XP."

"Okay, then we do the merchant quest first," Ris said.

They split up, each heading to a different merchant stall. Damien sauntered over to a weapons dealer, his fingers trailing along the edge of a plasma rifle that looked suspiciously like military surplus. The moment his hand made contact with the weapon, a familiar blue glow pulsed in his peripheral vision, and his quest log updated with a small but satisfying burst of experience points. He noticed the others doing the same - Reyes was practically drooling over some engineering tools, while Mic was attempting to "stealthily" examine a rack of armor that was clearly meant for someone half his size. After they'd all finished poking through the merchandise and collecting their easy XP, they regrouped near a central fountain.

"That seemed pretty easy to me," Ris said. "Watch your quests closely and most of all don't attack anything the tracker identifies as red."

They found the largest tent and entered. At the center hovering over a table of maps and artifacts was a man with a short white beard, wrinkles, and tufts of white hair protruding out from under a straw hat.

"Professor?" Ris asked the older man. The man shook his head and pointed to a dark-haired fellow with glasses and a magnifying glass looking over a piece of parchment. The professor appeared to be no more than twenty-five years old. "Professor?" Ris asked.

The man looked up from his parchment, "Yes, I am professor Dent. Who might you be?"

"Recruits. We were told you needed help with your expedition." Ris said.

He looked at each one of them and seemed particularly unsettled at Mic, "I don't need any help with the main expedition, but I do have need of a team to explore a new underground chamber discovered in some interesting ruins we thought previously to be unremarkable."

"What about the Alteri Dominion?" Damien asked. "Aren't they trying to thwart your mission?"

The professor huffed, "They were at one point. I took care of them. They work for one of the families who rule around these parts, House Davosi. The Davosi have been trying to get their hands on the artifacts I have uncovered for a while now. It's because there is a rumor about an ancient power source or artificial intelligence, or some nonsense these ancient people once used. I know a few people in a rival family. I made a few communications and lo and behold the Alteri left on their own accord, empty handed." He gestured toward Ris' scanner, "May I?"

"Certainly." Ris handed the professor his scanner.

"Here are the coordinates of the ruins. I noticed your wrist devices. They should be able to record and map the area. Explore the ruins, find the underground chamber and investigate it. Return to me when you are done and I will compensate you."

Each one of their wrist devices made the ding sound and indicated they had advanced to level 3. Ris checked the display and the professor's quest had been added as Professor quest part 1. It was blue. "All right, I understand this. The professor quests have several parts so it is an episode of the story. I am assuming each quest will fall under that heading until we complete them all and the final reward is a full set of new tenth level equipment."

"Where do you see that," Reyes asked.

"It's at the bottom when you scroll. Here, let me show you."

"Oh, okay, so we do these quests in order," Reyes said.

"Yes, exactly," Damien replied.

"What in the devil are you talking about? The professor asked. "Get going or I will find someone else who will."

Ris spoke up, "Yes, sir, come on guys." He led them toward the coordinates on the scanner.

"Reds and blues and such...." He rambled on about it until he was out of earshot.

Ris pointed the scanner, "Now that we have that out of the way, let's get to the ruins."

Damien trudged behind Ris, watching him fumble with the scanner. The device beeped and chirped as Ris swung it back and forth like a metal detector.

"Are you sure you know how to use that thing?" Damien asked.

"Of course I do. I put a point in tech expertise."

"One point," Cornelius snickered. "That's like giving a monkey a typewriter and expecting Shakespeare."

"I know what I'm doing," Ris protested, shaking the device. "The readings are just... complicated."

"We've been walking in circles for twenty minutes," Amelia said. "My fucking feet are killing me."

Mic stomped ahead and peered over Ris's shoulder at the scanner display. "You hold upside down. Even baby could see!"

"No I'm not!" Ris flipped the scanner around. "Oh."

"Some tech expert," Damien laughed. "Maybe you should have saved that point for something useful, like learning which end is up."

Ris stopped walking and glared at them. "Fine. You want me to prove I can use this thing?" He activated his wrist interface and navigated through the menus. "I was saving this point, but clearly you all need a demonstration."

The interface chimed as Ris allocated his saved skill point into advanced scanner operations. The device in his hands hummed and projected a detailed holographic map of the surrounding area.

"There," Ris said smugly. "The ruins are half a kilometer that way, through those trees."

"Isn't that kind of cheating," Cornelius muttered.

"How is it cheating?" Ris asked. "I legitimately leveled the skill."

Cornelius shrugged but said nothing.

They followed Ris through a dense patch of forest. The trees thinned out after a few minutes, revealing crumbling stone structures covered in vines and moss. Ancient pillars rose from the ground at odd angles, their surfaces carved with strange symbols.

"These must be the ruins," Damien said, running his hand along a weathered wall. "But where's this underground chamber the professor mentioned?"

"According to the scanner..." Ris adjusted some settings. "There's a hollow space beneath that central structure. Looks like it extends pretty deep."

"How do we get down there?" Reyes asked.

"There has to be an entrance somewhere," Ris said, walking the perimeter of the ruins while studying the scanner readout. "The professor wouldn't have sent us if there wasn't a way in."

"Unless he's fucking with us," Amelia suggested. "Sending the newbies on a wild goose chase."

"No, wait." Ris held up his hand. "I'm picking up an anomaly. Some kind of energy signature coming from under that fallen column."

Chapter 7: Ruins

Damien approached the fallen column. The weathered rock bore intricate carvings that spiraled across its surface in an alien script. He knelt down to brush away centuries of dirt and vegetation.

"Be careful," Ris warned, adjusting settings on the scanner. "The energy readings are strongest right where you're standing."

"When has Damien ever been careful?" Cornelius smirked.

"I'm plenty careful," Damien protested, continuing to clear debris from the column.

"Who are you kidding? You are as clumsy as they come."

Damien's hand brushed against a circular depression about the size of his palm. "Hey, look at this."

"Don't touch it!" Amelia called out.

But Damien had already pressed his hand into the depression. The stone hummed beneath his fingers, and lines of blue light raced along the carved symbols. The ground shuddered.

"Nice going, hotshot," Cornelius said as he stumbled backward. "What were you saying about being careful?"

"Shut it, Corny!" Damien retorted.

The column split lengthwise with a grinding of stone on stone, revealing a dark passage leading down into the earth. Cool, stale air wafted up from the opening. "See, I did just what needed to be done. We're in!"

"If scared, Mic go first," the alien declared, shouldering past the others. "Check for traps."

"Since when are you our trap finder?" Reyes asked.

"Since Mic put points in sneak." He puffed out his chest proudly.

"You're about as stealthy as a drunk elephant," Cornelius muttered.

Mic ignored him and began descending the steep stone steps, his massive frame barely fitting in the narrow passage. The others followed, with Damien bringing up the rear. Their footsteps echoed off the close walls.

The stairway opened into a vast chamber supported by towering pillars. Unlike the ruins above, these structures showed no signs of decay. Their surfaces gleamed as if newly carved, covered in the same mysterious script they'd seen on the column.

"This architecture," Ris breathed, sweeping the scanner around the room. "It's not like anything in the professor's records."

"That thing has the professor's records?" Reyes asked.

"Yeah, he must have uploaded them along with the coordinates. There are also instructions on what to look for in here."

Damien wandered toward the center of the chamber where a raised platform held what appeared to be some kind of control panel. As he approached, lights flickered to life along the floor, creating a path of illumination.

"Don't even think about touching that," Cornelius called out.

"Too late," Damien replied, already reaching for the panel. Before his fingers made contact, a holographic display sprang to life above it. Strange symbols and diagrams rotated in the air.

Mic stood to the side looking miffed he didn't think to press it first.

"For once in your life, could you not press every button you see?" Amelia asked.

"Hey, it worked with the entrance, didn't it?" Damien studied the floating symbols. "Besides, look at this - it's a star chart."

Ris hurried over, scanner whirring. "He's right. These are astronomical calculations, but they're using reference points I've never seen before. This is incredible!"

The chamber lit up as more systems activated. Lights raced along the walls, illuminating previously hidden doorways and alcoves.

"Uh, guys?" Reyes pointed to one of the newly revealed alcoves. "We're not alone down here."

Damien turned to see a humanoid figure step out of the shadows. It wore the uniform of the expedition team, but something about its movements seemed wrong, too rigid and mechanical.

"Are you here to rescue Stanic?" He was shaking from nerves and his wiry frame made him appear frail.

"Who is Stanic?" Amelia asked clutching her med kit.

"My expedition partner. He went down those stairs a few hours ago and has not returned."

"We will look for him. We are about to venture into the chamber." Amelia told the strange man.

"Oh, thank you, ma'am." His pleading face became almost jovial.

"Is there something amusing?" Ris asked.

The man's demeanor showed he had recently experienced some trauma, "Oh no, I'm only smiling from relief. I have been too frightened to go down there again and look for him."

"Again? You've already been? What's down there?" Cornelius asked.

"Darkness! I couldn't bring myself to go back, even to find my friend."

Cornelius nodded, "Point taken. The professor sent us here on purpose, making it all sound like it was a quick survey, nothing to worry about. I get the feeling that no one else would come here for him so he sent us."

"Cynical," Mic said. "I protect you." The alien smiled with a toothy grin.

"Funny!" Cornelius said.

One by one they traversed down the stairs into the darkness until the light faded out and it was almost pitch dark.

"Great, I can't see a thing," Reyes said.

A voice echoed up from the darkness, "There is a box with high-powered hand-held lights on a stone table just at the bottom of the stairs. Be careful not to step on me when you descend. I am at the bottom step."

"Stanic, I presume?" Ris asked in the direction of the voice.

"Yes, that is my name. My partner must still be up there."

"He is. Hold fast and we will bring medical attention to you should you require it." Ris said.

Amelia felt her way ahead of the others and found the man at the bottom of the stairs. Ris found the lights and clicked them on providing her with illumination. The man required minor medical assistance. He had scrapes and cuts all along his legs and arms from running fast, mostly blind, through the cavern. He had finally twisted his ankle only moments before the party began descending the staircase. Ris heard the now familiar sound from Amelia's wrist that she had been awarded experience.

"I am forever grateful for your assistance, but I cannot allow you to explore the cavern. It is too dangerous. I barely made it back." Stanic said.

"We are a group of six, we can make it through just fine," Ris said.

The man stared at each one of them in turn, assessing them, "very well, but let me warn you of what you face. There are three obstacles in your way. The giant spider is first. You have to kill her fast or she will rampage and destroy you all. The second is the arachnid queen. She is poisonous and twice as powerful as the giant spider. Watch out for her acid bath. She will spew it all over the floor and it will kill you before you realize it. Last is the ghost of the ruins. He is the spirit of one of the original aliens and he doesn't want you to enter the final chamber. Good luck and thank you again for helping me."

"It was my pleasure," Amelia said. "She ascended the staircase and brought down Stanic's partner to help him get out of the cavern. The man seemed nervous but okay enough to help his friend move closer to the entrance.

As soon as Stanic cleared the entrance, each one of their wrist devices chimed again. Each one of them had gained some experience for completing the quest to rescue Stanic, but it had not been enough to level any of them.

Ris handed out the lights and readied his power sword hilt, "All right, here's the plan. Mic, you get out in front and we will back you up. You keep whatever we are fighting occupied and Cornelius, Damien, and I will do as much damage as we can as quickly as we can. Reyes, you stay back and protect Amelia while she does her job keeping us alive. Amelia, I hope you are well stocked. We will probably need something to counter venom."

"I am fully stocked."

"Mic can do it, but first Mic needs stim."

Amelia rummaged through her metal medical case and produced a hypo-spray. She dosed Mic with it and he flexed his rippling muscles.

"Don't take unnecessary risks just because you are all juiced up, big guy!" Reyes said.

Mic made a sound that closely resembled grunting. Ris followed behind him closely. The cavern was barely wide enough for one person sometimes and Mic, in particular, had a difficult time navigating through the narrow openings at times.

Damien wondered why they had agreed to enter the dank place until he heard the occasional soft chime of the wrist band telling him he was getting exploration experience. The early levels might not have much significance as far as skills or loot, but they were necessary to advance. Upon studying his wristband, he found that advancing every five levels tended to have the most significance.

After they had made their way into the cavern for about fifteen minutes they emerged into a chamber the size of a small chapel, Damien estimated. He held his blaster ready when he heard the skittering noises coming from somewhere up ahead. Ris and Mic shined their lights in the direction of the sound and illuminated a spider about the size of a pony. It screamed and charged toward them.

What is it with all the fucking spiders on this planet!" Amelia lamented.

Cornelius and Damien opened up fire while Ris powered his sword. Mic grabbed the spider by the head and began to try to crush it. As far as Damien could tell, the blaster shots only angered it and Ris couldn't get close enough to use his sword on it with the limited space between him and Mic. Killing the huge beast proved almost impossible with the resources available to them, in fact, each time they fought the spider with their pitiful blasters, it took almost no damage. The timer would expire and it would rampage and stomp them all into dust. They had to retreat and regroup over and over again, depleting Amelia's precious medical resources.

"This is stupid," Damien said. "We need to kill it to get gear but we need better gear to kill it."

Reyes had begun to harvest crafting nodes along the way. These nodes glowed a pale blue when they passed them and only required the wrist device to harvest, "That's why I started harvesting. Maybe I can craft us something better."

"Well, screw this!" Ris said. "We can't keep doing the same thing over and over. We need a new plan."

"We need more powerful weapons," Damien said.

"Here I think I have everything I need according to my wrist device to upgrade my blaster." He took out his blaster and placed in on a rock in front of him. He took the material from the nodes and placed them next to it. He pushed some buttons on his wrist console and waved his wrist over the blaster several times. With each pass, there was a gnashing noise followed by the materials disappearing. The wristband made several dinging sounds.

When the sounds halted, Ris scanned the blaster. "It's a mark VII blaster now, up from a Mark II. Can you do my power sword as well?"

"I only had enough material for one upgrade. It took me all day to harvest that."

"Well, we can try to get by with one new blaster or we can try to harvest our own materials," Ris said.

"I think I will harvest my own materials, we're never going to kill that spider," Damien said. "There is supposed to be an even stronger one after that. He looked at his wristband, "and the quest here is blue. We should be able to do this. It's time to upgrade our equipment."

"I suppose it is time. We haven't upgraded almost any of our stuff." Cornelius agreed.

Reyes was gauging his wristband device, "I got quite a bit of experience harvesting and then making the upgrade. We might even be able to reach level 5th or 6th."

"It's settled then. Screw banging our heads against the wall. We will harvest materials and upgrade our weapons." Ris commanded.

Chapter 8: Mr. Ris Goes to Swashingtown

Damien and the others began to backtrack their way through the cavern picking and scraping the materials off the floor and walls where the nodes appeared. Finally, they exited the cavern and began moving around the ruins looking for the most lucrative nodes. They let Reyes upgrade their blasters since his crafting skill was the highest and increasing with each upgrade, however, after a time, Reyes noticed his experience dwindle. At that point, Ris began to work on crafting and increasing his experience.

It was well into the night cycle of the planet before they had enough of the material and completed work on all the weapons.

"That's the last of the weapons," Ris said handing Damien's blaster back to him. "But we still have this shabby armor to contend with. I don't think we are doing this right. Our equipment should be closer to our levels."

Damien scratched his head. "I don't see how we could have done anything different. Maybe we missed a bunch of quests."

"That's likely," Cornelius agreed.

"Why don't we find a spot and make camp here," Ris suggested. "We can get started on the armor materials again in the morning."

"You want to camp out here in these ruins?" Cornelius asked.

"Sure, why not. We can take watch if it will make you feel better."

"I will see about gathering some firewood," Reyes said and he wandered off with his light.

"I will see what food we have available," Amelia said. She began rummaging through the food stores they picked up at the visitor's center.

It wasn't long before they had a fire going and food in their bellies. Ris and Reyes began to do the maintenance work of going over their experience gain of the day. Soon, the other joined them.

"It just isn't fun," Damien was saying. "Even when we role-play back home with pen and paper it isn't fun if the odds are always stacked against you."

"Yeah, like the time I was trying to figure out what was going on with the villagers and no matter what I asked or suggested,

Dr. Thomas Bright would say things like, you find nothing or you don't see anything. Man, dude, give me a freakin' clue! I guess I was supposed to ask or see the one thing that would lead me on or he was just going to let me just stand there endlessly," Cornelius said.

"Well, what I mean is getting so close to dying over and over again and having to constantly regroup. I think we are supposed to repair this armor occasionally as well. Also, I have always hated going through a dungeon where you have to take two steps to the right on Tuesday and four steps forward or fry in the dragon's breath. It just gets too hard, frustrating, and not fun. Just like the instance today. We were underpowered, under geared, under skilled in crafting, but in order to gain anything we needed to kill something almost impossible for us, a venom spitting monster!" Damien said. "Are you supposed to have the gear and equipment first? Do we need a higher-level guy with us to get stuff?"

"Man, complain much?" Reyes said.

"What, you like this. Reyes?"

"No, Damien, but complaining about it does nothing to help us get through it. Strategy is what we need not complaints."

"Strategy would be great! I think we are supposed to work together and just let the healer heal the tank," Amelia said. "There isn't enough to go around all the time and I only have so much I can give out or I will run out of supplies too quick. I can't be healing you all at once if you draw the attention of the monster on yourselves. That spider was all over the place and the first thing the tank starts yelling at me is heals!, heals!"

"Well, important to heal tank." Mic said. "Can't hold it off if dead!"

"No doubt, we need better communication," Ris said. "Heal the meat shield first or we all die!"

"I no meat shield. I have feelings!"

"It's okay, big guy, it's tough to keep that spider's attention when Ris and Damien are doing so much damage to it. Maybe they should slow down and do the damage in increments ping ponging the beast back and forth." Reyes said.

"Get some sleep, we'll see about getting our armor upgrades done and getting back in there to take out those bosses in the morning." Ris said. "Be thinking of a strategy while we work. We can do this!"

Damien woke to the sound of Amelia cursing at her wrist interface. The sun had just barely crept over the horizon. He sat up, rubbing sleep from his eyes.

"What the hell, Amelia?"

"These fucking plant nodes are everywhere," Amelia said. "I can't believe I didn't notice them before." She waved her wrist over a glowing green vine, harvesting its essence.

"What are you making?" Damien asked, stretching.

"Stims. Healing, strength, speed - you name it. The wrist interface shows me how to combine the materials." She held up a freshly crafted hypo-spray. "Much better than the basic shit we started with."

The others stirred as the smell of breakfast wafted through camp. Reyes had managed to find some edible fruits, and Mic had caught something that looked vaguely rabbit-like.

While they ate, Ris and Cornelius worked on upgrading their armor. The crafting process went faster now that they understood the mechanics better. Damien watched as his shabby flight jacket transformed into reinforced combat gear.

"The armor rating is much higher," Ris said, checking his interface. "Should give us better protection against that spider's attacks."

"And I've got plenty of anti-venom stims now," Amelia added. "Plus some strength boosters for Mic."

"Mic ready to smash bug!" The alien flexed his newly armored muscles.

They packed up camp and made their way back to the cavern entrance. Damien felt more confident with his upgraded gear, but his stomach still churned with anxiety as they descended the dark steps.

"Remember the plan," Ris said as they approached the spider's chamber. "Mic draws its attention while we coordinate our attacks. No one goes off script this time."

"And wait for my fucking signal before you use your stims," Amelia added. "I need to time them right."

Damien checked his Mark VII blaster one last time. The weapon hummed with power, its energy core pulsing with a steady blue glow. He took position behind a fallen pillar as Mic stepped into the chamber.

The spider's screech echoed off the stone walls. In the beam of their lights, its eight eyes gleamed with malevolent intelligence. Damien's hands trembled slightly as he lined up his shot, but he forced himself to wait for Ris's signal.

"Now!" Ris shouted.

Mic charged forward, drawing the spider's attention while Amelia injected him with a strength stim. Damien and Cornelius opened fire from opposite sides, their upgraded blasters punching through the creature's thick carapace. Ris circled around with his power sword, looking for an opening.

The spider reared up, preparing to rampage, but this time they were ready. Amelia's anti-venom stims kept Mic going as he grappled with the beast, while their coordinated fire prevented it from focusing on any single target.

Damien's upgraded blaster sang with each shot, its enhanced power core delivering devastating hits to the spider's carapace. The creature thrashed and screeched, but couldn't break free from Mic's iron grip. Ris darted in with his power sword, severing two of the beast's legs in a single swing.

"Keep it steady!" Damien called out, lining up a shot at the spider's head. His blast struck true, and the monster collapsed with a final shriek.

Their wrist interfaces chimed in unison - level 4. Damien approached the fallen creature and found a piece of reinforced chest armor embedded in its hide. Similar pieces of gear lay scattered around the chamber, which the others quickly collected.

"All that crafting yesterday and now we get better gear anyway," Damien grumbled. This is exactly what I was complaining about!" But he had to admit the new armor was superior to what they'd made.

"It's the nature of things." Reyes said.

They pressed deeper into the cavern until they reached a vast chamber dripping with acid. The arachnid queen towered above them, twice the size of the previous spider. Before they could react, she sprayed acid across the floor.

"Move!" Ris shouted as they scrambled for higher ground.

This fight proved far more challenging than any of their previous encounters. Even with Amelia's enhanced stims coursing through their veins. Mic struggled to hold the queen's attention, his usual tank tactics failing against the massive arachnid. Damien kept accidentally drawing her off with his high damage per second. She also repelled off the walls making it difficult for Ris to land his blows with his power sword.

Acid burns ate through their new armor despite the improved protection, making Damien regret his earlier complaints about the gear. He was definitely glad to have the upgrades now, wasted day or not. The acrid smell of dissolving metal filled his nostrils as he dodged another spray, watching helplessly as Mic took the brunt of an attack meant for him. Thankfully, Amelia was there to heal the brute before he took on too much damage.

Eventually, their combined efforts brought the monster down. The spider queen's legs curled beneath her massive body as she collapsed with an ear-splitting shriek that echoed through the chamber.

Their interfaces chimed again - level 5. Beside the queen's corpse lay an array of advanced weapons. Damien selected a sleek Mark X blaster that made his crafted weapon look like a toy.

"A whole day wasted," he muttered, holstering his new gun, secretly happy to have the upgrade after the battle they had just hard fought.

"At least we learned the crafting system," Ris offered, choosing a quantum-edge power sword.

The final chamber held their strangest challenge yet but it was weirdly much easier to dispatch than either of the monstrous spiders. The ghost of the ruins materialized in the chamber before them - a translucent alien figure crackling with ancient energy. It spoke in an unknown language while hurling bolts of energy at the group.

Damien's new blaster proved its worth, the enhanced energy beams actually affecting the spectral enemy. Mic's attempts to grapple the ghost proved futile, but he provided enough distraction for Ris and Cornelius to flank it.

Working together, they dispersed the spirit's form. In its place floated a small crystalline artifact covered in the same symbols they'd seen throughout the ruins. Their interfaces chimed one final time - level 6.

"This must be what the professor needs," Ris said, carefully securing the artifact.

"Better be worth all this trouble," Damien replied, examining a acid burn on his sleeve.

"I think I have something for that attitude in my bag." Amelia said.

"No need," Damien replied, "We just need to find a bar."

Chapter 9: Carousing

"Hey, what was that?" Amelia said. "Something just bit my leg."

"Ouch, mine too," Cornelius said. He flicked on his light and all over the cavern floor were black bugs about the size of grasshoppers scurrying about.

The black bugs swarmed over their feet and legs, biting and causing sharp stinging pains. Damien jumped up, stomping and kicking at the insects. "We need to get out of here!"

"Yeah, screw these bugs. Maybe we can head back to The visitor's center and look for that bar!" Cornelius said, rushing to leave the cavern.

Damien nodded, "I could use a drink after this little excursion."

"Of all the things you could be thinking about, Damien." Ris said. "Do you have to chase after alcohol?"

Damien pointed to himself, "Duh, character flaw, remember."

They all scrambled to get out of the cavern as soon as possible, gathering their gear while swatting at the biting insects.

Mic simply stomped through the swarm, crushing dozens with each step. "Why bugs? They come after ghost die?"

"Maybe it's to get people to leave after the boss is defeated." Amelia said.

"This way!" Ris led them back out of the cavern and in the direction of the visitor's center, their lights bouncing wildly in the darkness.

Once they reached the safety of the center's lit interior, Damien found the place did indeed have a bar easily enough. It was a dimly lit establishment called "The Event Horizon." A few NPCs lounged at scattered tables while soft alien music played in the background. Once inside, he slid onto a barstool, his legs fresh from the stinging of bug bites. "Two Centaurian brandies," he called to the bartender. He glanced at Cornelius. "You're drinking, right?"

"After the killer spiders and those bugs? Hell yes." Cornelius settled onto the stool next to him.

The bartender, a green-skinned humanoid with four arms, deftly poured their drinks. Damien took a long sip, feeling the warm burn of the brandy. His wrist device dinged softly.

Social skill increased. Alcohol tolerance +1

"Great, even drinking gives us experience now," Cornelius muttered, then he took a healthy swallow of his drink. *Ding!* His own alcohol tolerance increased.

"You know what bugs me?" Damien swirled the amber liquid in his glass. "How are we supposed to level up if we can't even kill bosses our level? I mean, the rewards of armor and weapons are the same level as the quests to obtain them. We can't get the rewards without the equipment to get the rewards. There has to be an easier way."

"Maybe we're going about it wrong." Cornelius signaled for another round. "Remember in the old tabletop days? Sometimes the solution wasn't fighting at all."

"You think we can sneak past it?"

"Or trick it somehow. We've got better gear now with the upgrades. Maybe there's something in the environment we can use."

Their wrist devices dinged again as the bartender brought fresh drinks.

Strategic planning skill increased

"At least we're getting something out of drowning our sorrows," Damien said. He noticed his speech was already slightly slurred - apparently the alcohol tolerance skill wasn't high enough yet.

"Tell me about it." Cornelius leaned back, studying the exotic bottles lining the bar's back wall. "You know what's really weird? I'm starting to forget things. Like, I can't remember what I did for a living before this. But I remember every detail of my character's backstory."

"Same here." Damien frowned. "That hologram said something about memory scrubbing. You think that's what's happening to us?"

"Has to be. The question is, do we fight it or just go with it?"

"Like I said before, I don't think we have much choice." Damien drained his glass. "We either play along and level up, or we stay stuck here forever."

The bartender approached with another round they hadn't ordered. "Compliments of the gentleman in the corner," he said in a gravelly voice.

They turned to see a cloaked figure sitting alone in the shadows. As they watched, he raised his glass slightly in acknowledgment.

"Think we should go talk to him?" Cornelius asked.

"Could be a quest giver." Damien stood, only slightly unsteady. He wavered for a moment then caught himself.

Their devices dinged again.

Quest opportunity detected

Damien and Cornelius approached the cloaked figure, their steps less coordinated than usual thanks to the Centaurian brandy. The figure gestured to the empty chairs at his table.

"Please, join me." His voice had an odd metallic quality to it. "I couldn't help but overhear your discussion about memory loss."

Cornelius slid into a chair. "You know something about that?"

"How'd you hear us all the way over here?" Damien asked.

"Perhaps." The figure leaned forward slightly, but his face remained hidden in shadow. "I have many such enhanced abilities. I can hear across a room among other things." He leaned in further still, "Tell me, what do you remember about Earth?"

Damien opened his mouth to respond, then froze. Earth. He knew the word, knew it was important, but the details were hazy. Images flashed through his mind - tall buildings, ground vehicles, something called television - but they felt distant, like memories of a dream.

"I..." He shook his head. "I was a pilot. I remember that."

"Were you?" The figure asked softly. "Or is that just what your character sheet says?"

Cornelius rubbed his temples. "This is wrong. We're supposed to be here. Aren't we?"

"The line between game and reality becomes quite blurred when dealing with the Jaddus Collective's technology." The figure's metallic voice took on a thoughtful tone. "Their neural interface systems are incredibly sophisticated. Perhaps too sophisticated."

"What do you mean?" Damien asked, but found himself distracted by memories of his first solo flight through the Rigel system. The rush of acceleration, the gleam of distant stars... except that hadn't really happened, had it?

The figure produced a small device and placed it on the table. It projected a holographic display of complex code sequences. "The system is designed to temporarily overlay character memories and abilities onto the user's consciousness. But something has gone wrong. The overlay is becoming permanent. You, my friends will never return to your former lives on Earth. Soon, you will be a permanent part of *this* world."

"That's impossible," Damien said, but even as he spoke, he found himself reaching for memories of his life before. They slipped away like water through his fingers, replaced by vivid recollections of battles against space pirates and negotiations with alien diplomats.

"Is it?" The figure gestured to their wrist devices. "The system is actively rewriting your neural patterns. Your original memories are being overwritten with the game's lore and backstory."

"But why?" Damien asked. "Is it a malfunction?"

"Or sabotage," the figure suggested. "The Alteri Dominion has been trying to acquire Jaddus Collective technology for years. Perhaps they succeeded in compromising the system."

Cornelius started to object, then paused. "Wait... how do we know you're not part of this? Another NPC giving us a quest?"

The figure sat back. "An excellent question. But can you trust your own judgment anymore? How much of your critical thinking is still yours, and how much belongs to your character?"

Damien tried to focus, but his thoughts kept drifting to starship specifications and hyperspace calculations. He knew these weren't his real memories, but they felt more solid, more real than anything else he could recall. He suddenly realized that every moment they were around the stranger the new memories increased in frequency. With the aid of the intoxicating beverage, they were being altered on the fly. This stranger was trying to change them permanently.

Their wrist devices hummed softly, and text scrolled across the displays:

Memory integration proceeding... Original cognitive patterns degrading... Character template stabilizing...

"We have to stop this," Cornelius said, but his voice lacked conviction. The memories of his character's life felt right, natural. Fighting it seemed increasingly pointless.

"If you still can," the figure said quietly. "The question is, do you truly want to?"

"Who are you?" Damien asked, hid mind becoming a fog of old and new memories.

"I am but a humble servant of the Ataris. Welcome. Space Lords of Strata.

Damien's hand instinctively moved to his blaster as the figure revealed his allegiance. The Ataris were supposed to be extinct, wiped out centuries ago in the great purge. Yet here sat one of their servants, casually buying them drinks in a bar.

"That's impossible," Cornelius said. "The Ataris were destroyed."

"Were we?" The figure's metallic voice held a note of amusement. "Or is that simply what the history books claim?"

The room seemed to spin around Damien, though he couldn't tell if it was from the brandy or the continuing erosion of his memories. He could clearly remember learning about the Ataris in flight school, their advanced technology and mysterious disappearance. But flight school had never really happened, had it?

"The spider," Damien blurted out. "The one in the ruins. It's not just a monster, is it?"

"Ah." The figure nodded slowly. "You begin to understand. The creatures you face are guardians, placed there by my people long ago. They do not respond to brute force, but to specific frequencies."

Cornelius leaned forward. "Frequencies?"

"Your weapons. The mark VII blasters you so painstakingly crafted. Their power cells emit a particular resonance when fired. But alone, it's not enough." The figure produced a small crystal from within his cloak. "Combined with this, however..."

Their wrist devices hummed:

New quest available: The Ataris's Gift

Reward: Weapon modification crystal

Warning: Accepting this quest may alter current storyline progression

"And what do you want in return?" Damien asked, his pilot's instincts - real or programmed - telling him this was too good to be true.

"Want? Nothing. Consider it a gift from those who came before." The figure placed the crystal on the table. "Though I would suggest examining the archives carefully once you gain access. The truth of your situation may be hidden within."

Amelia burst into the bar, her face flushed. "There you are! You need to see this." She thrust her wrist device forward, displaying a message:

Warning: Critical system instability detected
Memory integration accelerating beyond safe parameters
Recommend immediate action to preserve core consciousness

"The interface is breaking down," she said. "Whatever's happening to our memories, it's getting worse."

"The crystal," Cornelius reached for it, but the figure had vanished, leaving only the small gem on the table.

"Did anyone else see where he went?" Damien asked.

"Where who went?" Amelia looked confused.

"The Ataris. He was just here…"

"Damien, the Ataris have been extinct for centuries. Everyone knows that." She paused, frowning. "At least, I think they have. I can't quite remember where I learned that."

Damien picked up the crystal. It felt warm in his hand, pulsing with a faint inner light.

His wrist device beeped insistently:

Accept quest: The Ataris's Gift? Y/N
Warning: This action cannot be undone
Time remaining to accept: 5:00

"Well?" Cornelius asked. "Do we trust it?"

Damien stared at the crystal, unable, or unwilling, to make the decision.

Chapter 10: The Archives

Damien's finger hovered over the interface. "We're out of options." He pressed 'Y' and the crystal pulsed brighter.

"Give it here." Amelia snatched the crystal and the small device the Ataris had left behind. She examined both with practiced precision, "The crystal has an insertion point. Hold on."

She slotted the crystal into the device. It hummed to life, projecting lines of complex code into the air before dissolving into nothing. Their wrist interfaces chimed in unison.

Core consciousness preserved
Original memory patterns stabilized
Integration protocols modified

"I feel... clearer," Cornelius said. "I can remember things now. Not everything, but enough."

"Me too." Damien took another sip of his brandy. I remember the Jaddus Collective being attacked and leaving us here to work through the game until we beat it in order to get our old memories back."

"Yeah, and now we're stuck here until we complete it." Amelia checked her medical scanner. "Our neural patterns are stabilizing, but we're still locked into the game's framework. I think we just avoided a disaster."

"At least now we know what we're dealing with," Damien said. "We need to get that artifact back to the Professor so we can get access to the archives."

Their devices hummed again:

Quest updated: The Archives

New objective: complete professor quest for advancement

"Well then." Cornelius stood, "Shall we go finish this quest?" He immediately slouched back into his chair.

"First thing tomorrow," Damien said. "I need to sleep off this brandy."

"Good call." Amelia gathered her med kit. "We should all get some rest. It's been a long day. Ris and the others have already turned in."

Their interfaces chimed one final time:

Tutorial complete

Main quest line activated

Current objective: Retrieve the Archives

Warning: Failure to progress will result in permanent neural pattern lock

"We'll just have to make certain we don't fail." Amelia said.

* * *

Damien and the others followed behind Ris as they approached the professor's tent the next morning. His head throbbed from the previous night's brandy, but at least his memories felt more stable now.

The professor looked up from his work as they entered. "Ah, you've returned. What did you find?"

Ris produced the crystalline artifact. "We found this in the ruins after dealing with the guardians."

The professor's eyes lit up as he examined the object. "Extraordinary! The craftsmanship, the symbols - this confirms my theories about the ancient civilization." He set the artifact carefully on his desk. "You've earned your reward."

He opened a large trunk and began distributing equipment - advanced armor, upgraded weapons, and specialized gear tailored to each of their roles. Damien whistled as he examined his new flight suit, complete with built-in shield generators.

Their interfaces chimed: *Equipment level increased to 10*

"We're still only level 9," Cornelius noted, adjusting his new armor.

"What else can I do for you?" The professor asked.

Ris approached him. "Perhaps extend us access to the archives?"

The professor stroked his chin. "The archives? Hmm. Yes, I suppose you've proven yourselves trustworthy." He took Ris's scanner and entered a series of commands. "Show this to the guard. He'll let you in."

"Thank you," Ris said. "This will help our research considerably."

"Just be careful in there. Some knowledge is best left buried."

"Will do." Ris said.

They made their way back to the cavern entrance where the guard still stood watch. Mic gave a friendly wave to his fellow alien.

"Back again?" The guard asked. "What purpose this time?"

Ris held up his scanner, displaying the professor's authorization. The guard examined it carefully before nodding.

"Very well. You may enter." He stepped aside and pressed his hand to a panel. The vault door slid open with a pneumatic hiss.

"That last level should come from exploring the archives," Damien said as they stepped through the doorway.

The massive door sealed behind them with a resounding thud, leaving them in the dim glow of an ancient lighting system.

"I hope those doors can be reopened." Amelia quipped.

"Come on, this way." Ris said leading them down a hallway toward another light source. Ancient data terminals lined the walls, their screens flickering with strange symbols. The air smelled musty, like old books left too long in a damp basement. "This place gives me the creeps," he muttered, checking his wrist interface for radiation readings.

A hunched figure emerged from behind a bank of computers, startling them. The elderly woman wore the traditional robes of an archivist, her silver hair pulled back in a severe bun.

"Welcome to the archives," she said, her voice thin and reedy. "I am Keeper Vennah. What is your purpose here?"

"We're looking for information about the Jaddus Collective," Ris explained. he looked at Damien and shrugged.

"Ah yes, the professor mentioned you might come." She shuffled over to a terminal and began typing. "But I'm afraid the main data core containing the information you seek is located in the auxiliary archives."

Damien groaned. "Let me guess - back to the ruins and the spiders' lair?"

"Indeed. Just beyond where you encountered the guardians." Vennah nodded. "The data core is essential for accessing the deeper archives."

"You've got to be kidding me." Damien kicked a nearby console in frustration. "We just came from there! Why didn't anyone give us this quest before?"

"Careful with the equipment," Vennah scolded.

"Sorry, but this is ridiculous. We could have grabbed it while we were fighting those spiders if someone had bothered to tell us what the next quest would entail."

Their interfaces chimed: *New Quest - The Data Core*
Objective: Retrieve auxiliary archives data core
Reward: Access to restricted archive sections

"This always happens," Damien continued ranting. "Every single quest giver sends us back to places we've already cleared out. It's like they enjoy wasting our time."

"I'm getting a little tired of your complaints," Cornelius said. "If it happens every time as you say, then you should be used to it by now."

"The professor knew we were going to need archive access. The guard knew where the data core was. Hell, even those expedition guys probably knew about it. But no one thought to mention it to us so we could retrieve it while we were there?"

"You done?" Amelia asked, checking her medical supplies.

"No, I'm not done! This is terrible quest design. We're supposed to just accept that everyone here has selective amnesia about important information until the exact moment we need it?"

Mic placed a massive hand on Damien's shoulder. "Mic think you need drink less brandy. Make you cranky."

"I'm not cranky, I'm annoyed. There's a difference."

"Still, don't make Mic smash your face until you shut up."

Damien cleared his throat, "point taken." Mic removed his massive hand.

Ris consulted his scanner. "The auxiliary archives are showing up now. Damien called it. It Looks like a straight shot back to the ruins and the spiders' lair."

"Of course it is," Damien muttered. He quickly shot a glance at Mic who was already frowning. "I'm not complaining!"

"If you're quite finished complaining," Vennah interrupted, "the data core is a delicate piece of equipment. You'll need these containment fields to transport it safely." She handed Ris several small devices.

"Thank you," Ris said. "We'll return as soon as we have it."

"Just try not to break anything else," Vennah called after them as they headed back toward the cavern entrance.

"I barely touched that console," Damien grumbled.

Mic pushed him along with his massive hand on the middle of his back, "Yep, no brandy for you."

Damien squinted against the harsh sunlight as they emerged from the archives. His head still pounded from last night's brandy, making the brightness of the day particularly unpleasant. They had barely made it twenty paces past the guard when a flickering blue figure materialized before them.

The hologram showed an Alteri, his translucent form crackling with static. "Space Masters, you must listen quickly. House Davosi has tracked your location. Their destroyer enters this system as we speak."

"And why should we trust an Alteri?" Damien's hand instinctively moved to his blaster despite him knowing it would have no effect on a holographic projection.

"Because a mutual friend sends warning." The hologram flickered. "There is a shuttle waiting at the spaceport. Our operatives have equipped it with sensor masking codes - you'll be able to slip past the destroyer's detection grid."

Damien exchanged looks with the others. A mutual friend could only mean one person - Dr. Bright. But how had he gotten mixed up with the Alteri?

"The codes are temporary," the hologram continued. "You must reach the shuttle before the destroyer enters orbit."

"What about the data core?" Ris asked. "We need that information."

"The archives will still be here after the Davosi leave. But you won't be if you don't evacuate now."

Mic growled. "Mic no like running from fight."

"We don't have much choice," Cornelius said. "A destroyer could turn this whole area to glass."

"He's right," Damien said, though it pained him to agree with Cornelius. "I've seen what those ships can do. We need to move."

Their wrist interfaces chimed: *Emergency Quest - Planetary Evacuation*

Objective: Reach spaceport before destroyer arrives

Warning: Quest failure will result in character death

"Well that's motivating," Amelia muttered.

"How long do we have?" Reyes asked the hologram.

"Minutes at most. The destroyer will achieve orbital position soon."

"Then we better run," Damien said. "Which way to the spaceport?"

The hologram projected a map showing their position and the spaceport location. "Follow this path. The shuttle is in hangar seven. May fortune favor you, Space Masters." The figure flickered once more and vanished.

"Some friend Bright turned out to be," Cornelius said as they broke into a run. "Consorting with the Alteri."

"Maybe he didn't have a choice," Damien replied between breaths. "Or maybe the Alteri was talking about someone else."

"Like who? Bright is the only one we would know around here that's not present and accounted for." Cornelius said.

"Less talk, more run!" Mic shouted from behind them.

They sprinted along the marked path. Damien's hangover protested every step, but survival instinct pushed him forward. The spaceport's control tower rose in the distance, a silver needle against the blue sky.

Chapter 11: Master of Disguise

Damien crouched behind a stack of cargo containers at the spaceport entrance, sweat beading on his forehead despite the sophisticated cooling system in his flight suit. The promised shuttle sat in hangar seven, its sleek form beckoning them to safety. But something wasn't right. There were guards milling around the ship.

"Those aren't our Alteri," Ris whispered, peering through his scanner. "Their energy signatures don't match the hologram's."

"The hologram didn't mention anything about guards being around the ship either." Reyes said.

"They could be House Davosi plants," Cornelius suggested. "Waiting to ambush us."

"You think they might have gotten word that we would be looking for a shuttle to leave the planet?" Ris asked.

"Could be." Cornelius nodded.

Damien studied the guards' movements. Four of them patrolled the hangar in a standard sweep pattern, their weapons ready. Their uniforms marked them as Alteri, but their bearing screamed military precision. "I knew we couldn't trust that damned Alteri hologram!"

"We need a plan," Amelia said, checking her medical supplies. "That destroyer will be here any minute."

"Plan? We're level nine now." Reyes pulled out his blaster with a wild grin. "We can take these guys."

Before anyone knew what was on his mind, Reyes burst from cover. Damien lunged forward, grabbing the back of his engineering jacket and yanking him behind the containers. They tumbled to the ground in a heap.

"Are you insane?" Damien hissed. "You want to get us all killed? You read the failure result."

"But, we have upgraded weapons," Reyes protested. "And Amelia's new healing stims-"

"Shut up," Ris commanded. "That was the kind of reckless stuff that used to get us wiped in the old days, Dean." He suddenly stiffened, "Where's Mic?"

Damien scanned their group. The massive alien was nowhere to be seen. A movement caught his eye - Mic's hulking form slipping between shadows toward the shuttle, attempting to be stealthy despite his massive size.

"Oh no," Cornelius groaned. "Not this again. He thinks the few points he has in stealth makes him invisible or something."

"What's he doing?" Amelia asked.

"Sneaking! He put all those points in stealth," Damien explained, watching in horror as Mic tried to sneak past the guards. "He thinks he's actually good at it."

They watched helplessly as Mic pressed himself against a wall, his massive frame completely visible to anyone who looked his way. The alien sidled along the wall like a child playing hide-and-seek, utterly convinced of his own invisibility.

"Should we create a distraction?" Ris asked. "Give him a chance?"

"Too late," Damien said. "If we move now, we risk drawing attention to him."

Mic reached the outside of the shuttle bay, still performing his absurd attempt at stealth. The guards continued their patrol, seemingly oblivious to the giant alien's presence.

"Are they blind?" Cornelius whispered. "Or maybe he *is* staying hidden."

"No," Ris replied. "They're pretending not to see him or something. They're too disciplined to miss something that obvious. This is definitely a trap."

"Great," Damien muttered. "Now what do we do?"

* * *

Mic entered the shuttle bay. He hunkered down and moved sideways in small careful steps.

One of the guards on duty in the shuttle bay finally spotted him and trained his weapon on him, "Hey, stop right there!"

Mic brought all his intimidation skills to the forefront of his mind and stared down at the guard as he approached, "You no see Mic."

At first, the guard seemed confused. "I see you, halt!"

"No, you no see Mic," Mic repeated, touching the blaster at his side before doubling his intimidation efforts. A hapless guard from around the corner abruptly found himself face to face with him. Mic extended his fist and pounded the Alteri to goo with one thrust of his giant hand. He turned and glared at the other guard.

"Uh, nope, I no see Mic." The guard said as he began to back off. Mic cautiously slinked by. He settled on the shuttlecraft platform and pointed a finger ominously at the other guard who turned and ran away. Mic waved the others over as they watched from the hangar doors in awe.

Nice work, Mic," Damien said patting the big alien on the back as they entered the craft.

"According to these scans, more guards are on their way," Amelia said.

"Are you sure you can fly this thing, Damien?" Ris asked.

Damien cocked his head while still preparing the shuttlecraft for takeoff, "Of course I can. I have been working on the skill since level 3."

"But you've never flown one of these not even in a simulation."

"Have faith, my friend, I feel like I've been flying one for years." He powered up the engines and entered the code that would override the bay doors and cloak them from the destroyer's sensors. The doors slowly opened, "of course, we are alerting several spaceport personal right now. I bet their consoles are lighting up like a Tau-Ceti gambling den." He pressed a few more buttons and then took hold of the wheel and joystick, "Hold on. Here we go." The ship lurched forward and then jerked back. A warning siren went off in the hanger. "Shit! Sorry about that, I forget to release the moorings." He reached down and flicked a switch, releasing the ship from its tether. The shuttle craft soared out the open hanger doors and moved quickly upward through the atmosphere. "See, perfect," A red light lit up in the control panel.

Ris reached out with his newly acquired telepathy, "They know we're out here in one of their shuttles.. I can feel them scrambling to regain control.

"They're hailing us," Damien said. "What do you mean you *feel* them?"

"Oh, I have leveled my telepathy up to level 5."

"Level 5!" Mic was shocked, "When get telepathy skill to level 5?"

"Wait, the spaceport tower is hailing us. They're insisting we talk to them." Amelia's voice raised a little with the urgency of the situation.

"Let me hear," Ris said.

"Unauthorized shuttlecraft, power down and return to base. This is your only warning."

"Shut it off," Ris said. "There's nothing they can do or they would have done it already.

"They're signaling the destroyer to intercept us," Damien said.

"What else is out there?" Ris asked. "Any ships that might aid them with pursuit?"

Damien activated the short range sensors, "An escort class vessel. It has a minimal crew. Most of the crew must have gone down to the planet. It won't come after us."

"Get us to a safe distance and punch it. Does this shuttle have a hyperdrive?"

Damien pressed some buttons and the display blinked. "Yes, and it's ready.

"Get us out of here as soon as you can," Ris said patting Damien on the shoulder.

"About to leave the atmosphere." Damien stated.

"Mic just realized Mic no like space!" Mic said as he braced himself in the shuttle. The craft lurched and sputtered in the atmosphere but excelled as soon as they left the ionosphere.

"When we are clear, scan for a mining planet with long range sensors, Amelia. I heard some scuttlebutt about it back in the bar." Damien said. "It's supposed to be a house Harne planet. Ris, can you get us in if we go there?"

Ris shuffled uncomfortably, "We will have to fake it. I may be a Harne, but I have not really had any contact with the Harne family since we were placed here."

"They will be your family just as your background says. You have nothing to fear." Damien said. "If we can shake the destroyer, the mining planet will be the perfect place to get supplies and regroup. The rumor in the bar says that there is a secret shipyard there too. If the rumor is true, maybe we can get a new shuttle and scrap this one."

"All right, as soon as you are clear, scan for it, Amelia." Ris instructed.

Chapter 12: Galactic Empire Unlocked

Damien guided the shuttle through space, his hands steady on the control. The destroyer's signal was still visible on the scanners, though they'd managed to put some distance between them. Just as he was about to plot a course to the mining planet with the coordinates Amelia had given him, all their wrist devices chimed simultaneously with an urgent tone.

Warning: Archives auxiliary quest incomplete
Critical story progression blocked
Return to complete quest recommended

"Well, that's not good," Damien said, studying the flashing red text. "Anyone else getting this?"

Ris frowned at his device. "Can we come back to it later? Maybe after we're even better equipped? I'm not sure what we are going to find there. The quest color is yellow. I'm not even sure what that means? Is it one level higher than blue?"

Amelia shook her head, checking her own interface. "I don't know about the level of the quest but technically yes, we could came back to it, but if we level up too much in the meantime before completing it, the quest will become trivial. The rewards won't scale with our level."

"That's not the real problem," Reyes cut in. "Remember the warning about the story progression? If we skip this, we might lock ourselves out of completing the expansion properly and therefore be stuck here forever."

Damien watched the destroyer's signal growing fainter on the scanner. They'd almost lost them. "So what's the call?"

Ris sighed. "Circle back around. Once we lose the destroyer's signal completely, find us somewhere to set down and hide the shuttle. We need those archives and to get this quest completed before we move on."

"You got it." Damien banked the shuttle in a wide arc, keeping an eye on the sensors. The destroyer's signal faded to nothing as they passed behind one of the planet's moons. He flew low as to not get back on the destroyer's long range sensors and aimed for the planet. He brought them down through the atmosphere, searching for a suitable landing spot no too far from the ruins.

A clearing in the dense forest caught his eye. The shuttle's landing struts touched down softly on the mossy ground.

Damien powered down the engines, quite pleased with his improved piloting skills.

The familiar ethereal form of the Ancient Alteri materialized in the shuttle's cabin before they could even stand. Its usually serene features were twisted in anger.

"What are you doing?" the being demanded, its translucent form flickering with agitation. "I gave you clear instructions to leave this planet!"

"We have unfinished business," Damien said, turning in his pilot's seat to face the spirit. "The archives-"

"The archives are meaningless compared to what awaits you! The bones showed me your path clearly. You must reach the mining planet before-"

"Before what?" Ris interrupted. "You haven't actually told us why it's so urgent we leave."

The Alteri's form pulsed with frustration. "There are forces at work here beyond your understanding. The longer you remain, the greater the danger."

"Oh yeah, we'll take our chances." Ris replied.

"Our wrist devices say differently," Damien countered. "Whatever's in those archives, we need it to progress."

"You still think this is just a game?" The ancient being's voice took on a harsh edge. "That you can simply follow quest markers and level up until you return home? The reality is far more complex."

"Then explain it to us," Damien said, but the Alteri's form was already fading.

"You were warned," its voice echoed as it disappeared. "The consequences are now yours to bear."

"This is maddening. Isn't this what the Jaddus Collective told us to do to get home?" Damien asked.

"I don't think they really want that to happen, Damien. I think this is something they want us involved in forever. I think they had hoped we would lose the ability to remember home by now."

"You may be right. I still can't tell if there was really a breakdown in the game or if it was written this way on purpose."

"Regardless, we have to see it through." Ris lamented.

* * *

Damien powered down the shuttle's systems one by one, keeping only the essential life support and cloaking systems active in order to conserve energy in case they had to make a break for it. The dense forest canopy provided decent cover, but he wasn't taking any chances. Through the viewport, shadows moved through the trees as a slight breeze blew across them. At first, Damien thought someone was using the trees as cover but he soon realized the shadows were just extensions of the oddly shaped tree branches moving from the wind.

"The cloaking field should hold for about six hours," he said, checking the power readings. "After that, we'll need to route power from auxiliary systems."

"Let's hope we don't need that long." Cornelius pulled up a map on his wrist device. "The archives are about three clicks northeast of here."

Damien grabbed his upgraded blaster and checked the charge. The weapon hummed with energy, far more powerful than the basic model they'd started with. "Anyone else wondering what's so important in those archives that both the Ataris and the Alteri are interested in them?"

"Could be anything," Ris said, adjusting his power sword. "Ancient tech, weapon schematics, star charts..."

"Or just another fucking quest item," Amelia muttered, sorting through her med kit. "Either way, we need it to progress."

"There's that foul mouth!" Reyes observed, "I almost thought you had forgotten about that character trait."

"Hell no, I just haven't been saying much."

They exited the shuttle single file, Mic taking point while Damien brought up the rear. The forest was eerily quiet, except for the occasional rustle of unseen creatures in the canopy above.

Damien's wrist device pinged softly as they walked, updating their position relative to the archives. The familiar interface was oddly comforting - a reminder that whatever else was happening, they still had some control over their situation.

"Hold up," Ris whispered, raising his fist. Ahead, voices carried through the trees. Damien crouched behind a fallen log, peering through the foliage. A patrol of Alteri soldiers moved through a clearing about fifty meters away, their weapons glowing with an ominous blue-green light.

"They're searching for the shuttle," Ris said, his telepathy picking up surface thoughts. "House Davosi wants it back."

"Can we go around?" Damien asked.

Reyes checked his scanner. "There's a ravine to the east. Might take longer, but it'll keep us out of sight."

They backtracked and circled around, adding nearly an hour to their journey. By the time they reached the ruins, the twin suns were high overhead.

"No bugs this time," Cornelius noted as they approached the entrance. "Maybe they only come out at night."

"Or maybe something scared them off," Damien said, not liking the implications. He checked his wrist device again - the quest marker pointed them deeper into the ruins, past where they'd fought the spiders.

The auxiliary archives themselves turned out to be housed in a circular chamber beyond the spider's lair. Just like in the main archives building, ancient technology lined the walls here too, most of it dark and silent. They moved to the center of the room where a pedestal glowed with a soft blue light.

"That's what we need," Damien said, approaching the pedestal. A crystalline data core sat in a recessed slot, pulsing with the same inner light as the Ataris's crystal from the bar.

His wrist device chimed:

Archive data core located

Warning: Removal will trigger security systems

Proceed? Y/N

Damien glanced at his companions. "Ready?"

They nodded, weapons raised. He reached for the data core.

* * *

"Dr. Bright, I can't tell you how good it is to see you. Did you bring the item?"

"Of course, I brought it," Bright said.

"Excellent, the Emperor is most anxious to see it."

"I bet he is," Bright said.

The Emperor was seated on his throne when Bright entered. He spun around with a grim expression on his face. He was not an inviting man. He was balding, toad-like man with a slack jaw and dead eyes.

"The Laucnar?" The emperor mused. "Interesting name for it."

"I like it. It reminds me of something from my past."

"May I see it?" The emperor said almost salivating.

"You may." Bright removed it from its container but still kept it in a containment field.

"May I touch it?"

"It tends to kill all those who touch it, your highness."

"Can you touch it?" He scowled.

"Yes, I can, but I warn you. I am not like the others. I have a special bond with it. It's deadly, I assure you."

"I am the emperor of the galaxy. If you can touch it I may touch it as well"

"Suit yourself. I warned you." He took the Laucnar out of the containment field and held it in his hand. It felt cool to the touch belying it's true nature. He moved closer and presented it to the emperor. The toad-like man took it in his hands and smiled, "See I am not affected by something so trivial. The emperor's hands began to melt and he dropped the smooth gem, The rest of him methodically fell apart and disintegrated shortly thereafter.

Bright picked up the blue-green orb and held it high above his head. It began to glow ominously. The Laucnar's light shined down on all the onlookers. "Behold, I am your emperor now!" Bright declared.

The courtiers and guards stood frozen, their eyes fixed on the glowing orb in Bright's hand. He could sense their fear - not of him, but of the mysterious artifact that had just dissolved their emperor into a puddle of organic matter on the throne room floor.

"Well?" Bright challenged, his voice carrying across the vast chamber. "Does anyone else wish to question my right to rule?"

The head of the imperial guard stepped forward, his ornate armor gleaming in the light of the Laucnar. "My lord, the succession laws clearly state-"

"The laws?" Bright laughed, holding the orb even higher. Its glow intensified, making several courtiers step back. "I hold absolute power in the palm of my hands. Your laws mean nothing now. There is only *my* law."

The guard captain hesitated, then slowly sank to one knee. One by one, the others followed suit until the entire court knelt before him. Bright ascended the steps to the throne, careful not to slip in what remained of his predecessor.

"Clean this up," he ordered, settling onto the golden seat. "And summon the imperial council. I have new decrees to issue."

As servants rushed to remove all traces of the former emperor, Bright studied the orb in his hand. Such a small thing to hold such devastating power. He remembered finding it in the mines, remembered the way it had called to him. Now it felt like an extension of his own body, its energy pulsing in sync with his heartbeat.

The council members filed in, their elaborate robes rustling as they bowed deeply. Bright noted the fear in their eyes, the way they avoided looking directly at him or the Laucnar. Good. Fear will keep them in line.

"My emperor," the chief councilor began, his voice trembling slightly. "We await your commands."

Bright leaned back on the throne, savoring the moment. "First, all planetary governors will reaffirm their loyalty to me personally. Any who refuse will be... replaced."

"Of course, my lord. It shall be done immediately."

"Second, I want a complete inventory of all military assets, including ships, weapons, troops - everything."

The military adviser stepped forward. "The imperial fleet stands ready to serve, my emperor."

"Good." Bright smiled, though there was no warmth in it. "Because we're going to need them."

As the council scurried to carry out his orders, Bright couldn't help but marvel at how smoothly everything had gone.

One touch of the orb, and an entire galactic empire fell into his lap. These people, so bound by their traditions and hierarchies, simply transferred their loyalty to whoever sat on the throne. Of course, his power *was* absolute as long as he possessed the Laucnar.

"Too easy," he muttered to himself, turning the Laucnar over in his hands. "They're all so eager to please their new master."

A servant approached him with a datapad. "The governors' responses are already coming in, my emperor. All pledge their complete loyalty."

"All of them?" Bright raised an eyebrow. "Without a single objection?"

"Yes, my lord. They seem most... enthusiastic about serving under your rule."

Bright dismissed the servant with a wave. Something wasn't right. No resistance, no challenges to his authority, not even a token protest from the dead emperor's supporters? People didn't just roll over and accept new leadership like this, especially not in an empire spanning dozens of worlds, did they? No, of course they didn't!

He studied the faces of the courtiers and officials milling about the throne room. Their fear seemed genuine enough, but there was something else in their expressions. Anticipation? Relief? As if they'd been waiting for this very moment.

Bright's wrist device chimed:

Galactic Empire unlocked
Emperor of Galaxy protocols and skills engaged

Warning: Ruling the galaxy is not for the faint of heart, You will face constant challenges to your throne and your life
Warning: Failure will result in assassination
Proceed? Y/N

Amused, Bright casually pressed Y.

Chapter 13: Conscription

D amien's wrist device chimed:

Archive data core located
Warning: Removal will trigger security systems
Proceed? Y/N

Damien glanced at his companions. "Ready?" They nodded, weapons raised. He pressed Y on his wrist device and lifted the glowing data core from its pedestal. Alarms blared through the archives, their piercing wails echoing off the ancient walls. Red warning lights strobed across the chamber.

"Here!" Ris pulled out the containment units Vennah had given them. He activated the first one, creating a shimmering energy field. "Quick, before the security systems kick in and trap us in here!"

Damien carefully placed the core into the containment field. The crystal pulsed brighter for a moment before settling into a steady glow.

"How are we supposed to read what's on this thing?" Reyes asked, eyeing the core.

"Thinking like a true engineer!" Ris mused, "the wrist devices should interface with it once we get it secured on the shuttle," he said. "At least, I think they will."

The ground shook beneath their feet as hidden machinery ground to life within the auxiliary archive walls.

"Time to go!" Damien shouted. They sprinted back through the ancient tech lined chambers and up the stairs, the alarms growing fainter behind them.

Damien's lungs burned as they raced through the forest toward the shuttle. He sucked in the pine scented air with every step. His newly upgraded flight suit helped regulate his temperature, but his muscles still protested the sustained sprint. Too much drink and not enough exercise was catching up with him.

They burst into the clearing where they'd left the shuttle. Amelia stood at the entrance ramp, waving them forward frantically. "Get in! We've got company!"

Damien vaulted up the ramp, the others close behind. He slid into the pilot's seat where Mic had already powered up the engines.

"The cloaking device isn't working against their sensors," Amelia reported, checking the scanner readouts. "The Davosi destroyer detected us as soon as they entered orbit. They're moving to intercept us if we try to escape the planet."

"How long until they're in position?" Damien's hands flew across the controls, bringing systems online.

"Minutes. They're already landing troops in the area."

The shuttle's engines whined as Damien pushed them to full power. The craft lifted off, branches snapping against the hull as they rose through the canopy. He angled the nose up sharply, aiming for space.

"Strap in!" He called back to the others. "This is going to get rough!"

The shuttle shot upward, breaking through the atmosphere at a steep angle. Warning lights flashed across his console as the inertial dampeners struggled to compensate. Damien ignored them, focusing on putting as much distance between them and the surface as possible.

"Davosi destroyer is zeroing in on our descent," Amelia said.

Damien turned the shuttle sharply and increased speed through the upper atmosphere. "I'll lose them by punching into space at a different angle."

"They are compensating." Amelia reported.

Damien made few adjustments and exited the ionosphere. The second he was in space he did a quick burst with the hyperdrive. They propelled forward.

"Ugh, Mic get sick. What that maneuver?"

"Dangerous is what it was." Reyes scolded, "You could have buckled the engines or ran us straight though something."

"Or I could have saved all our asses which is exactly what I did." He worked the buttons on the console as the alarms screamed at him.

"Destroyer still in pursuit. They altered their course to follow." Amelia said while adjusting the short term sensors.

Damien pointed to the navigation station, "Ris, or whomever, does anyone have any skill at navigation? I cant make the hyperdrive calculations and keep us alive and away from that destroyer at the same time."

Ris shook his head, "I don't have a clue."

"I know how to do it." Amelia said. She moved to the navigation controls and Reyes took her spot at the sensors.

"Why is our medical doctor so good at sensors and nav control while the rest of you can't do anything on board ship?" Damien chided.

Amelia chuckled, "Hypochondriacs tend to have a lot of contingency plans in case they have to get out of some place fast."

The shuttle lurched and complained every time Damien tried to coax more power and speed from the engines. "This shuttle is a POS!" He said. "It has almost no power."

"Destroyer bearing 774 mark 6 and closing," Reyes said.

"They are powering weapons," Amelia said. "Long range sensors confirms there is a mining planet but we will never reach it before the destroyer catches up with us."

"Punch it, Damien," Ris said.

"I'm giving her all I've got, Ris. This thing doesn't have a very reliable hyperdrive and I'm not a miracle worker."

"I think those are my lines," Reyes said.

"Stop the joking around, guys. We are in real trouble here." Amelia scolded.

Reyes slid to the edge of his seat, "What the hell? The destroyer is breaking up. I am detecting explosions throughout the ship on all decks. There is another ship coming into orbit. It's an Imperial escort packing enough firepower to level a planet."

"They're hailing us," Amelia said.

"On speakers.' Ris commanded.

"Shuttlecraft, this is the Imperial star escort ISS Machina. Prepare to land in our shuttle bay."

"Out of frying pan into fire," Mic said.

"We can't have them chasing us to the mining planet," Ris said. "Confirm the landing."

"ISS Machina, what is the purpose of landing in your shuttle bay?" Damien asked.

"We are in need of medical personnel. We would like to borrow yours for a few hours."

"Negative, ISS Machina. We need our science and medical officer where she is." Damien said. he flipped off the comms, "Hell, she's the only one of you who can co-pilot!"

"It is not a request, Shuttlecraft, you will comply."

"How did they even know we had a doctor?" Ris asked.

"Uh oh, we are caught in a tractor beam," Damien said as he tried to reverse the engines and break free. "I can't resist it. It's too powerful and we might as well be made of tissue paper." He released the engine throttle before the alarms started up again.

The Imperial ship guided the shuttle in to its shuttle bay. Troopers were waiting to force the door open but Damien opened it before they could tear it down. The troopers entered the shuttle and grabbed Amelia. They began to escort her kicking and screaming out the shuttle hatch.

Mic made a move but Ris stopped him, "You might get her hurt or killed." Mic nodded and relented.

Ris stepped up to the troopers instead. "Hey, how do you know for sure she's the medical personnel. I am the doctor of this ship." The trooper ignored him and still took Amelia with force by the arm. The extra troopers aimed their guns to keep Damien and the others at bay until Amelia was completely escorted off the shuttle. Once they had her, they buttoned the craft back up.

"Open the door," Ris said.

"I can't it's not responding. The bay doors of the Imperial escort are opening. I think they're about to forcibly throw us off the ship." The shuttle began to slide out the back of the bay. "Yep, they are using a repulsor beam to shoot us out of the bay and away from the ship."

The shuttle drifted out into space as the ISS Machina went to hyperspace.

"Someone knew exactly who she was," Ris said. "Pursuit course."

"No way. This shuttle would never make it. I am detecting micro fractures all over the hull now. The tractor and repulsor beams have ruined this shuttle's structural integrity. We might not even make it to the mining planet now." Damien said.

"Set a course for the mining planet. Best speed that will allow this piece of crap to stay together. We will have to make repairs and trace their route afterward."

"And then what?" Reyes asked. "That's an Imperial ship and it blew the Devosi destroyer away without so much as a skirmish."

Ris sighed, "We have to go after her."

Cornelius put his hand on Ris' shoulder, "Don't listen to Reyes. He's just scared and short sighted. We will think of something."

Ris nodded while Reyes sat back in his seat crossing his arms.

"All right," Damien said, "I'm powering up the engines and navigation, but I am going to have to do some clever flying to get us to any nearby planet."

"What about hyperdrive?" Ris asked.

"I will work on stabilizing it if Damien can hold things together." Reyes told him.

"Okay, I am engaging the engines and setting a course so I can activate the hyperdrive." The ship began to move and once he had the navigation programmed, Damien engaged the hyperdrive. Immediately red warning lights came on and he began his hour long dance of compensating for system failures.

At the halfway point, Damien's knuckles whitened on the shuttle controls as yet another warning light flashed across his console. The hull integrity was down to 23% and dropping.

Every slight course correction sent shudders through the damaged frame.

"How much longer?" Mic asked through clenched teeth, his massive hands leaving dents in the armrests of his seat.

"We're approaching the mining planet's atmosphere now," Damien said, trying to sound more confident than he felt. "Just hold it together a little longer." He wasn't sure if he was talking to the shuttle or himself.

The mining planet loomed large in their viewport, its surface scarred by countless excavation sites. Damien checked his instruments again - the approach angle had to be perfect or they'd burn up on entry.

"Hull breach on deck two!" Reyes called out from the engineering station. "Emergency force fields are failing!"

"This thing has a deck two?" Ris commented.

"More like a luggage cargo hold." Reyes answered.

"Reroute power from non-essential systems," Damien ordered, his eyes fixed on the rapidly approaching atmosphere. The shuttle groaned as they hit the outer layers, the hull temperature began climbing rapidly.

Mic muttered something that sounded like a prayer in his native tongue. The alien warrior had faced down countless enemies without flinching, but space flight nearly did him in.

"Life support is critical," Cornelius reported. "We're losing atmosphere faster than the system can compensate."

Damien nodded grimly. "We'll be on the ground before it matters - one way or another."

The shuttle bucked violently as they entered the lower atmosphere. Warning klaxons blared as multiple systems failed simultaneously. Damien fought the controls, trying to maintain some semblance of stability as pieces of the outer hull began tearing away.

"Landing thrusters offline!" Reyes shouted over the clatter of multiple alarms.

"Of course they are," Damien muttered. He diverted what little power remained to the maneuvering thrusters. It wouldn't be enough for a proper landing, but it might keep them from becoming a smoking crater.

The ground rushed up to meet them through breaks in the cloud cover. Damien could make out the sprawling complex of a mining facility below.

"Structural integrity failing!" Reyes' voice cracked with panic. "We're breaking apart!"

"Mic no like this!" The alien warrior had his eyes squeezed shut, his massive frame trembling.

Damien ignored them both, focusing entirely on keeping the dying shuttle airborne for just a few more seconds. The hull screamed in protest as he pulled back on the controls, trying to level their descent. More warning lights flashed across his console as critical systems failed one after another.

"Life support failure imminent," the computer announced in an eerily calm voice.

"Shut up!" Damien snapped at the machine. He could see individual buildings now as they continued their barely controlled plummet toward the surface. The shuttle's frame groaned ominously, pieces of the hull continuing to tear away in their wake.

"We're not going to make it!" Cornelius muttered between clinched teeth.

"Yes, we are!" Damien fought the controls as the shuttle started to roll.

"Hull breach on deck one!" Reyes called out. "Force fields completely offline!"

The shuttle lurched violently as another section of hull tore away. Warning lights flashed across every console as the life support system gave out completely. Damien could hear the wind howling through gaps in the failing structure as they plummeted toward the mining planet's surface.

Chapter 14: Mining Planet

Pieces of the ship continued to shear off in the heat of the atmosphere, ripping away in sheets of burning metal. Some pieces from the fore twisted and gouged the sides of the ship as they bent back taking new chunks of metal with them as they sailed by. Superheated air began to blow through the cracks. The only thing that kept them from being burned to a crisp was the secondary forcefields that had kicked on after the failure of the main structural fields.

"I'm not sure this thing is going to hold together," Damien said as they set course for the main mining platform.

"Mining platform A, this is Ris Harne of house Harne. Come in please."

"This is platform A. Please submit House Harne transmission code."

"I don't have the bloody house code. Emergency, emergency, please comply."

"Sorry unknown vessel. Without the code, I can't identify you or authorize your landing at our facilities. Please alter your course and leave Harne Mining."

"I am Prince Harne of House Harne. If I am not who I say I am you can arrest me on the platform, but if I am who I say I am you are going to be in a shitload of trouble. We are landing!"

There was a long silence on the other end, "Status, Harne ship?" the voice was a different person.

"Damaged and coming in hot."

"Proceed to platform D, away from anything that might be volatile. Are you able to land?"

Ris looked at Damien who nodded, "Yes, we can land...maybe." He looked at the landing controls and noticed an alarm flashing on that system as well.

"Emergency crews will be on standby," The voice said.

Damien pulled on the controls and managed to get most of the landing fins and vents deployed. A couple of vent covers flew off in fiery defiance. "Retro thrusters at maximum." He said as he headed for platform D. The ship tilted sideways as the landing gear literally broke out of the damaged ship and extended. Damien let out a sigh of relief, "Landing gear locked, thank God."

The ship shuttered as he brought it to a full stop above their destination. At the last second, the engines failed and cut out dropping the ship from a height of twenty feet. It slammed hard onto the surface of the platform. A few seconds after impact, one of the landing pods gave way and the ship fell lopsided to the left.

"You know what they say. Any landing you can walk away from is a good one." Reyes said with a smile. Damien just glared at him.

They exited the ship to the mining planet authorities waiting for them. Ris looked back at the ship and inspected the damage. It was much worse than he imagined.

"Sirs," one of the men in uniform said, "which one of you is Master Harne?"

"I'm Harne, Ris Harne."

"Sir, we have instructions to take you to the administration building. It's just up the way from here."

"I'll stay with the ship and effect repairs," Damien said. "She's junk, but she's all we have."

"I'm sorry sir but all of you are required to come with us." The uniformed officer said.

"Can your men fix that ship? We need it to go after one of our own as soon as possible." Ris asked.

The man looked back at the ship. "I'm not part of the platform repair crew, sir."

"Make an educated guess then," Ris said sarcastically fighting his frustration and irritation and losing.

"From what I have seen, our crews could rebuild it and then some." The man said. "Is that answer more satisfactory to you, sir?"

"We'll discuss that attitude of yours before this is all over," Ris said. "I know you don't believe I am who I say I am but you're going to find out soon enough."

The officer thinly grinned and lead them into the station. They took an elevator to a huge corner office with a massive picture window facing the platform presumably so the administrator could keep an eye on the entire area from his desk. Damien and Mic were shown to a seat opposite the window while Reyes and Ris sat facing the desk. The uniformed officers took positions at the door like guards. An administrator entered the room a few minutes later. He was portly and balding. He wore what must have passed as a business suit on this planet. It was a dark fabric similar to the suits from back home but it had about four more pockets sewn on the breast.

"I am administrator Felder. I oversee this facility. One of you claims to be a prince of House Harne?"

"I do not claim it. I am a prince of the house Harne." Ris said. He looked at Damien who was now standing with a hand over his forehead.

"Um, Ris."

"Not now Damien. Sit down" Ris said. He addressed the administrator. I demand you repair the ship we came in on as soon as possible."

"Ris, I really think…"

"I'm handling this, Damien," Ris said. "Where was I?"

"You were demanding." The administrator said.

"Right, what do I have to do to convince you I am who I say I am?"

The administrator motioned to one of the officers and he left. "We have a simple blood test if his majesty would not mind."

"I don't think I like your tone, administrator."

Damien was fidgeting, "Ris!"

"What is it?" Ris turned to Damien angrily.

"Ship being salvaged." Mic stated. "Crew dismantling it now."

"What?" Ris turned to the window to see a horde of crew members covering the ship like ants with all sorts of equipment dismantling the ship. In fact, in the short time, they had been talking to the administrator the crew had managed to get all the external covering off it and were cutting into the metal frame. "Wasn't that ship scalding hot? How are they crawling all over it like that?"

"My crew is very efficient. They are also very good with hot metal." The administrator said. "Now, what were you demanding?"

Ris could feel the blood in his veins boil, "where is this test?"

The door opened and a man in a white lab coat came in with a tubular contraption. The administrator nodded to him and he placed it at Ris's neck. A sharp prick and it was over. The man put a bandage on the small incision. He looked at the tubular machine and his eyes went wide. He bowed immediately.

"Well?" The administrator asked.

The man in the white coat nodded, "He is of house Harne, sir. Also, there is a ninety-nine point two four probability he is the prince."

Felder went ashen as the blood drained from his face and he bowed, "Forgive me, majesty. I doubted you. The way you carry yourself, what you are wearing, and the company you keep all seemed wrong for one of the royal house."

"My ship?"

Felder pressed a button on his desk.

"Platform D."

"This is Felder, status of the salvage?"

"We will have it completed in under an hour, administrator."

"Reverse it and put the thing back together."

"Administrator?"

"You heard me."

"But sir, that would be impossible. We have cut the frame into pieces, reassembly at this point can't be done. We would have to rebuild it from the ground up."

Felder's face became even more ashen, "Very well then, take the salvaged material to processing and have fabrication and construction contact me immediately."

"Yes, sir."

Felder bowed again, "We have many plans and specs, your majesty. We can build you a brand-new ship from your salvage."

"How long will that take?"

"If we allocate the entire team we can do it in two solar months."

Reyes cleared his throat, "We can't wait that long."

"This facility has a shipyard?" Ris asked. "The rumors Damien heard are true?"

"We do not have a ship yard officially, your majesty."

"What does that mean?"

"You are unaware of what we do here?"

"Why don't you enlighten me?"

"Well, you see, your majesty, we are close to territory owned by house Davosi. We have certain...objectives... your family wants us to complete."

"And one of them is shipbuilding?"

Felder glanced at the others, "Well..."

"You can tell us all. I trust all of my friends here."

Felder sniffed, "very well." He pushed some more buttons on the glass top of his desk and the window changed into an opaque screen. Mechanical schematics appeared in 3D. "This mining facility is a ruse. We do mine here but we use the vast resources to build armaments and ships for house Harne. In fact, recent intelligence suggests we are in for an attack by house Davosi very soon. This is the reason for the way you were treated when you arrived. We almost blew your ship out of the sky but we feared the Davosi spies might take that as a sign of war and we are not quite ready for that yet."

"Do you have any ships near completion?"

Felder's face lit up, "Yes, we do. I see. You want us to complete one for you."

Ris smiled at Damien, "Yes, I do but with a few modifications of our own."

The door opened and a man dressed in an all-black uniform entered. He carried what looked like a horse riding crop with him. His face was sucked in like he had just died by lemon sucking. A thin mustache on the edge of his upper lip made him appear like a 1930s villain. He took a moment to examine the schematics on the window before he glared ominously at Felder, "What is all this, Felder?"

"He is the prince, Desmond," Felder replied.

"And you are?" Ris asked. The man glared at him but said nothing.

"He is Desmond Styne, head of security for this facility," Felder said. "He considers himself overseer of all that goes on here."

"Turn it off. Turn it all off immediately!" Styne said. "We don't know this is our prince."

"We tested him, Desmond."

"Tested him how?"

"By blood, DNA. He is of house Harne."

"I don't know him."

Ris made a point to stand close and overbearing, "As far as you are concerned, I might as well be the emperor."

"As far as I am concerned, you are my prisoner here." He went to Felder's desk and cut the signal to the screen. A green light began to blink. "Ah, here is my communication with the patriarch. He pressed the green button and the screen turned to an older man with grey in his temples and beard. Ris knew it was his grandfather from the background information Dr. Thomas Bright had told him back home. Ris swallowed hard as Styne addressed the man as your majesty. He wasn't sure if he would be recognized by the family. He had rolled high on his background and Bright said he was a prince of the Harne family but he had never tested it face to face before.

"Do you recognize this man, your majesty?" Styne was saying. Ris stood closer to the screen as the man squinted.

"What the devil are you doing there, Ris?" The man asked. "I thought you were on a diplomatic mission to Davosi Prime."

"I got sidetracked, grandfather. I decided to oversee the progress here at the mining facility."

The old man frowned, "Sidetracked! Well, I can see by whom. Storm! I thought I told you to... no, I commanded you to cease your gallivanting around or this would be your last mission with my grandson."

"Um, sorry sir," Damien said.

"Sorry indeed!" He took a drink of something from a mug that said world's greatest grandfather on the side in big red letters, "So, what do you want so badly you had to call me away from breakfast, Styne, or did you just make the mistake of contacting me only to identify my own grandson for you? Don't you have the standard blood tests we sent you for that?"

"Forgive me, your majesty, He arrived without knowing the house Harne family code. You told me to inform you if that ever happened."

"All right, Ris. What is the problem?"

"I must have forgotten it, grandfather."

"Forgotten it?" He looked concerned now.

"Aye, sir."

The old man put down his mug, "What is the code I gave you personally for this occasion then? Tell me that."

Ris began to sweat. He didn't know the code. Out of desperation, he guessed, "It's mother's name, Moira."

"And?"

"I am the third child so Moira 3." It wasn't completely a guess, he vaguely remembered Bright saying something similar in one of their gaming sessions.

The old man squinted and picked up his mug once more, "Styne, my grandson had better have a pleasant visit at you facility or I will be personally offended. I am quite certain you would not want to offend me on purpose."

"No, your majesty." The old man had already cut the feed.

Styne bowed, "Forgive me, your majesty, but surely you realize I was only doing my job."

"Of course, Styne," Ris said. "You may go now."

"Yes, sir, if you need anything, please don't hesitate to send for me."

Ris nodded and turned to Felder, "All right, now that we understand each other, we have work to do. We have a ship to finish building and a friend to rescue."

"Mic hungry now," Mic said. "When we eat?"

"I will send a message to the kitchen at once. We shall have a feast prepared fit for the prince and his companions," Felder said.

Chapter 15: Revelations

The kitchen staff arranged a magnificent meal for the five of them but Damien, in particular, worked harder on the plans for the new ship than he did eating the food. It wasn't just the urgency of getting back out there to rescue Amelia, it was also to make the ship tougher so it could stand up to more firepower. He wanted more redundant systems as well in case of failures or damage. The others left it up to him to choose from the nearly completed ships in the shipyard and he chose a nimble, fast ship with ample cargo space and room enough to accommodate all of them. Now, it was really just a matter of implementing the upgrades since the ship was so near to completion when he selected it. In fact, it was just a few weeks from its initial shakedown. He estimated the modifications, if the crews worked with him as a priority, would only extend that time maybe a month or two.

He chuckled when he looked up from his schematics to see Mic wolfing down enough food for the both of them. Reyes seemed preoccupied with the workings of the mine and he could see Ris remained anxious to go after Amelia. His friend felt guilty because he couldn't do more to prevent her abduction. He knew Ris also struggled with the question of who would want to take her and why? Damien knew the answer and so did Ris he surmised. It had to be someone who knew her, what she was, and who they were. It had to be their one missing friend, the one they had not met up with yet, who had a different path laid out before him. It had to be Thomas Bright. The question they pondered most was what happened to him and how did he view the others. He had to be the antagonist of this story somehow. Damien knew he would eventually need to get Ris to face that possibility. It would be difficult, because one of the threads of memory he still had from his former life was that Ris and Thomas had been best friends since they were very young.

"I noticed a triple lockdown system on all the doors. What's all that about?" Reyes was asking Felder.

"Styne tripled our security due to an incident with our former administrator, my predecessor."

"Oh?"

Felder glanced at Ris, "Don't you know the story? Is your house so good at keeping secrets from its own members?"

"I have been on assignment in space. I haven't had contact with the family for some time. What's the story?" Ris asked.

"The former administrator went berserk and killed three people down in the mine. Supposedly he was corrupted by an artifact buried deep underground. The indigenous people of this planet claim an ancient space faring race once crashed a ship here and buried something deep in the ground before they all committed suicide. It's an old superstitious tale. I didn't put any stock into it until one day a miner sent word up here that they had stumbled upon a glowing blue-green orb about the size of a baseball in the shaft. The administrator went to see in person. The next thing I knew, I was being called to the mine. Administrator Bright had killed two people and was heading for the shipyard. He was gone by the time I got there. Being second in command, I was elevated to administrator."

"So, the locks are to prevent people from leaving the mines if they discover any more artifacts," Reyes asked. Felder nodded.

"Bright!" The name Damien was just thinking about almost made his ears burn. "Thomas Bright?" He glanced at Ris who was shaking his head in disbelief.

"Yes! I am surprised you know him. Then again, we are in the presence of Prince Harne, surely he knows who runs his family's clandestine facilities."

"Is there any security footage of this glowing ball or the Administrator?" Ris asked.

"I believe so. I will call Styne to bring it here if there is." He went to the communications console. "Styne, can you bring the footage of Dr. Bright and the laucnar to the dining hall? His Majesty would like to see it."

There was a grumble at the other end, "Very well, give me a few minutes to locate it."

Reyes whispered in Ris's ear, "The laucnar? You don't think?"

"Yes, that it sounds a lot like loc-nar, the evil gem from that weird cult movie Heavy Metal," Ris said. "Yeah, it crossed my mind. If something like that exists here, then I know why the professor was digging on the first planet and why the empire is so interested in us all of the sudden."

Cornelius was chuckling, "I knew it. I knew he would end up with an evil gem someday. It has to be him, it's so appropriate he would name it something like the Laucnar with a soft vowel sound. I wonder why he didn't just blatantly call it the Loc-nar?"

"Because he's Thomas," Damien said, "He had to put his own spin on it. He would never have just outright copied the name."

"True." Cornelius agreed.

Styne entered the dining hall and went directly to the communications console. He typed in a few commands and then sent the image to the large glass two-way screen at the side of the hall. The images became clearer and then he froze the image on a glowing blue-green ball. It was difficult to see because of the angle, but it was there.

"Can you show us the former administrator's face?" Ris asked.

After his usual grumble, Styne played the image again and stopped on the face of Administrator Bright.

"That him. Dr. Thomas Bright." Mic said.

Felder responded, "There was doubt? I don't understand."

"We know him very well but we have not seen him in a very long time is all," Ris assured him. "We didn't know where he ended up after we got separated the last time.

"I'll be damned. Thomas really does have the evil gem!" Cornelius said. "I was just joking about it, but now that I see it's real I can't believe it." He turned to the others, "We are screwed."

"I thought it was just a joke too," Reyes said. I always thought Bright was..."

"Dr. Bright." Ris corrected casting an uneasy eye at Felder.

"Dr. Bright was always a bit of a goody goody." Reyes finished.

"Except when gaming." Cornelius stated, "It was like he let all his pent-up frustration of everyday life come to the fore. He is ruthless when playing villains. That's why I made the joke of the evil gem in the first place." He laughed nervously while glancing at the image on the screen.

"He is good person. Not sure he would turn bad so easy." Mic said.

Ris sighed and met Damien's gaze as he looked back at him. He knew at that moment what Ris was thinking. He was thinking the same thing he was. The books the game was modeled after included the dreaded evil gem from all the play sessions of Space Lords of Strata they invented back home. The Laucnar was a playoff of the green gem in the movie and therefore it would be just as evil if not, even more, corrupting like the one ring. It would corrupt the gentlest of souls...eventually, and it was tailored to Thomas as his own special backstory.

"We have to rescue him," Reyes said.

"I think I know what happened to Amelia now," Damien spoke up. "Dr. Bright once confessed to me that he had a crush on Amelia. With the evil gem in his possession, he would finally have the confidence to pursue her."

"Damien!" Ris scolded.

"What? We all already knew it. It had to be him."

"Remind me never to tell you any of my secrets." Ris said.

"Oh, so you think I'm ratting out secrets. May I remind you this might have started off as a game but it has very real consequences. It's better we face the possibilities."

Felder shook his head, "I don't know what you are talking about with games and evil gems. You are all a confusing lot. We do not play games here, I assure you."

Ris coughed, "We should not be speaking of this here."

Cornelius nodded, "I don't think so either."

"it's a bit of a stretch that Bright would want Amelia because if a schoolyard crush don't you think," Reyes said. "Why would he fixate on her when he has all that evil power to command. I don't think he would worry at all about her. That was an Imperial ship and Imperial troopers who took her."

"Quiet Dean," Ris commanded.

"The Imperials took your friend? Felder asked.

"See what you have done now, Dean?" Cornelius asked.

"Yeah, sorry. Well, I guess the cat is out of the bag now, Dean said. "Yes, Imperials took her. Does Bright have any connection to the Empire?"

Felder put his hand to his chin, "hmm, I don't know. He took the Laucnar and left for parts unknown. I guess it's possible." He turned to his chief security officer. "Do you have any idea, any intel?"

"No, I have no idea," Styne said. "He left here and we have not heard another word about or from him since. Although, I did get a strange report from the Imperial channels that there was some sort of altercation on their home world. It might have been our man. I only glanced at the communique."

"Not everything is adding up. We need to get off this planet to investigate." Ris moved to the window viewscreen to look again at the image of Dr. Thomas Bright frozen upon it, "We need to investigate what happened to Bright. Felder, I want a crew rotated on our ship day and night until it's done. In the meantime, I want to tour the weapons and planetary defense facilities. I have a feeling we have more than just house Davosi to worry about now." He turned to Styne, "and if you can find that communique, I would also like to read it."

"Yes majesty, I shall endeavor to find it." Styne said.

"Good, let's see if we can get moving on this. I have the feeling things are about to heat up."

Chapter 16: Repair, Rebuild, Level Up!

Damien leaned back in his chair as Styne and Felder left with Ris, the remnants of their feast spread across the dining hall table. His mind wandered to Amelia, hoping she was safe wherever the Imperials had taken her. He didn't think Bright would ever hurt her but he was unpredictable now that he had his evil gem.

"Anyone else notice our memories are getting clearer?" he asked, swirling the remains of his drink. "I mean, not our real memories - those are fading. But I remember my first solo flight through the Rigel system like it happened yesterday."

"Tell me about it," Reyes said, tinkering with some mining equipment he'd picked up. "I can recall every detail of the engine modifications I made to the Stellar Wind, but I can't remember what I did for a living before... before all this."

Mic grunted, he had resumed demolishing his forth plate of food. "Mic remember crushing space pirates on Centauri Six. Good fight."

"That never actually happened though," Damien pointed out. "Those are just character backstories we made up."

"Real enough now," Cornelius said darkly. He'd been unusually quiet since seeing Bright's image and realizing what he was becoming due to the Laucnar.

Damien stood and walked to one of the vast windows overlooking the mining facility. Workers scurried about like ants far below, already beginning to ramp up production to complete the modifications to their new ship in record time as Ris commanded. "You know what's weird? I actually feel more comfortable in space now than I do on solid ground." He scanned the rooms below their vantage point. This *is* real! It exists now, Why should we not embrace it?

"You're saying that because you're becoming your character," Cornelius said, joining him at the window. "We all are. The question is, how much of us will be left when this is over?"

"If it's ever over," Damien muttered. He checked his wrist device - still level ten, but new skills and memories seemed to be unlocking constantly now. "At least for now, this is our reality. Remember when we used to joke about how I always got lost and fell off things? When I think about it, I am clumsy because my attitude toward life is fuck it!"

"Used to?" Cornelius smirked. "You literally tripped getting off the shuttle earlier, and that was always your attitude toward life as I recall."

"That was different! The landing gear was broken."

"Sure it was." Cornelius's grin widened. "Just like that time on Proxima B when you 'accidentally' walked into the women's decontamination chamber?"

"That never-" Damien stopped himself. "Wait, did that actually happen or is that just part of the backstory?"

"Sheez dudes! Does it matter anymore?" Reyes asked, not looking up from his tinkering. "What was so great about us before anyway. Look at where we are! Look at how far we have come!"

"I guess it doesn't matter, does it." Damien returned to his seat, nearly missing it in the process. The others snickered. "Oh shut up."

"At least your piloting skills are improving," Cornelius offered diplomatically. "Even if your basic coordination isn't."

"Speaking of skills," Damien checked his interface again. "Anyone else notice we're gaining them faster now? I've got three new pilot specializations I don't remember learning."

"System's probably accelerating the integration," Reyes suggested. "The more we accept our new memories, the faster it can overlay the skills."

"Mic just want to smash things," the alien warrior grumbled. "Too much talking."

"You're developing quite the vocabulary there, big guy," Damien said. "What happened to the broken English?"

Mic straightened. "Mic... I mean, I find proper grammar emerging with increased neural integration." He immediately slumped back. "But smashing still better."

They all stared at him for a moment before bursting into laughter. Even stick- in-the-mud Cornelius cracked a smile.

"Well, at least we haven't lost our sense of humor," Damien said, wiping his eyes. "Though I'm pretty sure I never used to laugh this much at near-death experiences."

"That's your pilot personality coming through," Cornelius said. "Always making light of danger."

"Maybe." Damien stood again, more carefully this time. "I just hope whatever's happening to us, whatever we're becoming, we can still help Amelia and Bright. They're our friends, even if I'm starting to forget how we met. We don't have to accept everything, do we?"

"We'll find them," Reyes assured him, finally setting aside his project. "Though I have to admit, I'm more worried about what we'll find when we do." He wrinkled his forehead, "It feels like I am forgetting something. Didn't we have an archives data core with us earlier?"

"Come to think of it, yes. Where is it now?: Damien asked.

"Containment?" Reyes asked.

"We'll have to aske Ris where he put it. You don't think it's what's messing with our memories do you? You're the engineer."

"It could be. I'm pretty sure the idea was for us to have completely forgotten everything of our lives before and to have fully embraced our rolls here by now. The Jaddus Collective underestimated the human need to hold on to things especially memories."

"It not worry others we are losing fight to hold on to old selves?" Mic asked.

Cornelius smacked his lips as he used a toothpick to dislodge some of the food sticking from earlier, "Nope, it doesn't worry me. I don't believe every memory will ever be completely erased from before. I think we are meant to get to a certain level of memory loss in order to be successful here. I say we stop fighting it an embrace it. We will be better off for it and if the Alteri are true to their word, I think once we complete this thing, they will return us to normal."

"If they are still in control." Damien added. "Still, the data core is part of the story in this reality. Our wrist devices wouldn't let us skip out on it. I think it's linked to our memories."

Reyes began tinkering again, "I for one don't miss what I can't remember."

Damien watched the construction crews again through the window. The new ship was taking shape, its sleek lines already visible in the skeletal framework. His wrist device chimed, indicating another skill upgrade was available.

"Again, is anyone else getting these constant updates?" he asked, scrolling through the interface. "I just unlocked advanced atmospheric entry protocols and something called 'stellar drift compensation.'"

Reyes looked up from the workbench where he'd been modifying their weapons. "Tell me about it. I've got quantum harmonics and temporal shield modulation now. Not sure what half of these even do."

"I suspect you soon will." Damien said.

"Temporal shields?" Cornelius whistled. "That's high-level tech."

"Says the guy who just got enhanced infiltration and diplomatic immunity," Damien said, looking at his display over his shoulder.

Reyes snapped his fingers, "You know what our ship needs?"

"What?" Damien asked.

"A female artificial intelligence assistant. Some kind of android maybe."

"Ah, someone or some thing who can help maintain the ship and even fly it in emergencies." Damien agreed. "Can you find something like that and program it to the ship?"

"I don't see why not." Reyes said as he made his way to the computer console to research it.

"Hey, this are useful skills!" Cornelius said. "I can feel it. I can't wait to use some of my new diplomatic and subterfuge skills. "

Mic flexed his massive arms, which seemed even larger than before. "Mic get strength boost and new armor skills. Can wear heavier plate now."

"Your grammar's slipping again, big guy," Damien noted.

"Mic choose when to talk proper," the alien warrior grinned. "More fun this way."

"At least the skills are useful," Reyes said. "I've already applied the quantum harmonics to boost our weapon output. Should give us an edge when we go after Amelia." He typed something into the computer, "Ah, here was go, android tech."

Damien's device chimed again. "Zero-G maneuvering just unlocked. That could come in handy." He scrolled through the interface. "Anyone else notice we're getting these upgrades faster now?"

"You said that already." Reyes said, "You're repeating yourself." He stiffened, "Wait, is this normal? What is happening to us?"

"The system's probably compensating for our accelerated timeline,"Cornelius suggested. "We're not following the normal leveling curve anymore. It might be our decision to accept the backstory memories. I do remember the hologram in the visitor's center saying he tried to level us to ten but couldn't advance us properly. He said we would get a flood of skills, remember?"

"Did he say that?" Reyes asked.

"Ugh, this messing with our heads in maddening and it's getting old. I think to get through this and beat this thing we need to just embrace it and play it through. I am making my decision now. I'm not going to fight it anymore." Damien said.

"Good," Cornelius said, checking his own device. "I'm not going to keep fighting it either. Oh, Advanced stealth protocols just came online. I can practically turn invisible now."

"Show off," Damien muttered. He turned back to the window, watching the crews work. Their new ship would be ready soon, and with these enhanced abilities, they might actually have a chance at whatever came next.

"Hey, check this out," Reyes called from the workbench. I found out how to do this from the droid tech archives just now. He held up one of their blasters, now modified with glowing blue circuits along its barrel. "The quantum harmonics let me tap into the weapon's power core directly. Should triple its output."

"Nice work," Damien said, holstering his own newly upgraded blaster. The weight felt different now, more natural. Like he'd carried it for years instead of days. "Between your upgrades and our new skills, we might actually survive this."

"Cool!" Reyes said, "Now back to the android situation." He returned to the computer console.

"Mic crush anything that get in way," the alien declared, then paused. "Also, Mic now certified in advanced battlefield medicine."

Everyone turned to stare at him.

"What? Mic like to help." He shrugged his massive shoulders. "Not just about smashing."

Damien laughed. "Well, with Amelia gone, it's good to have a backup medic. Even if he does talk like a caveman."

"Mic's bedside manner probably needs work," Cornelius smirked.

"Patient complain, Mic sedate. Very effective."

The others chuckled, but Damien noticed Reyes remained focused on researching android tech. He must have found something. "Anything interesting, Reyes?"

"Yeah, there's a new technique for programming older recreational androids for more useful tasks. it's very interesting."

"New technique?" Damien asked.

"Some of the most sophisticated positronic systems were developed to mimic human companionship. It turns out in order to make androids more human it takes a lot of clever innovation. This could work."

"We're all still getting used to these changes," Damien said. He felt the familiar surge of a new skill unlocking - something about solar wind navigation. The knowledge settled into his mind like it had always been there. "I hope we can handle learning at this pace."

"No worry about it. This meant to happen. We talk too much. Time to fulfill destiny." Mic commented.

"Well said, my friend, well said." Damien agreed.

Chapter 17: Arsenal

Using the crafting experiences and practices they had earned, Damien, Cornelius, and Reyes worked on fabricating much of the ship's materials as they could. Ris even helped so he would not fall behind in tech level. Damien's pilot skills were important to him and he leveled little else except for blaster and carousing. He had the reputation as a drinker and he wanted to make certain he could hold his liquor.

Each one of them had finally finished most their tenth level skill updates and when Reyes completed his advanced sensor array skill, he noticed several Davosi scout cruiser were headed their way on long range sensors. The mining planet was also equipped with an arsenal of weaponry and Ris surmised they may be coming to raid it. There was nothing to indicate anyone knew they were there, but it was also a possibility that the Davosi had been informed via spies of their whereabouts and had dispatched the scouts to intercept or apprehend them.

"Brace yourselves. This is it. The Davosi scout cruisers are entering orbit." Damien said.

"How much longer on our ship?" Ris asked.

Damien rolled his chair over to the nearby console and used the touch screen to check, "Primary systems are coming online but the engines still need adjusting. Looks like it's still a ways out at this point."

"I assume the Imperial probes are still out there searching, too."

"Yep," Reyes said adjusting the sensor array, "and they will likely have one or two following the Davosi ships in case they find us."

Damien adjusted in his seat and touched the screen again, "The techs are stress testing the engines. Maybe the ship is further along than I thought."

"Damn, I hope so. We had better get the ship ready or we will be in a world of trouble. Once they find this arsenal, the Empire will become very interested in this little mining planet." Ris said.

Damien nodded, "We are working on it as fast as we can. I don't see how we can move any faster and have a viable ship to fly. We have to trust it's construction and put it through a good shakedown."

"There might not be time for that. We may be putting it through its paces on the fly." Ris said.

"Crap," Reyes cursed, "Two battlecruisers just entered planetary space. Where the hell did they come from? They weren't on long range sensors. Several other vessels are now popping up on short range sensors as they come out of hyperspace as well. It's a surprise attack."

From his office, Felder opened facility-wide communications. The message came over the loudspeaker. "Battle stations, Davosi fleet ships have entered our space. Repeat battle stations." Crews began moving very quickly throughout the base. A klaxon began to sound the attack. "Activate planetary defenses."

Damien watched on the monitors in their makeshift control room as long gun barrels began to protrude from the nearby hills and the mountains to the south of the installation. The noses of drone missiles popped up out of the hillsides. Fighter ships were manned in the hangers.

As the Davosi ships came into range the missiles fired on them destroying then and raining down Davosi ship debris on the planet. A few ships broke through the defenses and started a ground assault, but were quickly taken out by the defenses as well.

Cornelius smirked, "Dumbasses, don't you know what the word arsenal means?"

Reyes manipulated the sensor control, "Don't celebrate too early. They are just throwing everything they got at us so that they can land those troop carriers."

Damien watched through the command center windows as Davosi troops poured from their landing craft. The installation's defense forces engaged them with blaster fire, but the enemy kept advancing. His fingers danced across the console, bringing up status reports on their new ship. It was getting close to now or never.

"How bad is it?" Ris asked, strapping on combat gear. "Can it fly yet?"

"Primary systems are at 80%. Life support, weapons, and engines are functional but untested. Navigation's still buggy." Damien studied the readouts. "We can fly, but it won't be pretty."

"It'll have to do." Ris powered up his sword. "Get the technicians you need for on the fly maintenance and prep for launch. I'll coordinate the defense."

Blaster fire erupted in the corridor outside. Ris rushed out to join the fighting while Damien prepared to leave for the ship. "Reyes, grab your team and meet me on the ship. We're leaving ahead of schedule."

"Are you insane? The power grid isn't properly calibrated yet!"

"Would you rather stay and explain our unauthorized construction project to the Davosi?"

He paused. "Fair point. Go, we're on our way."

Damien gathered what gear he could carry and headed for the launch bay. The sounds of combat echoed through the facility - screams, explosions, the distinctive whine of blaster fire. He rounded a corner and nearly collided with Mic, who was carrying three unconscious technicians over his shoulders.

"Found more help for ship," Mic grunted. "They try to run wrong way, so Mic... convince them."

"Good thinking, big guy. Get them aboard."

The new ship loomed before them, sleek and deadly despite its unfinished state. Reyes and his engineering team were already swarming over it, making final adjustments. Damien climbed into the cockpit and began the pre-flight sequence.

Warning lights flashed across his console as systems came online. The reactor hummed to life, but the power readings fluctuated wildly. Damien adjusted the settings, trying to stabilize the output.

"We've got company!" Cornelius shouted from the launch bay entrance. He fired several shots down the corridor. "Davosi troops, at least a dozen!"

"Ris, we need to move!" Damien called over the comm.

"Little busy!" Ris's voice crackled through static. "Hold them off for two minutes!"

Damien switched to external cameras. Ris was leading a counter-attack against the Davosi forces, his power sword carving through their ranks. But more troops kept coming.

"Reyes, how close are we?"

"Don't rush me! These power couplings could blow mid-flight if I don't balance them properly."

A blast struck the ship's hull, leaving a scorch mark. Damien's fingers tightened on the controls. "We're out of time. Get inside and finish enroute."

"That's not how engineering works!"

"It is today." Damien fired up the engines. They coughed and sputtered before settling into an uneven rhythm. "Ris, fall back now!"

The launch bay doors began to close as Ris and his men retreated inside. Cornelius provided covering fire while the engineers scrambled aboard. Damien watched the power levels spike dangerously as Reyes tried to stabilize the systems.

"Everyone strapped in?" Damien asked.

"No!" several voices shouted.

"Too bad." He punched the throttle. The ship lurched forward, nearly throwing them all off their feet. The inner launch bay doors weren't fully open, but Damien squeezed the ship through the gap, paint scraping off the hull. "One set of doors down, one set to go."

"I knew these engines were too big powerful for this ship, Reyes griped, "But you insisted."

"They'll be fine, The reactor I had installed could power a ship twice this size. You'll think me when I am able to out maneuver those ships out there." Damien yanked the controls hard as the ship careened through the outermost launch bay doors. Metal screeched against metal, and warning lights blazed across his console. The inertial dampeners weren't fully online, making every maneuver feel like riding a bucking bronco.

"Reyes! I need more power to the stabilizers!"

"I'm trying! I'm still working out the bugs in these systems!" Reyes shouted back from engineering. The deck plates rattled beneath them as the ship climbed through the atmosphere. "This is what you get with a two month refit."

"More like a two month modification." Damien corrected.

"Whatever!"

A Davosi cruiser loomed ahead, its weapons already tracking them. Damien rolled their ship into a spiral, narrowly avoiding the first volley of energy blasts. The hull groaned in protest.

"We're losing structural integrity on the port side," one of the conscripted technicians called out.

"Mic not like this flying!" The alien warrior gripped his seat with white-knuckled intensity.

Cornelius stumbled forward, barely catching himself on Damien's chair. "Can't you smooth it out a bit?"

"Sure, I'll just ask the mostly finished ship to fly better!" Damien wrestled with the controls as another blast rocked them. "Reyes, how's that cloak coming?"

"Working on it! The power grid's all wrong - we're pulling too much power from the engines! Rerouting power to pull from that ridiculously oversized reactor."

Ris maintained his composure despite being thrown against the bulkhead twice. "Those cruisers are launching fighters. We won't last long against a coordinated attack."

Damien pushed the engines harder, weaving between enemy ships. The controls fought him every step of the way, like trying to pilot through molasses. Another hit sent sparks flying from a nearby console.

"Hull breach on deck three!" someone shouted.

"Emergency force fields holding," another technician reported. "Barely."

"Got it!" Reyes's triumphant voice rang out. "Cloaking device online... now!"

The ship shimmered and vanished from view. The pursuing Davosi vessels broke off their attack, their sensors unable to track their target.

Damien's relief was short-lived as new alarms blared throughout all the bridge consoles. The engine readouts were climbing into the red zone. "Reyes..."

"I see it! The power draw from the cloak is overloading the engines. The power is not rerouting to pull from the reactor properly. We need to shut down either the cloak or the engines or the engines will blow!"

"If we cut engines, we'll be stranded," Cornelius pointed out.

"Better than exploding," Damien said, already powering down the drives. "I'll cut the inertial dampeners and we will continue at speed through the frictionless vacuum of space. The ship's momentum carried them forward as the engines fell silent. "At least the cloak is stable. How long can we maintain it?"

"Power levels are good," Reyes reported. "We've got maybe four, five hours before we need to risk starting the engines again. We'll get to work on them." I'll come to the bridge and monitor the progress from the engineering console."

Damien slumped in his chair, his hands shaking slightly from the adrenaline. "Well, that was fun. Anyone else want to try flying the unfinished ship next time?"

"No thanks! I think ground better than space!" Mic said.

Damien watched Ris pace the bridge, his friend's agitation visible in every step. Through the viewscreen, the mining facility grew smaller as they drifted away under cloak. Damien steered by thruster to keep them on course.

"What's the deal, Ris?" Damien asked.

Ris inhaled sharply, "It's just the arsenal we worked so hard to protect is now subject to enemy forces. There is a lot of firepower we're leaving there."

"You should have set charges and blown the place sky high!" Cornelius said.

"Too late now. Damn, we can't just abandon it," Ris said, "Those weapons could shift the balance of power in this entire sector."

"What do you suggest?" Damien asked, monitoring their minimal power usage. "Our ship barely made it out of there intact."

"Maybe we could rally some of House Harne's forces," Ris continued. "Stage a counter-attack before the Davosi can secure their position."

Reyes looked up from his engineering console. "The structural integrity field is still fluctuating. We'd need at least two days of repairs before we could even think about combat with this ship."

"And that's assuming we can find somewhere safe to make those repairs," Cornelius added from his tactical station.

Ris opened his mouth to respond but froze, staring at the viewscreen. Damien followed his gaze and felt his stomach drop. Three massive Imperial capital ships had just dropped out of hyperspace, their massive hulls shimmering in the starlight.

"Well, that complicates things," Damien muttered, checking their cloak's power levels again.

"The Empire must have detected the Davosi attack," Ris said quietly. "They'll crush the invasion force easily. Davosi ships will be no match against those cruisers."

"And they will claim the arsenal for themselves," Cornelius finished.

Damien watched more Imperial ships arrive, their weapon systems already powering up. The Davosi fleet looked tiny in comparison. "Sorry man, it looks like your grandfather's facility is about to become Imperial property."

"Along with all those experimental weapons," Ris gripped the back of Damien's chair. "The emperor will absolutely control the entire sector once he has that kind of firepower."

Through the viewscreen, they watched the first salvos of Imperial turbolaser fire tear into the Davosi ships. The battle was quick and completely one-sided.

"Mic think we leave at good time," the alien warrior observed from his station.

"The Empire's moving ground forces in already," Damien reported, reading the sensor data. "They're not wasting any time securing the facility."

"My grandfather's going to be furious," Ris said. "Generations of House Harne research and development, all of it falling into Imperial hands."

"Someone leaked the secret of the planet to either the Davosi, the Empire, or both." Reyes said.

"Better the Empire take it than House Davosi," Cornelius suggested. "At least the Empire maintains some pretense of law and order."

"Tell that to the planets they've subjugated," Ris shot back. He watched another Davosi ship explode under Imperial fire. "You were right, Cornelius, we should have found a way to destroy the arsenal before we left."

"There wasn't time," Damien reminded him. "We barely got ourselves out."

"Patch us in to internal sensors, Dean." Damien commanded.

"Okay, got the facility internal sensors on screen."

Internal sensors revealed the Imperial forces moving with practiced efficiency, securing the facility level by level. Damien could almost picture the Imperial troopers sweeping through the corridors they'd fled just hours ago.

"The emperor will have everything," Ris said softly. "The weapons, the shipyards, the research data. All of it."

Chapter 18: Friday the 13th

"Additional imperial vessels have joined the fray and are engaging the Davosi fleet," Ris announced.

Damien watched another explosion bloom against the starfield as the Imperial forces methodically decimated the Davosi fleet. His fingers tapped and flipped the buttons on and above the control panel, their minimal power usage leaving most systems offline.

Ris's face suddenly lit up. "Wait - the repair station! My family maintains a hidden facility on the dark side of the third moon."

"You're just mentioning this now?" Damien raised an eyebrow.

"I didn't remember until..." Ris tapped his temple. "The memories are still settling into place. But we can use the maneuvering thrusters to drift there without compromising our cloak."

Damien adjusted their trajectory with short bursts from the RCS thrusters. The battered ship responded sluggishly, but he managed to guide them into the moon's shadow.

"There." Ris pointed to what appeared to be nothing more than a crater-pocked section of the lunar surface. He rattled off a string of coordinates and Damien spotted it - a barely visible seam in the rock face.

"Doesn't look like much," Cornelius observed.

"That's the point." Ris transmitted a code sequence. Ancient machinery groaned to life as massive doors split the rock face, revealing a cavernous hangar bay beyond.

Damien eased their ship through the opening, relying more on instinct than instruments in the darkness. The landing struts creaked as they touched down on the dusty deck plates. Behind them, the camouflaged doors rumbled shut.

Warning lights shifted from red to green as the bay repressurized. Damien released a breath he hadn't realized he'd been holding as life support readings stabilized.

"This place has seen better days," Reyes said, examining the corroded support beams and outdated equipment scattered throughout the bay.

"It's perfect," Ris replied. "No one would think to look for us in this relic. You and your team can make repairs while we monitor the situation at the arsenal."

"Come on," Damien waved over the technicians they'd "recruited" from the facility. "Let's see what we can salvage from this rust pile."

"Mic help carry heavy things," the alien offered, already hefting a replacement hull plate.

"Just try not to break anything else," Reyes called after him. "We've got enough repairs already."

Damien watched the others file out toward the station's observation deck, leaving him and the engineering team to their work. Through the hangar's force field, he could still see flashes of weapons fire in the distance as the Empire secured their newest acquisition.

After a time, Ris reappeared, "What about those engine calibrations, Reyes?" he inquired. "Seems like we should make ourselves scarce. How much longer do you and the technicians need?"

After consulting his displays and his assistants, Reyes responded, "Propulsion systems are functional but remember they are still fresh off the line. They need a gentle touch to break them in. Damien, No more of those hard maneuvers like before."

"Yeah sorry, those maneuvers were necessary to keep us alive, but they were a one time thing, I hope." Damien responded.

"So, we can be underway soon?" Ris asked.

"Working on it." Reyes said with a thumbs up. "Give me a moment and I'll come back with a progress report." He turned and went with the technicians and began giving instructions.

Damien and Ris left the ship and joined the others in the control room of the station. "What does it look like out there now?"

"Fighting slowed, but Empire still winning." Mic said. "Davosi holding up better than expected."

Reyes entered the room and went to one of the consoles.

"What do you say, Dean? Can we get out of here?" Ris asked.

"Like I said, all systems are online. We will have to do some adjustments as we get out of the system, but yeah, I think we're ready. If Damien can ease us out of here undetected."

"The battle between the fleets gives us perfect cover to sneak away," Cornelius observed. "If we can restart the engines and Damien can keep us under the cover of the cloak."

Visibly annoyed, Damien snapped, "You are both speaking as if this ship is piloted by an amateur. Remember, I'm handling the controls here. Trust me to navigate us out." He promptly stumbled over his own seat. "These chairs in this control room are just old. Anyone could have stumbled over one!"

"No stress," Mic quipped, prompting chuckles from the group.

Reyes left his console, "Everything's prepped and charged. I think we can get moving."

The group made their way back into the hangar bay. Ris paused to take in the vessel's distinctive nose art - Iron Maiden's mascot Eddie appeared to crash into the hull. Below the cockpit, the numerals 666 were emblazoned alongside "Friday the 13th" and an inverted horseshoe. The vessel itself was breathtaking -

nearly filling the hangar, bristling with weaponry at every wing junction. Its design merged aeronautical elements up front with a unique rear section.

"Why Friday the 13th?" Ris questioned as they boarded.

"Named for a British bomber from the Second World War on Earth. Crews were superstitious about F-designated craft due to high losses, so one captain chose Friday the 13th to change their luck. Worked too - completed over a hundred missions safely. Given our streak of misfortune, it seemed fitting," Damien explained.

"And Eddie's presence?"

"Come on now - Iron Maiden rocks!"

A deafening blast partially collapsed the hangar entrance. From engineering, Reyes reported, "Someone's targeting the hangars - could be either side. Doors are jammed."

"Not for long," Damien declared, activating weapons systems to target the obstruction. "Brace yourselves!" A volley of energy beams and cannon fire preceded their forceful acceleration forward.

"So much for ease out of here," Mic said.

"Hey! Easy does it! Remember what I said about those engines!" Reyes protested.

The ship burst through the wreckage and climbed sharply skyward, outpacing pursuing fighters. The automated defenses eliminated one that ventured too close.

"Mic realize again. Mic hates space!"

"We know," Cornelius acknowledged.

"Damien's flying awful," Mic grumbled.

Grinning back, Damien retorted, "But I'm all you've got!"

"Crap, cloak's down," Reyes said, jumping to help a technician get it working again.

"Never mind that, we don't need it. The ships' fighting out there will provide cover. Divert the power to the engines." Damien commanded.

Breaking atmosphere revealed the imperial capital ship battling the Davosi fleet. Damien and Cornelius were right, the chaos provided perfect cover - no vessels could disengage long enough to chase them.

"Hopefully Styne loaded those coordinates from his informant in time. If his information's good, we might rescue Amelia before Bright turns that sinister gem against us," Ris said.

Cornelius verified his screen, "Coordinates confirmed. Transferring to your navigation system, Damien."

"Received. Target's a planet deep in empire space according to the star charts."

"Flight mode activated," came a feminine voice from a beautiful blonde attendant at the rear of the bridge. "Welcome aboard. May I get you something to drink?"

Startled, Ris asked, "Who's this?"

"That's just Mira, our android crew member. Mira stands for Medical Interfacing Recreational Android - she handles medical care, backup piloting, and more." Reyes said.

"Recreational!" Ris repeated, "She's a sex bot!"

Reyes chuckled, "Not anymore. We reprogrammed her. She is more like a co-pilot, flight attendant."

"No need Mic's field medic skills?"

Reyes shook his head, she's not for the field. You are still our field medic while Amelia's away."

Mic beamed, "Good."

"Although, I don't know how you are going to be healing us and smashing things at the same time." Cornelius said.

"Mic find way."

Damien eased back in his pilot's chair as Mira gracefully moved through the bridge, serving drinks to the crew. Her movements were fluid, almost human-like, but with a precision that betrayed her artificial nature.

"Centaurian brandy for you, Captain Storm," she said, placing the glass beside his control panel. "Although it is frowned upon to pilot a vessel while drinking alcohol, and mineral water for Mic - you prefer non-alcoholic beverages during flight?"

"Mic appreciate. Yes, Mic like to be sharp in space, no alcohol." The alien warrior took his drink without looking away from the tactical display.

Damien sipped his brandy, watching the stars streak past. "It's for sipping, Mira, I can drink it and pilot just fine."

"If you say so, Captain."

"I do!" Damien took another sip. The new ship handled beautifully now that the initial kinks were worked out. Reyes and his technicians had done a fine job.

"Your medical facilities are fully stocked," Mira announced, her voice carrying that slight synthetic undertone. "I've prepared emergency kits for the rescue operation and calibrated the auto-doc for human and non-human physiology."

"What about combat capabilities?" Ris asked, studying the android with a mix of curiosity and suspicion. "Do you have any protective and self preservation abilities?"

"I am equipped with advanced combat protocols and can operate all ship's weapons systems," Mira replied. "However, my primary function is medical support and ship operations. I can serve as backup pilot or backup engineer if needed."

"She's also got some impressive hand-to-hand combat skills," Reyes added returning to monitoring his engineering station. "We modified her original... recreational programming... into something more practical."

Damien noticed Mira's expression shift slightly at the mention of her former purpose. The android's emotional responses were remarkably sophisticated.

"I prefer my current duties," Mira stated firmly. "Would anyone like refreshments? The galley is fully stocked."

"Some food would be good," Cornelius said. "We haven't eaten since before the escape."

"I'll prepare a proper meal," Mira said. "The crew needs to maintain optimal nutrition levels before combat operations."

As she left for the galley, Damien checked their course. Still on track for the Imperial world where they believed Amelia was being held. The ship's enhanced sensors hadn't detected any pursuit - either they'd made a clean getaway, or the Empire was too busy with the Davosi to chase them.

"She's different from most androids I've encountered," Ris observed. "More... alive somehow."

"The Jaddus Collective's technology is incredibly advanced," Reyes explained. "Their neural networks are practically indistinguishable from organic brains. Mira's probably more self-aware than most humans."

Mira returned with trays of hot food - some kind of meat and vegetable dish that smelled amazing. She distributed plates to each crew member, making sure everyone had utensils and napkins.

"I've also prepared the medical bay for potential casualties," she reported while serving. "The stasis pods are ready if we need to stabilize serious injuries, and I've programmed the surgical suite for emergency procedures."

Reyes frowned, "Hmm, she's repeating herself. I will have to look at her subroutines when I get the chance."

"What about our weapons?" Cornelius asked between bites. "Do we have backup blasters should we need them?"

"The armory is fully stocked. I can assist with equipment selection and tactical planning." Mira's eyes flickered briefly, accessing internal data. "My combat protocols include strategies for infiltration, extraction, and ship-to-ship warfare."

"Good to know," Damien said. He had to admit, having a capable android crew member would be invaluable for the rescue mission. Especially one who could handle both medical emergencies and combat situations.

"I've also taken the liberty of analyzing the Imperial facility's likely security measures," Mira continued. "Based on available data, I can suggest several potential infiltration routes."

"We'll need all the help we can get," Ris said. "The Empire doesn't take kindly to uninvited guests."

Chapter 19: The Death Moon

Damien adjusted the ship's navigation, "We should be in visual range in a few moments. According to the database, this planet is called Andronia Prime. It's an industrial planet with a newly discovered, high functioning renewable power source technology. The planet's spinning core has something to do with it."

Ris sat down in the co-pilot seat. He felt woozy and dizzy.

"What's wrong with you?" Damien asked.

"I can feel her. Amelia is near. I can also sense Bright and the Laucnar. We are in the right place."

"Did you put more points into telepath?"

"I did. I thought it might come in useful but I never imagined the skill would feel like this. I thought it would be more tangible and less nauseating."

The ship exited hyperspace before a green planet, which looked remarkably clean and inviting for an industrial planet. Ris had pictured the old industrial age of Earth, all black, sooty, and billowing plumes of black smoke. Andronia Prime had none of that. As they approached, what looked like a close moon from a distance began to resemble a half-completed space station.

"Oh, come on! You have got to be kidding me. He is building a Death Moon!" Ris said.

"You mean star?" Cornelius corrected.

"No, I mean moon. It's a freakin' moon. I never understood what they called it a star." Ris said. "It orbited a planet!"

"Probably because it moved on it's own like a ship." Reyes said.

"That makes no sense either." Ris said.

"Who cares, It makes sense Bright would build one if he could. He was a huge fan of all the movies!" Damien said. "If I were evil, I would probably build one too! It's cool."

"How did he have time to construct this?" Cornelius asked.

"It's his evil gem," Ris said. "It's allowing him to do just about anything he wants. He was building this while we were building this ship. I'll see if I can counter it by getting into Bright's head when we get close enough to him so he doesn't just use the Laucnar to crush us."

Reyes touched the screen on his console, "Well, it should be easy to destroy then. All we have to do is hit its core reactor."

He frowned as he examined the scanners and sensors. He did not look happy.

"What is it?" Cornelius asked.

"The power core is not online. The station is drawing power from a link to a power source on the planet below."

"Is there force shield around it?" Mic asked. "Like in movie?"

"No, there is not a shield generator. Bright is a crafty one. He thought of the weaknesses from the movie and has eliminated them. We could attack the station and essentially nothing would happen. We would just be blowing small chunks of it into space. They could have a bunch of ships up here blasting us out of the sky long before we could do significant damage." Reyes said.

"He's powering everything with the evil essence from the Laucnar." Ris said. "I can feel its power. There is no need for conventional power systems. He really is dangerous when he has an evil gem!"

"Cornelius should never have made that joke about him. Now it's our reality." Damien observed.

"How the hell was I supposed to know?" Cornelius asked, "Who would have thought we would all be out here in space like this living something we just made up or saw once in a movie? You are all idiots."

"Hit close to home, did I?" Damien asked.

"Damien, slow us down and don't get any closer. Deploy the cloak." Ris said.

"Are you crazy? I activated the cloak as soon as we came out of hyperspace. We are invisible and running silent already."

"Good work," Ris said. "All right Cornelius, it's time to make a plan. I hope you have been putting points into all your espionage skills."

"Of course, I have."

"We over heads! Only tenth level skills." Mic said, looking at his wrist device.

"That's why we have to be smart, then. Cornelius has already proven he can disguise himself and act. We have to play and rely on our strengths."

"Good, I go with him. I sneak."

"Uh, sure thing, Mic," Ris said. "I guess we are going to follow the movies for now and see if we can land on the station."

"Screw that!" Damien said. "We are in stealth mode. I'm going to attach the 13th to the side and we can sneak on board the space station that way. I am not putting this ship in a hanger to get confiscated or torn down like before." He guided the ship toward the half-constructed space station, his hands steady on the controls. The massive structure loomed before them, its skeletal framework reflecting the starlight. He found a suitable docking point near what appeared to be a maintenance airlock.

"Extending magnetic grapples," he announced, carefully maneuvering the ship into position. The hull vibrated slightly as the grapples engaged. "We're locked on."

"Any sign they've detected us?" Cornelius asked, checking his weapons.

"Negative. Cloak's holding steady and we're running silent." Damien powered down non-essential systems to minimize their energy signature. "Mira, maintain ship readiness. We might need a quick exit."

"Understood, Captain Storm. Medical bay is prepped for emergency extraction. Piloting subroutines online and ready. I'll get us out of here should you need me too."

"Good." Damien said. "Stand by."

Ris stood at the airlock, his eyes closed in concentration. "Amelia's definitely here. Her presence is... strange though. Distorted somehow."

"The Laucnar's influence?" Reyes suggested, adjusting his tool belt.

"Maybe. There's something else too - like a shadow in my mind. Bright's watching, waiting."

"It's a trap," Cornelius stated flatly. "I think we all know it is."

"Of course it's a trap, lobster head!" Damien said, joining them at the airlock. "But we're going in anyway."

Cornelius chuckled, "I had forgotten the "It's a trap" line in the movie. Good one!"

"Mic crush traps," the alien warrior declared, hefting his massive weapon.

They cycled through the airlock in pairs, their magnetic boots engaging as they stepped onto the station's outer hull. Damien felt exposed despite their stealth gear, like eyes were watching from every nook and cranny. "Do you sense any cameras on us, Ris?"

"No, not mechanical eyes, but something is watching us somehow. I can feel it." Ris led them through the maintenance corridors, following some invisible thread only he could sense. The station's interior was a maze of half-finished passages and exposed circuitry. Their footsteps echoed oddly in the artificial gravity.

"Security's light," Cornelius whispered, scanning ahead. "Too light."

"He knows we're coming," Ris replied softly. "He's clearing the path."

They passed empty guard posts and disabled security cameras. Every door opened at their approach, every system conveniently offline. Damien's pilot instincts screamed that they were being herded around like cattle.

"She's close," Ris said, pressing a hand to his temple. "Two levels down, in some kind of medical bay. But..."

"But what?"

"The shadow in my mind - it's getting stronger. Bright's presence is everywhere, like he's part of the station itself."

"The Laucnar must be amplifying his powers even more than we thought," Reyes observed. "He's probably connected to every system."

They found a maintenance lift and descended deeper into the station. Damien kept his blaster ready, knowing it probably wouldn't help against whatever awaited them. The lift doors opened onto a sterile white corridor that wouldn't have looked out of place in a hospital.

"There," Ris pointed to a set of double doors marked 'Medical Research.' "She's in there."

"Along with who knows what else," Cornelius added.

"Only one way to find out." Damien stepped forward, but Ris grabbed his arm.

"Wait - something's changing. The shadow... it's moving."

The corridor lights flickered, and a cold laugh echoed through hidden speakers. "Welcome, my old friends," Bright's voice reverberated around them. "I've been expecting you."

Of course you have." Ris replied.

Bright's laughter echoed through the station's corridors as he materialized before them, his form shimmering with an eerie blue-green light. The Laucnar pulsed in his hand, its power visibly flowing through his body like liquid lightning.

"Thomas, this isn't you," Ris stepped forward. "Remember who you are - remember our gaming sessions, the stories we created together. The Jaddus Collective is behind this. We don't have to follow the path they have laid out before us."

Bright's eyes glowed with an unnatural azure fire. "Gaming sessions? Stories? Such trivial things. I am beyond such childish pursuits now. The Laucnar has shown me true power. It might have started off as some sort of game, but this is real enough now."

Damien watched as Cornelius and Mic edged around the confrontation, working their way toward the medical bay doors. Damien, partly out of curiosity, and partly to distract him from seeing his friends, fired a bolt from his blaster at Bright. As he expected, the energy bolts he fired simply dissipated against Bright's shimmering aura. He didn't even flinch as they bounced off him.

"Blasters are useless against me here." Bright said. "You can try to distract me, but I can feel what you are trying to do. Go ahead, take her. I have what I was after from her. She is of no use to me now. Take her, if you dare."

"You were our friend," Ris pressed. "Our Gamemaster. You brought us all together."

"That weak fool is gone," Bright snarled. "There is only power now. Look around you. I have the power to reshape reality itself!"

The Laucnar's energy surged outward in a wave of destructive force. Ris raised his power sword, the blade absorbing the blast as his telepathic shields deflected the rest. Damien felt the residual energy crackle past him like static electricity.

Behind Bright, Cornelius managed to slice through the medical bay's security panel. The doors slid open with a hiss, revealing Amelia strapped to an examination table.

"About fucking time you assholes showed up!" she shouted as Mic ripped through her restraints. "I've been stuck here for fucking months!"

Bright spun at her voice, but Ris seized the moment to attack. His power sword clashed against the Laucnar's energy field, sending sparks of blue and green light cascading around them. The two began a deadly dance, blade against mystical force.

"Get her out of here!" Ris called between strikes. "I'll hold him off!"

Bright laughed, "You will?"

"I'll damn well try!" Ris said with another swing of his power sword.

Damien provided covering fire, as useless as it was, as Mic carried Amelia toward the exit, Cornelius leading the way. Imperial troops finally began pouring into the corridor, but Mic's massive form simply plowed through them like bowling pins.

"You really think you can stand against me?" Bright taunted, hurling another blast of energy that Ris barely deflected. "I have transcended our former existence!"

"No," Ris countered, his blade weaving patterns of light as he parried each attack. "You've just forgotten who you really are. The Laucnar has consumed your true self."

But Damien could see in Bright's eyes that there was nothing left of their old friend to reach. He had not resisted the memory transfer as they had. The man who had guided their adventures, shared their victories and defeats, was completely gone. In his place stood something inhuman, corrupted by power beyond mortal understanding.

"Keep moving!" Damien shouted to the others as more troops appeared. Mic's massive fists sent soldiers flying in all directions while Cornelius picked off stragglers with precise shots. Amelia had already acquired a blaster from somewhere and was cursing like a drunken sailor as she fired at their pursuers.

Behind them, Ris and Bright continued their supernatural duel, power sword against cosmic force, telepathic shields straining against waves of corrupted energy. The Laucnar's glow had spread throughout the entire corridor, making the metal walls pulse like a living thing.

Chapter 20: Beyond Current Ability

Damien pointed the way to the 13th. "This way, down this corridor." Amelia was lagging behind but Cornelius was there to help her along. Mic was clearing the way, knocking any of the unfortunate troopers against the polished new walls or worse. They were just about to the door where Reyes had rigged one of the outward hatches to open at their command when there was a huge explosion and thick green energy poured through the hallways knocking them all down.

Damien held up his wrist device, "What was that, Ris? Come in Ris."

"Get to the ship, I'm near a shuttle at one of the bays." Ris's voice sounded shaken and rough."

"What the hell happened?" Damien asked again. There was silence at the other end and then Ris spoke again, "The Laucnar's energy just bounced off my power sword and disfigured Thomas. I know what you're going to say. We don't have time for the parallels. He is down at the moment, but not for long. I can't get to the Laucnar. There was another surge and a shift. Reyes and Damien fell down a corridor one way and Mic fell with Cornelius and Amelia the other direction.

Damien recovered near the hatch Reyes had rigged. "We got separated. Corny, Mic, can you get back to us? Amelia, where are you?"

Amelia's voice came over the comm, "I'm fucking stuck in this corridor."

"Near Mic and Cornelius?" Damien asked.

"They are separated from me by a fallen fucking bulkhead." Amelia said.

Reyes scanned in their direction, "I think we can get to them with the ship. There's a place not far from them where we can scoop them up." He clicked some buttons on his wrist device, "I am giving you the coordinates. Go there and wait for Damien and I to get to you in the ship."

Damien and Reyes sprinted the rest of the way through the corridors back to where they had docked the Friday the 13th. The ship's airlock cycled open at their approach, Mira's efficient programming already preparing for emergency departure.

"Power up all systems," Damien ordered as he slid into the pilot's chair. "We need to move fast."

"Systems are powered and ready, Captain." Mira said.

"I think I'm going to love that android!" Damien said as he began his flight procedures.

Reyes rushed to engineering, his fingers flying over the controls. "Releasing magnetic grapples now."

The ship shuddered as it detached from the station's hull. Damien engaged the thrusters, carefully maneuvering them away - but something felt wrong. The controls weren't responding properly.

"We've got a problem," Reyes called from engineering. "Energy readings are spiking all around us."

A shimmer of blue-green light rippled across space, forming a massive dome around the half-constructed station. The force shield sprang to life with a cascade of pure energy that made their instruments go haywire.

"Damn it!" Damien slammed his fist on the console. "Bright's using the Laucnar to power a containment field."

His wrist device chimed with an incoming transmission. "Damien, you copy?" Ris's voice broke through the static.

"I read you. We're off the station but there's a shield up now. Where are you?"

"Found Amelia. She's hurt but mobile. Can't reach Mic and Cornelius though - they're trapped behind some kind of energy barrier."

Damien studied his tactical display, plotting possible approach vectors. "I can get to them. The 13th's shields might withstand the Laucnar's energy long enough for an extraction."

"Too risky," Ris countered. "That force field could tear the ship apart. it's too much of an unknown."

"Got a better idea?"

A pause. "There's a shuttle bay near our position. If Amelia and I can get to it..."

"Gotcha, do it," Damien said firmly. "Get clear of the station. We'll find a way through to the others."

"The shield's energy signature is fluctuating," Reyes reported, examining his readings. "If we time it right, we might find a weak point."

Damien nodded, his hands steady on the controls despite the tension knotting his shoulders. "Ris, get to that shuttle. We'll handle the rescue."

"Copy that. Be careful - Bright's not done with us yet."

The transmission cut off as Damien brought the ship around, searching for any vulnerability in the shimmering barrier. Through the viewscreen, he could see Imperial troops converging on Mic and Cornelius's position. They needed to move fast.

"Mira, prepare the medical bay," he ordered. "We might have wounded coming aboard."

"Medical protocols engaged, Captain," the android responded smoothly. "Triage systems standing by."

Damien's fingers tightened on the controls until his knuckles hurt. They had to find a way through that shield - their friends were counting on them. "Anything Dean?"

Reyes made some more quick scans, "You are not going to believe this but I think there is some equipment down on the planet I can use to destroy the station."

"Why wouldn't I believe it?"

"Because of the movie with the force shield and...never mind." Get us to the planet.

"It's not the same at all." Damien said maneuvering the ship toward the coordinates Reyes was sending to him on the nav computer.

"I don't care. I misspoke. Just get us to the surface."

"Ris, come in." Damien activated his comm.

"What is it?"

"Can you go back to the station and get the others? Reyes says he found something that needs our ...attention... and it's will not be good for our friends up there."

"Understood, I don't think this force shield works on these imperial shuttles, Amelia and I should be able to get back through it and into the station. Send me their locations."

"Copy that." Damien said typing in Cornelius and Mic's last known location.

Damien guided the Friday the 13th through the planet's atmosphere, the ship's hull glowing red-hot during entry. The industrial landscape of Andronia Prime spread out below them - a maze of clean, efficient factories and power distribution centers.

"There," Reyes pointed to a complex of buildings near what appeared to be a massive power relay station. "That's where we need to be."

Damien brought them down on a landing pad, the ship's sensors detecting no immediate threats. The facility appeared deserted - probably evacuated when Bright took control of the station.

"What exactly are we looking for?" Damien asked as they descended the ship's ramp.

"The station's tethered to the planet's power grid through a series of quantum relays," Reyes explained, consulting his wrist device. "If I can access the main control systems, I might be able to overload the connection."

"Causing what, exactly?"

"Best case? The station breaks orbit and drifts away from the planet. Worst case? The power surge triggers a cascade failure in their systems." Reyes grinned. "Either way, Bright loses his toy."

Their wrist devices chimed with an incoming transmission. "We're back on the station," Ris's voice came through clearly. "No sign of Bright yet."

"How bad did you hurt him?" Damien asked, following Reyes into the facility.

"The Laucnar's energy reflected off my power sword - hit him directly. The damage... it wasn't pretty. I can't sense him clearly anymore. His presence is scattered, unfocused. I think he was trying to kill me with that blast and he ended up taking most of it himself. I think he will be out of it a while."

"Good," Reyes said, already working at a control panel. "That'll make this easier. Have you found Mic and Cornelius?"

"Not yet. The station's layout keeps shifting - like the Laucnar's power is warping the structure itself, another sign Bright isn't back in control of it yet."

Damien watched Reyes work, the engineer's fingers flying over the controls as he accessed the power grid's systems. "How long will this take?"

"Depends on how many security protocols I have to bypass. The basic infrastructure is standard Imperial design, but Bright's modifications are... unusual." Reyes frowned at his display. "It's like he's merged the Laucnar's energy directly into the power distribution network."

"Can you still trigger the overload?"

"I think so. The quantum relays weren't designed to handle this kind of power. If I can create a feedback loop..." Reyes trailed off, focused on his work.

Their devices chimed again. "Still no sign of Bright," Amelia's voice this time. "But something feels wrong. The whole fucking station is giving me the creeps."

"Just find Mic and Cornelius," Damien told her. "Reyes is working on getting you all out of there."

"The sooner the better. This place is seriously fucked up."

Damien paced while Reyes continued his modifications, checking his wrist device for updates from the others. The facility's emptiness made him uneasy - it felt too easy, like walking into another trap.

"Got it!" Reyes announced suddenly. "Primary power coupling is reconfigured. Now I just need to..."

A series of lights began flashing on his console. "What's happening?" Damien asked.

"The quantum relays are responding. The station's orbit is already starting to decay." Reyes's fingers danced across the controls. "If Bright doesn't notice in time, the whole thing will drift out of range of the planet's power grid."

"And if he does notice?"

"Then I trigger the surge and hope the system overloads before he can stop it."

The lights flashing on the console began to turn red and an ominous klaxon began to sound. Damien watched as Reyes began to get frustrated and he now appeared to be randomly pressing buttons.

"Um, what is all this?" Damien asked.

"It's..." Reyes was interrupted by several large explosions nearby and before he could utter another word, an explosion so powerful it rocked their location, boomed in the distance. Too far away to hurt them, but close enough to alert Damien it was a big one!

Chapter 21: Just Tenth Level

"Oh crap!" Reyes said, "Damien, I think we should get back to the ship as fast as we can.

"What the hell did you do?" Damien asked.

"Well, I don't understand this power technology, you can hardly blame me!"

"What did you do?"

"How fast can you round up the others?"

There was another explosion somewhere in the distance.

"Was that you?" Damien asked.

Reyes nodded, "What did you expect? I am level fucking ten!"

Damien held up his wrist, "Ris, come in. Are you there?"

"I'm here. What was that explosion?"

"You better get back to the shuttle, pronto. Abort the mission, abort the mission."

"We are already up in the space station."

Reyes shook his head, "No, bad idea. I think I started a power cascade that's causing surges in the power grid. It's causing the magnetic field of the planet to pull the death moon toward it."

"What?" Ris asked.

"I made the power station a huge magnet and it's pulling the space station out of space."

"Really?" Damien said.

"No, but that's close enough," Reyes told him. "I don't have time to explain it. Hell, I don't understand it myself. Just accept it's bad!"

"Did you understand anything you were doing to the power grid?"

"Shut up and let's get out of here.

Damien held his wrist up again, "Ris, can you get back to that shuttle?"

Another explosion went off. People who were indoors before began to scramble all around them.

"It's getting dangerous to move around here on the ground." Damien said, "Do we need to fly to you?"

"We can get back to the shuttle." Ris said.

"Okay, get to the shuttle and get back to the 13th. We are almost ready to attempt a risky rescue to get Mic and Cornelius. Standby for my instructions."

"We are? What did you not understand about the moon base crashing into this planet?" Reyes was almost panicked as usual.

"We are not letting Cornelius and Mic die on it! There are huge gaps in the construction of the base. They are probably held in place by flimsy force fields, we might be able to get the 13th close enough to blast through one."

"Your left your wrist comm on, Damien, I heard your plan." Ris said. I think we can rescue them that way just as easy as you. Does Reyes know if these shuttles can fly through the construction force fields.

Damien looked at Reyes, he shrugged, "Reyes doesn't know for sure."

"Okay, stand by."

"There are a lot of troopers heading this way." Reyes pointed out.

Damien took out his blaster and hunched down, "I think we can run for those crates by the supply shed."

"Lead on," Reyes said.

They took off for the crates. A soldier spotted them, "Halt!"

"No thanks!" Damien said and blasted the soldier off his feet. "Forget the crates and just run for the ship."

Damien's blaster fire got the attention of some other soldiers and they gave chase. They made it back to the cloaked ship all the while firing blasters back and forth. Reyes took a glancing blaster volley just as they began to close the doors. It started bleeding steadily.

"Are you all right?" Damien asked as he started manipulating the flight controls.

"No, I've been shot, dumbass."

"No need to be nasty. Mira, medical emergency."

"You get shot and see how cordial you are."

"Keep pressure on it. Mira, medical emergency!"

Mira exited the sickbay, "Acknowledged, can you walk?"

Reyes nodded, "I think so."

Damien waited until Mira helped Reyes move into the small sick bay before he took off. He calibrated the sensors to pick up the movement of the death moon. It was only moving a few centimeters a minute at this point.

"Computer, how long before the space station crashes into the planet?"

"At the current rate of descent, the station will contact the planet in twenty-six hours." Damien let out a sigh of relief. "However, the explosions on the planet are the result of a catastrophic power cascade. If the cascade continues, the station will be pulled in faster and collide with the planet in a matter of hours. If the system goes into massive overload, the planet and the station will be destroyed in a matter of minutes."

"Well, that's not good! Computer, How do we stop the cascade?"

"Cascade is currently too far into the systems to be halted. Stopping it now would require a complete reboot of the system."

"Okay, how do we do that"

"The rebooting system was destroyed in the first explosion. Full destruction is eminent."

"What about fail safes?"

"The emergency fail safe system control was destroyed in the second explosion."

"This is beginning to feel like the Titanic."

"I am unfamiliar with that reference."

"A ship that struck an iceberg. Men posted without binoculars, running too fast in the dark while ignoring ice warnings."

"I am unfamiliar with that reference."

"Never mind." He went down the corridor to the medical bay. Reyes was getting bandaged. "The computer says destruction is eminent. What do we do?"

Reyes sighed, "Thanks, Mira."

The android nodded, "My pleasure."

"We wait for Ris to tell us he rescued Mic and Cornelius. Then we hope we all can reach escape velocity before the massive overload explosion that's about to happen occurs and destroys the planet."

"Do we have any more of that weird bourbon from the pleasure planet where you found Mira?"

"Yes, but you can't drink right now!"

"The hell I can't!"

* * *

Mic used his intimidation sneak to the amusement of Cornelius until he had to knock a guard out cold who wasn't buying it. Once they got passed that station another checkpoint loomed ahead. Cornelius had already stolen a captain's uniform from one of the men they had to fight on the way. He strolled up the checkpoint.

"You men, what the devil are you doing here?"

The men snapped to attention, "Captain sir, we were ordered here to guard the control room after the explosions on the planet surface, sir."

"The explosions are pulling this station out of orbit. You four men should be on your way to the evacuation stations."

"No sir, we are Dr. Bright's personal guard. We must stay as long as he does."

"Dr. Bright? He is still here?"

"Aye, sir."

"Mic, we have some stubborn soldiers."

Mic De'gene moved remarkably fast for his size. He took the blaster fire easily into his leathery skin without a scratch. The first soldier got a hard knock on the head as the second caught Mic's fist in his face, the third got a head butt and the fourth ran like a scalded cat.

Ris appeared from the opposite direction. "There you are? Did you see Amelia come through here?"

"No," Cornelius said. "You're the only one we've seen since we got separated. What happened?"

"She was right behind me one second and gone the next. We need to find her and get out of here. Reyes screwed up something on the planet surface that's setting off power surges and explosions."

"Where do we go? Is Damien bringing the ship to get us?" Cornelius asked.

Ris held out his arm and stopped him. "Wait, I sense Bright behind this door. I also sense Amelia is in there with him."

The three of them entered the room with Mic leading the way. Amelia was seated on a sofa. Her terrified expression told Ris this was most likely a trap. He surmised Bright must have used the evil gem to move instantly to their location. He glanced around the huge room but did not see the glowing orb. The place was almost the size of an aircraft hangar. From the looks of the girders and beams up above, the room was really just an unfinished floor under a multitude of unfinished floors and not intended to be constructed into such a large space. Force fields separated part of the unfinished room from open space. Bright was standing at one of the finished windows with his back to the door.

"So, you have found me, now what?" Bright asked. Ris realized he could see him in the reflection of the window glass.

"We came for Amelia," Mic said.

"Where's your evil gem?" Cornelius blurted out.

"Ah yes, the infamous joke about me and the evil gem. Don't let Dr. Thomas Bright have an evil gem blah, blah, blah. I never really cared for that tired old joke. I just enjoyed being bad because I knew that no one was really getting hurt. It was just a game after all."

"Life's a game," Cornelius said. "We all play our roles and keep our secrets. This world is no different. In this world you can hurt someone."

"Come back with us. We are all worried about you," Ris pleaded. "We'll finish the quests and be done with it, together."

"But, I am having so much fun on my own. I have even escalated myself to emperor. You should bow down before me."

"Not happening." Mic said.

Ris stepped in to prevent an altercation, "All right, how about we take Amelia and you can keep your death moon and throne. We'll just leave and never look back. You can take the Laucnar and rule the galaxy or whatever."

"You know as well as I that the others have compromised my station. It's being pulled into the planet below."

"I'm sure you can save it." Cornelius said. "You have your evil gem."

Anger flashed briefly on Bright's face but he recovered, "Oh, I will save it. But first I need to get rid of you."

"Get rid of us as in help us get off this Station?" Ris asked.

Bright was not amused. He turned toward the group exposing his disfigured face, "Look at you. You had the first planet and the mining planet at your disposal and you have only reached level ten! Good lord, Ris, you could have been fifty easily by now."

Amelia winced at the sight of Bright's disfigured face. Ris saw that he had tried to get the Laucnar to repair it but it didn't do a very good job of it. He pointed his wrist at Bright to check his level. The display read forty-nine. A sinking feeling came over him. "You kill us and you level to fifty."

"Yes, there you go. That wasn't so difficult, was it."

"But why did you kidnap Amelia?"

"Isn't it obvious? I only needed her to lure you here. I thought you'd be higher level by now."

"I don't understand." Ris said. "Higher level? What does that have to do with anything?"

Bright smirked, "Funny thing, I found out by accident that player characters give twice the experience of non-player characters."

"And we last player characters." Mic said.

Bright touched his face, "At least you are decent with your telepathy for a level ten. I'll fix this accident with time. I was only around fortieth level and you took me by surprise. It was a valuable lesson for me."

"I have been strategic with my progression."

"Have you? Again, you're hilariously low level. You were always were a poor player. Look at the horrible gear you are wearing. It's sad for even a tenth level telepath."

"I had a lot more to worry about than my gear."

"How did you do it, scale to my level temporarily? Stims?"

"You don't know? You gained nine levels between the time of us fighting and now and you don't know about stims?"

"That's what I thought and yes, I know about them. There are also stims to increase experience gain. You should have used those."

"Where did you get stims, Ris?" Cornelius asked.

"I got the stims from Mira. I visited her sickbay back on the ship and found them.

"Thanks for telling *us* about them!" Cornelius said.

"There wasn't enough for everyone. I made an executive decision. Besides, they only temporarily leveled certain skills like power sword to fifty. They didn't affect my level. I was still tenth."

"I should have known you would go for the temporary fix instead of actually leveling up!" Bright said.

"Can we get more from Mira?" Cornelius asked.

"She can probably synthesize more. We have to get out of here and to the ship first."

"How? We have no chance. You no have more stims. He too high level for us to defeat." Mic said. "HEY, where he go?"

Ris look around, "He's toying with us." He activated his power sword. "Come on out, Thomas, we're not done yet."

Amelia sighed, "Don't waste your breath. He's long gone. I guess you have not realized what he was talking about yet."

"I guess not. What are you getting at?" Ris asked as he powered down his sword.

"He's right that player characters give more XP. But at tenth level we are gray to him. He'll get nothing from our defeat at the moment. He wants us to level up before he fights us."

"Huh?" Cornelius said.

"Look, we have been getting trivial amounts of experience, XP, with the little tasks and quests we've been doing. What we should have been doing is checking the level of the quests and the mobs we are supposed to defeat. The spider bosses we killed were blue, barely any experience for us. They got us this far but we should have defeated them earlier."

"We barely survived that at the level we were!" Cornelius reminded her.

"Because we were not doing the quests to up our gear first. We needed white and yellow colored quests and mobs. White is equal to our level and yellow is one level higher. Red is significantly higher and purple will just one shot you dead. The closer to our level the quests and mobs are the more experience we will get. The lowest designation is gray. Gray means too low level to bother with. You might get an item for dispatching them but no XP."

"So, Bright left because we are too low level?" Cornelius said. "How do you know all this?"

Amelia nodded, "Yep, he left because we are gray to him. we need to level before he will bother with us. I know all this because it took you assholes forever to find me and I had a lot of time to read the databases while trapped on this fucking station."

"It make sense gamemaster know how to play better. We suck." Mic said.

"It also means that we will have to level if we have any hope of getting to the end of this thing, which means we will all become vulnerable to him at some point. We can't stay at level ten and gray to him forever or we will never reach the end of this." Ris said. "We are going to have to stick together as much as possible as we level.

The station lurched and felt like it fell a few meters.

"It's getting worse. We don't have much time." Ris said.

"Won't Bright use the Laucnar and fix the power problem and save this station and the planet?" Cornelius asked.

"It doesn't look like it," Ris said. "Come on, we need to get out of here." He raised his wrist, "Damien come in."

"It's about bloody time. Sensors show the cascade is worse. The station is falling toward the planet at an alarming rate."

"Bright is gone. You don't have to worry about him. Just come to our location and get us."

"What the hell are you talking about? He's gone as in dead?"

"What? No! I'll explain on the ship. Just get here."

"All right, I'm on my way."

Chapter 22: Regroup, Reassess

"So, we have been doing this all wrong this whole time?" Damien said as Ris finished explaining what they found out on the station.

"Yep, he took off somewhere. He doesn't care about the station now or the planet. He was just trying to lure us here. Once he found out what level we were, he left."

"It's not the last we'll see of him, though." Reyes said.

"No, he will be waiting for us gaining levels and equipment. Amelia, did you read what the level cap was?"

"I don't think there is one." She responded.

Mira entered the bridge. "Captain, there is about to be significant loss of life on the planet. My programming parameters will not allow me to stand by while I have pertinent information."

"What is it, Mira?"

"She went to Reyes' engineering console, "May I?"

Reyes moved for her to sit down.

"I can program our sensor array to send a pulse with coded instructions for the network computer to reverse the polarity beam to repulsor. With your permission or course."

"We are terrible players!" Cornelius said. We were just chatting away, perfectly okay with the station crashing to the planet."

"I have a twenty seven point two chance and dropping, sir." Mira stated.

"Yes, yes, do it, you have my permission." Damien said.

Mira began to work at lightning speed. Her servos hummed as she pressed them to the limit as she programed the pulse. She sent the message to the planetary computer at the end of her toil.

"Nothing happened." Cornelius said. "The station is still in decay."

Reyes went to the sensor control, "Something is happening. The station is now being repelled away from the planet by the power cascade."

"Nice job, Mira." Ris said.

"It is my pleasure to please. Now, if you will arm the quantum missiles, you may destroy the station once it clears the atmosphere into space."

Reyes slapped his forehead, "Shit, i forgot about the quantum missiles, we had the fire power to destroy this thing the whole time."

Ris shook his head, "It wasn't evacuated then. It's better you forgot about the mistitles until reminded just now. "

Reyes armed the missiles.

"Wait, sirs. May I?"

"Yes, Mira, go ahead. If you know of any improvements to any of our situations just do it. You don't have to keep asking permission."

"Asking permission is my programming."

"Fair enough, you have permission." Damien said.

Mira manipulated the computer controls on the database console.

The groups wrist devices chimed:

Warning: Quest parameters altered

Experience for quest updated

Warning: new quest activated: Destroy the Death Moon

Proceed? Y/N

"YES!" Damien said and pressed Y. They all did.

Reyes watched the station as it cleared the atmosphere, "Now?"

"Wait, won't the debris still fall on the planet?" Ris asked.

"Most of it will be vaporized by the quantum field from the missiles. the debris will be minimum." Reyes said.

"Oh, then proceed." Ris said.

"Fire missiles," Damien commanded.

Reyes fired the quantum missiles. They all watched as the three projectiles flew through space and then began to strike the station one at a time causing white quantum fields that vaporized large chunks of the former Death Moon. Some of it broke into debris that largely burned up in reentry to the planet's atmosphere.

Their wrist devices chimed again.

Quest: Destroy the Death Moon completed
Reward: 6, 345, 674 Experience each

Their devices all chimed five more times indicating a level each, Ris chimed one additional level since he was the closest to level eleven.

"Now this is more fucking like it!" Amelia said. "I am going to wisely allocate my skill points this time!"

"Can you add more quests like that, Mira?" Damien asked.

"Sorry, captain, I can only add capital story quest like that when they present themselves. It is not something I can do creatively."

"Well, if you see another instance where you can do that, don't hesitate to let me know."

"Certainly, captain." Mira said.

Damien leaned back in his pilot's chair, studying the star charts while the others discussed their encounters with Bright. The destruction of the Death Moon had given them a significant boost, but they were still far behind their former gamemaster.

"He hesitated when I mentioned our gaming sessions," Ris said, pacing the bridge. "For just a moment, I saw recognition in his eyes."

"That's because he's not completely gone," Amelia replied. "The Laucnar hasn't fully corrupted him - it can't erase who he was, only suppress it."

Cornelius nodded. "Remember when he first found the gem in the mines? The reports from Felder said he killed those workers immediately, but then he waited months before making any other moves."

"Like he was fighting it," Damien added. "The old Thomas trying to resist its influence."

"I'm not sure he killed those workers." Ris said. "I got the sense from him that the Laucnar was similar to the one in the movie of it's origin. I think it killed the men and Felder attributed their deaths to Bright."

"Speaking of influence," Amelia said, pulling up data on her console. "I found references in the station's archives to ancient texts about artifacts like the Laucnar. The Alteri supposedly documented their effects on different species. The gem is part of the lore now. Other races have been searching for it."

"Where would we find these texts?" Ris asked.

"There's a repository of Alteri knowledge on Nelius Prime. It's the next logical stop anyway - plenty of level-appropriate challenges there to help us gain experience."

Damien checked his navigation charts. "Nelius Prime... that's in the outer rim territories. Lots of ruins, some indigenous life forms that could provide decent XP."

"And more importantly," Amelia continued, "the texts might tell us how the Laucnar works. How it bonds with its host, why it kills some but not others, what weaknesses it has. The more we understand it, the better chance we have of saving Thomas."

"If he can be saved," Cornelius muttered.

"He can," Ris said firmly. "You saw how his face was damaged when the energy reflected. The Laucnar couldn't fully heal him - that means it has limitations."

Mic, who had been quietly maintaining his weapons, looked up. "Bright also not kill Amelia when had chance. Part of him still good."

"The big guy's right," Damien said. "Bright could have killed any of us at any time with that thing."

"No, you're forgetting, he just spared us because he wants the maximum experience from defeating us," Reyes pointed out. "We're worthless to him at our current level."

"Maybe," Amelia said. "Or maybe part of him is still our friend, still the gamemaster who wants us to progress and grow stronger. The texts might help us understand which is true."

Damien pulled up the detailed stats for Nelius Prime. "The planet's got everything we need - ruins to explore, creatures to fight, mysteries to solve. Plus, it's far enough from Imperial space that we shouldn't have to worry about their patrols."

"Don't count on that." Ris said. "If Bright's the emperor, he will know where we are. We need to remain vigilant and ready to bug out of there at a moments notice if we're not ready to confront him if or when he shows."

"What level are the challenges there?" Cornelius asked.

"According to the database, most of the content is rated for levels 15-20. Perfect for us now that we're level 15." Damien highlighted several promising locations on the map. "Ancient temples, abandoned research stations, wild territories full of predators..."

"And the Alteri repository?" Ris asked.

"Here." Damien zoomed in on a massive structure partially buried in the jungle. "The Hall of Knowledge. The archives say it's guarded by automated defense systems and some kind of trials we'll have to pass."

"Level-appropriate trials, I hope," Reyes said.

"Only one way to find out." Damien began plotting their course. "The question is, do we focus on gaining experience first, or head straight for the repository?"

Chapter 23: Nelius Prime

Damien engaged the hyperdrive, watching the stars stretch into streaks of light. The Friday the 13th's engines hummed smoothly now, a testament to Reyes's repairs. He checked their heading to Nelius Prime - the journey would take several hours, giving them time to allocate their newly gained skill points.

"Alright people, let's make these levels count," he announced over the ship's comm. "We can't afford any wasted points this time."

He studied his own interface, carefully selecting pilot specializations. Advanced atmospheric entry, stellar drift compensation, combat maneuvers - skills that would keep them alive when things inevitably went wrong. He also put points into blaster combat and light armor proficiency, knowing from experience that trouble had a way of finding him even on the bridge.

In the medical bay, Amelia obsessively organized her hyposprays while reviewing her skill options. "Fucking skill trees are overwhelming," she muttered, but methodically selected advanced trauma care, xenobiology, and to everyone's amusement, three separate pharmaceutical specializations.

Mic sat cross-legged in the cargo bay, his massive frame dwarfing the crates around him. He focused on combat skills - heavy weapons, armor mastery, and something called "devastating impact." But true to his word, he also put points into field medicine.

At the sensor station, Ris meditated as he strengthened his telepathic abilities. His power sword skills increased dramatically, along with combat precognition and mental shielding.

Reyes practically bounced between engineering consoles, excitedly upgrading his technical expertise. Quantum mechanics, advanced robotics, weapon modifications - his fingers flew over the interfaces as he absorbed the knowledge. "This is better than Christmas!" he exclaimed.

In the shadows of the bridge, Cornelius silently worked on his infiltration and espionage skills. Enhanced stealth, disguise mastery, and something called "shadow step" that made him nearly invisible. He also increased his skill with blades and small arms, knowing stealth wasn't always an option.

Mira moved efficiently between stations, offering suggestions and monitoring their progress. "Your skill selections appear optimal," she observed. "Though I note several of you are neglecting defensive abilities."

"We're building on our strengths," Damien replied, adding one final point to his evasive piloting. "Better to be really good at what we do than mediocre at everything."

Their wrist devices chimed periodically as new abilities came online. Damien felt the knowledge settling into his mind - not just technical data, but muscle memory and instinct. He found himself understanding complex flight maneuvers he'd never attempted before.

"How much longer until we reach Nelius Prime?" Ris asked, opening his eyes as he completed his skill allocation.

Damien checked the navigation display. "About two hours. Plenty of time to get comfortable with our new abilities."

"Good," Ris stood, his power sword igniting with newfound energy. "Because I have a feeling we're going to need every skill we've learned."

"Whoa, do you have to turn that thing on in here?" Damien said alarmed. "What if we got bumped or something? That thing would tear through anything in this ship."

"Oh, sorry, I got a little excited." He deactivated the sword. 'If anyone needs me, I will be in the cargo bay."

"You better not be going down there to turn on that sword!" Damien scolded.

"Don't worry, I am just going to check on something and meditate." He left the bridge.

* * *

Ris entered the cargo bay, his footsteps echoing off the metal deck plates. He moved past the stacked crates and equipment until he reached a secure storage locker near the back wall. The containment field hummed softly as he retrieved the data core, its crystalline surface pulsing with an inner light.

He settled into a cross-legged position, placing the core in front of him. The device seemed to respond to his presence, its glow intensifying slightly. His newly enhanced telepathic abilities could sense something emanating from it - not thoughts exactly, but patterns of information, layers of coded data.

Ris closed his eyes and reached out with his mind. The core's energy felt familiar somehow, like an echo of memories just beyond his grasp. He tried interfacing it with his wrist device, but the system refused to recognize it. The screen simply displayed "Unknown Format - Unable to Process."

As he probed deeper with his telepathy, fragments of memories flickered through his consciousness - faces, names, places from their lives before. But each time he tried to focus on these memories, they slipped away like grains of sand through his fingers. The more he attempted to read the core, the faster these remnants of their past seemed to fade.

He sensed that the core contained more than just data - it held their original memories, their true identities, carefully preserved until they completed whatever trial the Jaddus Collective had designed for them. But something was preventing the complete memory wipe that should have occurred. They retained just enough awareness to understand their situation, to know they needed to progress through the levels and complete their objectives.

The core pulsed brighter as Ris concentrated, and for a moment he caught glimpses: a gaming table surrounded by friends, character sheets scattered across its surface, dice rolling across felt. But trying to hold onto these images made his head spin. His enhanced mental shields strained against some kind of feedback from the core.

Their partial awareness felt deliberate - not a malfunction, but a designed feature. Just enough memory to drive them forward, to give them purpose beyond simply playing out their roles. Without this lingering connection to their past selves, they might have fully embraced their new identities and forgotten their mission to return home.

Ris opened his eyes, watching the core's steady pulse. Each attempt to access it seemed to accelerate the erosion of their remaining memories. He carefully returned it to its containment field, knowing they would need those memories intact when the time came to complete their journey.

His wrist device chimed, but displayed only static when he tried to scan the core again. Whatever secrets it held would have to wait until they were ready -

* * *

Ris contemplated their next move as he returned to the bridge. Damien was about to bring the ship out of hyperspace.

Damien eased back on the hyperspace controls, watching the star streaks collapse back into pinpoints of light. Nelius Prime filled the viewscreen - a vibrant green and blue sphere wreathed in wispy white clouds. The planet's twin moons loomed in orbit around the planet.

"Quite a sight," he muttered, running preliminary scans. The readings confirmed what they'd found in the database - vast jungles covered most of the landmasses, broken only by the occasional mountain range or ancient ruin poking through the canopy.

"I'm detecting multiple energy signatures," Reyes reported from his station. "Some from the ruins, others from... life forms. Big ones."

"Can you isolate the level 15 areas?" Ris asked, studying the sensor displays. "We need somewhere to start building experience."

Reyes adjusted the scanners, filtering the data. "There's a cluster of ruins about twenty kilometers from the Hall of Knowledge. Energy readings suggest moderate difficulty - should be perfect for our current abilities."

Damien brought them into a low orbit, getting a better look at their landing options. The jungle stretched endlessly in every direction, but he spotted a clearing near the ruins that looked large enough for the Friday the 13th.

"Captain," Mira spoke up from her station. "With your permission, I would like to activate my defensive protocols while you explore. The ship's automated systems may require manual override in case of emergency."

"Good thinking," Damien nodded. "Full authorization granted. Use whatever skills you need to keep her safe or come get us if things go wrong."

"Acknowledged. Defense systems online. Pilot subroutines engaged."

Reyes highlighted a spot on the navigation display. "That clearing there - about two kilometers from the nearest ruins. Should give us decent cover while staying within easy walking distance."

Damien guided them down through the atmosphere, the ship's hull briefly glowing from the heat of entry. The jungle canopy rushed past below as he lined up their approach. Ancient stone structures peeked through the vegetation - temples, monuments, and what looked like the remains of a city.

The landing struts settled onto the mossy ground with a soft thud. Through the viewscreen, Damien could see exotic birds taking flight from nearby trees, startled by their arrival.

Their wrist devices chimed simultaneously:

New Quest Available: The Forgotten City
Explore the ruins and discover their secrets
Warning: Level 15-20 content
Accept? Y/N

"Well, that's convenient timing," Damien said, pressing Y on his interface. The others did the same.

"Convenient or suspicious?" Cornelius asked, checking his weapons.

"Does it matter?" Amelia shouldered her medical kit. "It's level-appropriate and gets us closer to catching up with Bright."

Damien ran through the ship's shutdown sequence, leaving key systems active for Mira. The humid jungle air hit him like a wall as they descended the landing ramp. Strange animal calls echoed through the trees, and something large crashed through the underbrush in the distance.

Damien followed Ris through the dense jungle, swatting at insects that seemed determined to explore his ears and nose. The humidity made his flight jacket stick to his skin, and he envied Mic's natural resistance to the climate. The alien warrior moved through the vegetation with surprising grace despite his size. He activated his flight suit's cooling system, hoping he still had enough power in the batteries he forgot to recharge.

"These readings are odd," Ris said, frowning at his scanner. "The energy signatures keep shifting, like they're trying to avoid detection."

"Maybe they are," Cornelius suggested from somewhere behind them. Damien turned but couldn't spot him - the infiltrator's enhanced stealth abilities made him practically invisible in the jungle shadows.

"I'm impressed." Damien said. "Your rogue skills are coming along nicely."

"They're shit. When I get to 50 then be impressed." He retorted.

The ruins emerged gradually through the foliage - first a fallen column here, a crumbling wall there. But as they pressed deeper into the ancient city, Damien noticed something unsettling about the architecture. The buildings weren't just weathered by time - they showed signs of violent destruction. Massive gouges carved into stone walls, blast marks that no natural force could have created.

"Hold up," Ris raised his hand, studying his scanner intently. "These markings... they're Alteri script."

"Can you read them?" Damien asked.

"Some. My telepathy's picking up residual impressions." Ris traced the carved letters with his fingers. "They're warnings. Something about... containment protocols?"

Amelia cursed under her breath. "I don't like the sound of that. The last thing we need is some ancient fucking disease or something. I better use a protective hypospray!"

"Not disease," Ris shook his head. "Something else. The impressions are fragmented, but I'm getting images of... combat? No, not combat. They were running from something."

The scanner's display flickered erratically. Damien's wrist device chimed with an alert:

Warning: Unknown energy patterns detected
Caution advised

"The energy readings are all wrong," Reyes said, checking his own instruments. "This isn't normal decay or residual power signatures. It's like the whole city is... alive somehow."

A distant crash echoed through the ruins. Damien's hand moved to his blaster as something large shifted in the shadows of a nearby building. The movement wasn't natural - more mechanical than organic.

"Mic no like this place," the alien warrior growled softly. "Smell wrong."

"This is fucking 15th level!" Amelia used the protective hypospray on her neck.

Damien cringed, the air felt charged, like the moment before a lightning strike. His instincts screamed they should retreat, but they needed the experience these ruins could provide.

"The script continues here," Ris moved to another wall. "It's a record of their last days. They were conducting some kind of experiment... something went wrong..."

The ground trembled slightly beneath their feet. In the distance, more crashes and the sound of stone grinding against stone. Whatever inhabited these ruins was definitely aware of their presence now.

"The Alteri didn't abandon this city," Ris's voice was grim as he deciphered more text. "They sealed it. Tried to contain whatever they created here."

Chapter 24: The Forgotten City

Damien's fingers tightened on his blaster as Ris held up his hand in warning. The scanner's display pulsed with increasing energy readings, and the ground vibrated with rhythmic tremors that shook loose debris from the crumbling ruins.

"Multiple signatures converging on our position," Ris reported, his voice tight. "The energy patterns... they're artificial. Some kind of ancient machines."

Through gaps in the fallen stonework, Damien caught glimpses of movement. The construct that emerged towered three stories high, its humanoid form a patchwork of Alteri technology and corrupted modifications.

"That's no maintenance droid," Damien muttered, backing away slowly. The machine's head swiveled toward them, sensor arrays glowing with malevolent intelligence. Its arms ended in what appeared to be weapon mounts, though centuries of exposure had warped the metal into grotesque shapes.

"Fifteen to twentieth level my ass!" Cornelius materialized beside him. "That thing's got to be at least level thirty."

"More incoming," Reyes called out, his own scanner beeping urgently. "Three... no, four more energy signatures approaching from different directions."

Mic hefted his massive weapon. "Mic smash robot!"

"Wait!" Ris's voice cut through their panic. "These aren't just security constructs. They're what the Alteri were trying to contain. Their experiment in artificial intelligence evolved beyond their control."

"Isn't that a cliche' by now?" Cornelius asked. "How many times has the artificial intelligence run a muck and overtaken its creators?"

"It's universal, people are scared of what they don't understand." Damien said.

"The fucking cliche' is about to pound your ass into the ground!" Amelia said as she prepared her newly made stims to hand out.

The first construct took a thunderous step forward, servos whining as it raised its arm-mounted weapons. Ancient targeting systems powered up with an ominous hum.

"Evolved is right," Damien said, noting the bizarre modifications covering the machine's frame. "Looks like it's been upgrading itself with whatever it could salvage."

Amelia prepped a combat stim. "If these things have been trapped here for centuries, no wonder they're pissed off."

The construct's sensors pulsed brighter as it analyzed them. Its head tilted slightly, like a curious predator studying potential prey. Or perhaps, Damien realized, like a machine recognizing something familiar in their technology.

"Our gear," Reyes whispered. "The wrist devices, the weapons - they're based on Alteri designs. These things might see us as..."

"As their creators," Ris finished. "Or their jailers."

The construct's weapons hummed louder, energy building to dangerous levels. Through the ruins, Damien could see the other machines converging on their position, each one unique in its corrupted evolution. Some moved on multiple legs like metallic spiders, others floated on antigravity fields that sparked and groaned with instability.

"Please tell me you have a plan," Damien said to Ris, his blaster suddenly feeling woefully inadequate against these monstrosities.

"Working on it." Ris's scanner beeped rapidly as he analyzed the approaching constructs. "These energy readings... they're not just machines anymore. The AI has merged with the city's power grid somehow. They're all connected, sharing a collective consciousness."

The lead construct's head snapped toward Ris at his words, its sensors focusing intently on his scanner. The weapon mounts adjusted their aim with mechanical precision.

The construct burst from the ruins in an explosion of ancient stone and vegetation. Its metallic frame gleamed with an unnatural sheen, energy pulsing across articulated limbs that seemed to shift and reform with each movement. Damien's enhanced combat reflexes kicked in as he dove behind a fallen column, drawing his blaster in one fluid motion.

"Those aren't standard defense robots," Reyes called out, his scanner whirring. "The energy patterns - they're evolving, adapting!"

"Catch up, you're behind. We already figured that out." Cornelius said.

More constructs emerged from the shadows, their forms a bizarre fusion of Alteri technology and organic growth. Damien's level 15 combat training along with the enhancements in his flight suit allowed him to identify weak points in their armor - joints, power cores, sensor arrays. His upgraded Mark X blaster felt comfortable in his hands as he took aim.

"Mic smash machines!" The alien warrior charged forward, his massive frame shrugging off energy blasts that would have vaporized him at lower levels. His new devastating impact ability sent the first construct flying into a stone wall with bone-crushing force.

Ris ignited his power sword, the blade came alive with enhanced energy. His combat precognition allowed him to dodge attacks before they came, weaving between the constructs with impossible grace. The blade carved through metal and stone alike.

Cornelius materialized from the shadows behind one of the larger robots, his shadow step ability making him nearly invisible. Enhanced blade skills guided his vibro-knife into critical systems, shorting out power cores with surgical precision.

"Their adaptive algorithms are fascinating," Reyes shouted, his upgraded technical expertise allowing him to analyze the constructs even as he fought. "They're learning from each attack, developing countermeasures!"

"Less studying, more shooting!" Damien called back. His new evasive combat training let him roll between cover points while maintaining accuracy. Energy bolts from his blaster found gaps in the constructs' evolving armor. He heard the distinct chime of his and the others' wrist devices as they registered XP gain during the fight. It was the most he had ever heard them going off at once. They were finally fighting at level.

Amelia moved efficiently between them, her advanced medical protocols keeping them in fighting shape. She was distributing stims while healing when needed. "These fucking things are radioactive! Everyone's getting decontamination shots after this!"

A massive construct, easily twice the size of the others, burst through a temple wall. Its form rippled and shifted, absorbing debris to enhance its armor. Damien's wrist device registered it as a level 18 elite.

"Focus fire!" Ris commanded, "we're going to need to work together to take this one down. Mic's devastating strikes staggered the machine while Cornelius's stealth attacks disrupted its systems. Damien's precision shots found vulnerable spots exposed by the damage.

The construct adapted quickly, its surface flowing like liquid metal to seal breaches. But Reyes's enhanced engineering knowledge spotted a fatal flaw. "Every third attack the construct's power core becomes unstable! Hit it now!"

Ris leaped forward, his power sword channeling maximum energy. The blade plunged deep into the construct's chest, finding its core. The machine exploded in a shower of parts and energy, its adaptive programming unable to compensate for the overload.

Their wrist devices chimed with earned experience as more constructs approached through the ruins. These moved differently, having learned from their fallen companions. Damien could see their forms already beginning to change, evolving to counter the group's displayed abilities.

"They're networked," Reyes reported, scanning the new threats. "Each one we destroy makes the others stronger. They're sharing combat data!"

Damien reloaded his blaster's power cell, the weapon's enhanced systems adjusting to compensate for the constructs' adaptations. "Then we better take them all down before they evolve beyond our current abilities." He fired another volley at an approaching construct. The machines were evolving faster now, their metallic forms rippling and reforming to patch damaged areas. His wrist device registered each hit, but the experience gains were diminishing as the constructs adapted to their tactics.

"We need to find their power source," he called out between shots. "Cut them off at the source before they evolve beyond our abilities."

Ris nodded, his power sword carving through another construct's legs. "The energy readings are strongest from that central temple." He pointed to a massive structure rising above the ruins, its ancient stone covered in pulsing lines of blue-green light.

"That color..." Damien's stomach dropped as recognition hit him. "It looks just like-"

"The Laucnar," Ris finished. "But smaller, less powerful. This is it! The Alteri must have been experimenting with similar artifacts."

Reyes's scanner beeped urgently. "The energy signature matches! It's definitely the same type of power source, just on a smaller scale. The constructs are drawing power from it somehow."

A mechanical screech echoed through the ruins as more machines emerged, their forms now barely recognizable as humanoid. Tentacles of living metal writhed from joints, and sensor arrays shifted like organic eyes. Damien's wrist device registered them as level 17, their rapid evolution pushing them beyond the group's current abilities.

"The Alteri weren't just building machines," Ris said, his telepathy picking up fragments of information from the ruins. "They were trying to create true artificial life. The power source let them bridge the gap between mechanical and organic."

"And it worked too well," Cornelius appeared beside them, his stealth field flickering. "These things aren't just evolving their bodies - they're developing consciousness."

Damien watched as one of the constructs paused to repair a fallen companion, its movements displaying something almost like concern. "They're not just sharing combat data anymore. They're actually learning, feeling."

"That's fucking ridiculous, they are not." Amelia said. They're just repairing like any Ai would do in this situation."

"The archives mentioned containment protocols," Ris said, deflecting an energy blast with his sword. "The Alteri must have realized their creations were becoming too powerful, too independent. They tried to shut them down, but-"

"But the machines fought back," Reyes finished. "They've been trapped here for centuries, growing, evolving, waiting for someone to find them."

Damien spotted a path through the ruins toward the central temple. "If we can reach that power source, maybe we can-"

A massive construct crashed through a nearby wall, its form a horrific blend of machine and something almost organic. Damien's wrist device flashed a warning - level 20, far beyond their current abilities. The machine's sensor arrays focused on them with terrifying intelligence, and for a moment Damien could have sworn he saw recognition in its gaze.

The construct's surface rippled as it absorbed nearby debris, its form growing.

Damien dove behind a fallen column as the level 20 construct's energy beam carved through the space he'd occupied moments before. He could feel the heat of the blast through his flight suit.

The machine towered above them, its form a nightmarish fusion of technology and pseudo-organic growth. Metallic tentacles writhed from its joints, absorbing debris to enhance its already formidable armor. Its sensor arrays pulsed with malevolent intelligence as it analyzed their tactics.

"This thing's different from the others," Damien called out, firing his blaster at exposed power conduits. The construct's surface rippled, sealing the damage almost instantly. "It's analyzing all our moves!"

Mic charged forward, his massive frame absorbing hits that would have vaporized him at lower levels. His devastating impact ability cracked the construct's outer shell, but living metal flowed to repair the damage. The alien warrior barely dodged a counterattack that left a smoking crater in the ground.

Cornelius materialized from the shadows, his enhanced stealth allowing him to slip past the construct's defenses. His vibro-knife found a gap in the armor, but the machine's tentacles lashed out with impossible speed, forcing him to retreat.

"The power core's unstable," Reyes shouted from cover, his scanner displaying complex energy patterns. "But it's protected by multiple layers of adaptive shielding!"

Ris's power sword carved through a tentacle attempting to crush him, his combat precognition letting him stay one step ahead of the machine's attacks. "We need to overload it somehow - force it to evolve beyond its own capabilities!"

Damien spotted a pattern in the construct's movements. Like flying through an asteroid field, there were gaps in its defense if you knew where to look. His blaster clicked as he adjusted its output.

"Amelia, got any of those combat stims left?" he asked, ducking another energy blast.

"A few vials," she replied, tossing him an injector. "Make it fucking count!"

The stim coursed through his system as Damien rolled to new cover. His perception sharpened, time seeming to slow as his enhanced reflexes kicked into overdrive. He could see the construct's attack patterns now, predict where its defenses would be weakest.

"Everyone hit it at once!" he called out. "Force it to adapt to multiple threats!"

They struck simultaneously - Mic's devastating blow, Cornelius's precision strike, Ris's power sword, and Damien's perfectly aimed shots. The construct's systems overloaded trying to counter every attack. Its surface rippled frantically as it attempted to evolve new defenses.

Reyes's voice cut through the chaos: "The core's exposed! Hit it now!"

Damien's final shot found the construct's vulnerable power source just as Ris's blade plunged into the same spot. The machine's form twisted impossibly as its evolution spiraled out of control. It exploded in a burst of energy that sent them all diving for cover.

Their wrist devices chimed repeatedly as experience flooded in. Damien felt the rush of new levels - 16, then 17, as the group's triumph over the boss construct registered. The remaining machines froze, their network connection to their leader severed.

"Holy shit," Amelia breathed, checking her own device. "That's what proper leveling feels like!"

Damien stood, his muscles aching despite the stim's effects. Around them, the lesser constructs began to power down, their evolution halted without their leader's guidance. His wrist device registered more experience as the quest to explore the forgotten city completed.

"Level 18," Ris announced, deactivating his power sword. "We're finally starting to catch up."

"And we learned something about the Laucnar," Reyes added, collecting salvage from the fallen constructs. "The Alteri were experimenting with similar artifacts. Maybe the texts in the Hall of Knowledge will tell us more."

Chapter 25: Passing the Trials

Damien wiped sweat from his brow as they approached the Hall of Knowledge. The ancient structure loomed before them, its weathered stone walls covered in pulsing lines of energy similar to the constructs they'd fought. The jungle had reclaimed much of the exterior, but the entrance remained clear - almost as if the vegetation deliberately avoided it.

"More Alteri script," Ris said, examining the doorway. "This place... it's different from the ruins. The energy patterns are more controlled, purposeful."

A holographic interface materialized as they approached, its display showing familiar text. Damien's immediately recognized the format.

"This isn't Alteri technology," he said. "Look at the interface - it's the same as the visitors center on the first planet. It's a Jaddus Collective design."

"Are you sure? Let me see." Ris pushed to get a better look. "Well, I'll be damned."

"They must have modified the original structure," Reyes agreed, scanning the entrance. "The power signatures match their engineering style."

The hologram flickered, displaying a message:

Welcome Seekers of Knowledge

To proceed, each must face three trials:

Mind, Body, and Spirit

Only through completion may the archives be accessed

"Three trials each?" Amelia checked her medical supplies. "That's going to burn through my fucking stims."

"At least we know it's level-appropriate content," Damien said, noting the white quest marker on his wrist device. "The Collective wouldn't design trials we couldn't complete."

"Don't bank in that." Cornelius countered.

Individual doorways appeared along the entrance hall, one for each of them. Damien approached his designated path, feeling the familiar tingle of a scanner analyzing his capabilities.

"See you on the other side," he called to the others as they moved toward their own trials.

The first chamber contained a complex holographic puzzle - a three-dimensional maze that shifted and reconfigured itself as he attempted to navigate through it. He used spatial awareness which proved critical as he manipulated energy streams to create new paths.

His wrist device chimed as he completed the Trial of Mind, registering both experience gain and rewards - enhanced tactical analysis protocols that would prove useful in combat, and something to use on his armor to enhance it to level.

The second chamber threw him into a zero-gravity combat scenario against shadow versions of himself. Each clone anticipated his moves, forcing him to develop new strategies on the fly. His recent combat experience with the constructs helped him prevail, earning another level and improved evasion techniques.

But the Trial of Spirit proved most challenging. The chamber stripped away his enhanced abilities, forcing him to confront fragmenting memories of his life before. Images flashed through his mind - a gaming table, friends laughing, rolling dice. The more he tried to hold onto these memories, the faster they seemed to fade.

Understanding dawned as he realized this wasn't just a test - it was preparation. The Jaddus Collective had designed these trials not just to challenge them, but to help them accept their new reality. By facing the loss of their old memories, they could better embrace their roles in this world. It was cool and cruel at the same time.

His device chimed one final time as he completed all three trials, pushing him to level 20. The others emerged from their own trials looking similarly drained but stronger for the experience.

"Did anyone else's Spirit trial feel... personal?" Cornelius asked quietly.

"Like it was designed specifically for us," Ris nodded. "The Collective must have mapped our consciousness when they brought us here. They knew exactly how to test each of us."

"And how to help us grow," Damien added. "These trials weren't just about gaining levels - they were teaching us to accept our new abilities, our new selves."

Ris blinked, "What they were for, if I'm honest, was to purge the last remaining memories in case any lingered. I have been studying the data core we retrieved from the auxiliary archives. I think the core is our stored memories. Someone or something is allowing us to hold on to our awareness in spite of the Jaddus Collective trying to rid us of it."

"What does that mean?" Cornelius asked.

"Well, I see two possibilities. One, if we don't wipe *all* the memories away as they are trying to do, when we finish this our old memories of who we were before and our memories of home will not and cannot be restored. They keep putting in quests to make sure the memories are wiped, which has me believing they have to be in order for the stored ones to be returned."

"What's the second reason? Amelia asked.

"The second reason is to give us the edge of awareness. Being aware of who we are and where we are and following the game-like dynamics give us an edge. We can recognize what to do in certain situations like elite boss fights etc. Getting rid of that edge could be the reason for the memory purge part of the story quests."

Amelia pointed to the door. "We are at the depository of the Alteri. Perhaps our answers are in there."

The central archive doors slid open, revealing rows of data crystals pulsing with stored knowledge. Their wrist devices registered the completion of another quest chain, but Damien barely noticed. His mind was focused on what they might find within.

As they entered the building, Damien stood before the towering shelves of data crystals, each one pulsing with stored knowledge. The archive seemed to stretch endlessly in every direction, its contents organized in ways that defied conventional logic.

"Where do we even start?" he asked, running his fingers along a row of crystals. Each one responded to his touch, displaying holographic snippets of information in ancient scripts.

Amelia pushed past him, her medical scanner already analyzing the nearest shelf. "We need information about the Laucnar. If we can understand how it works, maybe we can help Thomas."

"The Laucnar," Ris repeated thoughtfully. "Notice how the archives recognize that name? Just like they adapted to calling Bright's station the Death Moon."

Damien paused. "Yeah, the simulation's lore changes to match our contributions. Bright bastardized the name Loc-nar from that old movie, and now it's part of the official record."

"Exactly," Ris said. "Which means..."

"The emperor should be in here too," Damien finished. "Bright's fatal flaw was always trying to be the perfect player. He had to have the best character, the most dramatic storyline."

"By making himself emperor, he wrote himself into the lore," Cornelius added, materializing from between the shelves. "He's researchable now."

Damien moved to a central console, navigating the archive's interface. "If we can access records about the emperor, we might learn more about how the Laucnar has changed him. What abilities he's developed, what weaknesses might have emerged."

The console lit up as it processed his request. Data crystals shifted on their shelves, reorganizing themselves around some unseen pattern. A cluster near the center began pulsing more intensely.

"Here," Damien called the others over. "Imperial records, newly added to the archive. Look at the timestamp - they only appeared after Bright took the throne."

Ris examined the crystals, his telepathy picking up traces of stored information. "The lore is still being written. Every choice we make, every name we give things, it becomes part of this world's history."

"Which means we can influence it," Damien said. "We're not just playing through a pre-written story - we're helping create it."

"Like how the Death Moon wasn't originally part of the game's lore," Reyes observed. "But once we named it that, the simulation adapted. Added quest lines, experience rewards, everything needed to make it feel real."

Damien selected a crystal containing recent Imperial decrees. "Bright's doing the same thing on a massive scale. Every time he acts as emperor, he's adding to the story. And since he's such a perfectionist..."

"He's documenting everything," Ris finished. "Every power he gains, every decision he makes - it all gets recorded here because that's what a proper emperor would do."

Damien manipulated the archive's interface, scrolling through the indexed data crystals. The system vibrated as its internal processors accessed his request for information about Emperor Bright. Holographic displays flickered to life, showing fragments of Imperial records.

"Here's something," he said, expanding a recent entry. "After taking the throne, Bright's first act was to order a complete survey of all known Alteri ruins. He's searching for more artifacts like the Laucnar."

"That tracks," Cornelius said. "He always did love collecting powerful items in our gaming sessions."

The archive displayed footage of Imperial troops methodically excavating ancient sites. Damien noticed how the soldiers seemed to move with almost robotic precision, their actions perfectly coordinated. "Look at this - he's using the Laucnar to control his forces directly. They're extensions of his will."

Ris studied another data crystal. "The gem's power has limits though. These medical reports show his disfigurement isn't healing properly. The energy that reflected off my sword did permanent damage."

"And here," Amelia pointed to a biochemical analysis. "His cellular structure is... changing. The Laucnar isn't just corrupting his mind - it's altering his physical form, and not in a good way."

Damien pulled up another record, this one showing the emperor's private chambers. The walls pulsed with the same blue-green energy they'd seen in the ruins. "He's modifying the Imperial palace, integrating the Laucnar's power into the structure itself. Just like those constructs did with their city."

"Makes sense," Reyes said. "If the gem's power is limited, he'd want to amplify it however he could."

More records detailed Bright's increasingly erratic behavior - ordering entire planets surveyed for traces of Alteri technology, executing officials who questioned his obsession with ancient artifacts. But what caught Damien's attention was a psychological assessment from the Imperial medical staff.

"According to this, he's experiencing periods of lucidity," Damien said. "Moments where his original personality resurfaces. The Laucnar's control isn't absolute."

The archive's final entry was the most recent - a directive ordering Imperial forces to locate and capture any beings displaying "enhanced capabilities." Damien's stomach dropped as he realized what that meant.

"He's hunting other players," he said. "Looking for anyone else the Jaddus Collective might have brought into the simulation."

"Experience points," Amelia answered. "Remember what he said? Player characters give more XP than NPCs when defeated. He's trying to level up faster."

"He always out-leveled me in every game, even when we agreed to level together. He never stayed the same like we've been doing." Ris said.

Damien accessed another crystal, this one containing theoretical research on the Laucnar's properties. "The gem's power grows with its user's level. The stronger Bright becomes, the more control he has over its energy."

"So he's not just collecting artifacts and hunting players for power," Ris said. "He's trying to master the Laucnar completely, bend it fully to his will."

The archive showed the gem's influence spreading through the Imperial bureaucracy. Officials who spent too much time near the emperor began displaying similar signs of corruption - heightened aggression, obsession with power, physical mutations. Bright was slowly transforming the entire Empire into an extension of the Laucnar's will.

"Well, that's just perfect," Cornelius muttered. "Our gamemaster's turned into a level-grinding tyrant with a cosmic artifact of doom. Anyone else missing the days when we just rolled dice?"

Chapter 26: Secrets of the Alteri

Damien leaned closer to the archive's holographic display, interested in the new information as it populated and scrolled across the screen. The more he read, the more pieces began falling into place.

"This can't be right," he muttered, rechecking the data. "Amelia, take a look at this."

She moved beside him, scanning the ancient text. "What am I looking at?"

"The Laucnar - it's not what we thought. These records show it's some kind of advanced AI storage system. The Alteri created these 'gems' as repositories for artificial consciousness."

Amelia adjusted the display settings, bringing up detailed schematics. "You're right. The crystalline structure acts as a quantum computer, capable of housing complex neural networks. The blue-green energy we've been seeing? That's just a visible manifestation of the quantum processing power."

"And look here," Damien highlighted another section. "The gem controlling those constructs we fought? Same basic design as the Laucnar, just an earlier prototype. They were all part of the same research project."

The archives revealed more as they dug deeper. Diagrams showed how the Alteri had attempted to create truly autonomous artificial minds, using the crystals as both hardware and power source. Each gem was meant to evolve and grow along with its developing consciousness.

"This whole place is being run by one," Damien realized, noting the familiar energy patterns pulsing through the archive's walls. "That's why it can adapt and record new information so efficiently."

"But what does this have to do with the Jaddus Collective?" Amelia asked as she began a new search in the database.

The answer appeared in a genealogical database - a direct lineage linking the ancient Alteri to the modern Collective. "They're descendants," Damien said. "The Collective inherited all this technology, including the research into artificial consciousness. At the visitor's center, the computer said they suspected the Alteri Dominion as their attackers. If the collective is a descendant why would they attack themselves?"

"You're forgetting in that same message it said the modern Alteri are suspected of working exclusively for the nefarious

House Davosi. I assume that means they no longer have ties with the Jaddus Collective."

"Ah, yeah, they might not even realize they are related anymore."

Amelia's fingers flew across the interface as she connected more dots. "I'm going to go out on a limb here and make an educated guess based on this data. "The game - it's not just a simulation. They're using our brains, our memories and experiences, to help solve problems with the AI development."

"That's why they need our original memories stored separately," Damien said. "Our minds are processing power for their experiments. We're helping them understand how consciousness works by literally living through their tests."

The archives showed how the Alteri had struggled with making their artificial minds truly self-aware. They could create incredibly advanced programs, but true consciousness remained elusive. The Jaddus Collective had apparently inherited both the technology and the challenge.

"So Bright isn't being corrupted by some evil artifact," Damien said. "The Laucnar is trying to merge with his consciousness, create some kind of hybrid awareness. That's why he's having those lucid moments - two minds fighting for control."

"And why he's so obsessed with gaining levels," Amelia added. "More power means more processing capability, more control over the merger. He's not just playing the game anymore - he's becoming something entirely new."

"Nah, he's always been obsessed with leveling." Ris said. "I think you two are grasping at straws."

Cornelius frowned at the knowledge database. "Yeah, I don't buy it either. I think you are both making fairly big leaps in logic while piecing together what you're looking at here. If the Alteri can create this simulation and all these elaborate quests etcetera. why would they need our flawed human brains to fix problems? This game simulation is based on our games, it was for fun. The Alteri, or the Jaddus Collective, loved our adventures and wanted to be part of them. it doesn't add up. I think what you've found here is just lore for the game."

"Agree, it's just to fit quests." Mic said. "It does not have to make sense if just to advance game. It just need to sound good."

"Yeah, like it's plausible." Reyes agreed. "All this stuff in this archive could just be bullshit."

"Great!" Ris said, "we're second guessing our second guessing."

Damien spun at the sound of footsteps behind them. A familiar figure emerged from between the archive shelves - Thomas Bright, his disfigured face partially hidden in shadow. The Laucnar's energy rippling beneath his skin, giving him an otherworldly glow.

"Still fumbling around at level 20?" Bright's voice dripped with disdain. "I expected better from you all. You should be well past 50th by now."

Damien's wrist device flashed a warning - Purple- Level 60. His grip tightened on his blaster, though he knew it would be useless against someone that powerful.

"You've been here already," Ris said, studying their former friend. "You knew what we'd find."

"Of course I did. I've explored every archive, every ruin worth investigating." Bright gestured dismissively at the data crystals. "You're wasting time here. The real challenges, the true paths to power, lie elsewhere."

"Like where?" Damien asked, noting how Bright's form seemed slightly transparent in the archive's light.

"That would be telling." Bright smiled, the expression grotesque on his warped features. "Though I'm getting tired of waiting for you to catch up. Your incompetence is... disappointing."

Cornelius moved silently through the shadows, using his enhanced stealth abilities to circle behind Bright undetected. But when he struck, his blade passed right through their former friend's body.

"A hologram," Damien said as Bright's image flickered. "He's not really here."

"Just checking on your progress," Bright's projection smirked. "Or lack thereof." His form began to fade. "Don't take too long. I'd hate to have to find other players to harvest experience from."

The hologram vanished, leaving them alone among the archive's pulsing crystals.

"Damn it," Ris slammed his fist against a shelf. "He planted that information about the Laucnar. Led us right to it."

"You think it's all fake?" Damien asked, reviewing the archive entries they'd found.

"Maybe not all of it," Ris said. "But enough to mislead us. Make us waste time theorizing while he gets even stronger."

"He's at level 60 now," Amelia noted, checking her device. "We need to hit at least 50th before we can challenge him."

"50th?" Reyes whistled. "That's a lot of grinding ahead of us."

"Then we better get started," Damien said, holstering his blaster. "Bright's not going to wait forever."

"I'm sure he will continue to level as well. I can't imagine him stopping to wait on us. He doesn't have the patience for that." Ris said.

"At least now we know what we're up against," Cornelius added. "And what level we need to reach."

"Mic tired of talking," the alien warrior growled. "Time to find things to smash."

Damien nodded, already plotting their next move. Level 50 seemed impossibly far away, but they had no choice. They needed to catch up to Bright before he grew too powerful to stop.

"I am kind of sick of feeling like we are always behind." Ris said. "Well, what's next?"

"What you mean? We smash things to 30th." Mic said.

"Not here we don't." Cornelius said. "This place is level 15 to 20 remember."

"That's right." Reyes said. "We might as well go. I don't think any of us would trust anything else lore-wise we find in here."

"Okay, let's get back the ship and regroup." Ris suggested.

Damien led the way back through the archive's winding corridors and back outside. After a short walk, The Friday the 13th's familiar silhouette emerged through the jungle canopy as they approached the landing site. "Before we do anything else, we need to properly allocate these new levels," he said, activating his wrist interface. "No point rushing into more fights if we haven't optimized our skills."

Mira greeted them at the landing ramp, her android systems already analyzing their conditions. "Welcome back. I detect significant power increases in all crew members."

"You could say that," Damien settled into the pilot's chair, scrolling through his skill options. "It just doesn't feel all that productive now." As he scrolled, he *was* happy the jump to level 20 had unlocked several advanced piloting specializations he'd been eager to explore, though.

Amelia caught his eye, gesturing for him to join her and Reyes in the medical bay. Once they were alone, she closed the door.

"I think a lot of what we found in those archives was legitimate," she said in a low voice. "The technical specifications about the Laucnar's quantum processing capabilities were too detailed to be fake."

Reyes nodded, examining his own interface. "The engineering schematics matched known Alteri designs perfectly. Bright couldn't have fabricated all that just to mislead us."

"His hologram showing up was too convenient," Damien agreed. "Like he wanted to make us doubt everything we'd learned about his new toy."

"Exactly," Amelia pulled up data she'd copied from the archives. "Look at these neural interface patterns. They're consistent with how the Laucnar affects organic tissue. Bright's trying to keep us from understanding its true nature."

"Why don't you two keep researching this. You are both scientists and engineers so you can use points to enhance your skill people like me can't afford to waste."

"We were already planning to." Reyes said.

"So where do we go from here?" Damien asked. "We need somewhere to level up that he hasn't already stripped clean."

"What about further into the outer rim?" Reyes suggested. "There are plenty of uncharted systems out there. Places the Empire hasn't reached yet. We are already partially there."

"And more importantly, places Bright wouldn't bother with," Amelia added. "He's focused on ancient sites, places with obvious power. The rim worlds might have challenges he's overlooked."

Damien considered this as he allocated points into advanced atmospheric flight controls. The outer systems were dangerous, but they might be their best chance to gain levels without Imperial interference. "Do you think we can do this without jeopardizing our main story quests?"

"We just need to grind the levels. We can always do the story quests later experience or not. Amelia said.

"Speaking of grinding, don't we get more experience from the story quests? Why would we deviate from that?" Damien asked.

"Yeah, but the story quests take twice as long to complete and are very involved. On the outer rim we can just level." Reyes said.

"True grinding." Amelia agreed.

"We'll need to be careful though," Reyes said. "No more rushing into situations under-leveled. We do this smart, build our power steadily."

"Agreed," Amelia said. "And we keep studying what we learned about the Laucnar. Understanding how it works might be just as important as gaining levels."

"Okay. let's go tell the others where we think we should go next and see what they say." Damien suggested.

Damien followed Amelia and Reyes back to the bridge where the others waited. Mic had already begun cleaning his weapons while Cornelius studied star charts on the main display. Ris paced near the viewport, his power sword hilt tapping against his leg.

"We think we should head deeper into the outer rim," Damien announced. "Find somewhere Bright hasn't already picked clean."

Ris paused his pacing. "The rim worlds are dangerous. Lots of unknown variables."

"Exactly," Damien said. "Bright's focused on known power sources - ancient ruins, Alteri sites. He won't waste time with unexplored systems."

"Mic like unknown danger." The alien warrior looked up from his weapon maintenance. "Better than fighting emperor's armies."

"He's right," Cornelius added. "The Empire's influence barely reaches the outer systems. We could level up without Imperial interference."

Ris activated his scanner, studying the long-range star charts. "There are several candidates. Most are uncharted, but I'm picking up some interesting energy signatures."

The holographic display zoomed in on a particular system near the rim's edge. A green world orbiting a yellow star, its surface largely unexplored according to the database.

"This one," Ris highlighted the planet. "Preliminary scans show level-appropriate challenges - everything scales between 22 and 30. No signs of Imperial activity or ancient ruins that might attract Bright's attention."

Damien examined the readouts. The planet's atmosphere was breathable, its gravity close to standard. But something about the energy patterns seemed odd - not necessarily dangerous, just... different.

"What are those readings?" he asked, pointing to fluctuating power signatures.

"Unknown," Ris admitted. "But that's partly why I chose it. Whatever's down there, it's not something Bright would recognize or care about. No obvious power sources to tempt him."

"The scaling is perfect for us," Amelia noted. "We can start with the level 22 areas and work our way up as we get stronger."

"We'll have to work together at first, that's two levels above us and one above Ris. " Cornelius said.

"We can all solo twenty-second level with the armor upgrades and weapons we have. "Reyes said.

"There is nothing wrong with confidence." Ris laughed. "So much for not running in headlong."

"Well, if we run into anything too tough, the ship's not far," Reyes added. "Mira can have us out of there in minutes."

Cornelius studied the sensor data. "No settlements, no ruins, no signs of civilization at all. Just wilderness and whatever's generating those energy patterns."

"Sounds perfect," Damien said. "Natural challenges instead of artificial ones. Real experience instead of quest grinding."

"I agree," Ris nodded. " It might be a good change of pace and we can gain levels organically without worrying about Bright's interference. And if there are any discoveries to be made, they'll be ours first."

"Then it's settled," Damien moved to the pilot's station. "Everyone strap in. Let's see what the outer rim has to offer."

Chapter 27: Confrontation

Damien guided the Friday the 13th through hyperspace, the ship's enhanced engines running smoothly under his command. The outer rim world Ris had identified grew larger in their viewport as they approached. Its atmosphere swirled with weather patterns unlike anything Damien had seen before.

"These readings are getting stranger," Ris said from the sensor station, adjusting his scanner settings. "The energy signatures are multiplying as we get closer. They're everywhere, especially concentrated in the forest regions."

Damien brought them into a high orbit, running preliminary atmospheric scans. "What kind of power sources are we talking about?"

"That's just it - they don't match any known patterns. Not Alteri tech, not Imperial... nothing in our database." Ris studied his display. "It's like the planet's generating its own energy somehow."

The ship's sensors picked up massive storm systems moving across the surface. Lightning cascaded between clouds in unpredictable patterns, and wind readings showed dangerous gusts.

"The weather's as weird as the energy readings," Damien noted. "Those storms aren't following normal atmospheric patterns."

"The plant life is off the charts too," Reyes added from his station. "Biomass readings are incredible. The forests cover most of the continental landmasses."

Damien adjusted their orbit to avoid a sudden wind shear that rattled the hull. "Any signs of animal life?"

"Plenty," Ris replied. "Large creatures moving through the canopy, herds of something in the few plains there are... and these energy signatures seem stronger around concentrations of life forms."

Through the viewport, Damien could see the planet's surface more clearly now. Vast forests stretched to the horizon, their canopy occasionally broken by clearings or rock formations.

"The energy readings are definitely strongest in the trees," Ris continued, fine-tuning his scans. "It's like they're drawing power from somewhere underground and channeling it up through their root systems."

"Natural power conduits?" Damien said, intrigued. "That's good, Bright is looking for artificial power sources, not biological ones. It's not likely he would take interest in this place."

The ship's sensors chimed with new data as they began atmospheric entry. The energy patterns grew more intense, creating interference with their instruments. Damien compensated, keeping them steady despite the turbulence.

"I'm picking up thousands of distinct energy signatures now," Ris reported. "They're pulsing, almost like they're communicating with each other through the root systems. The whole planet's like one giant power grid. The thing is I am not reading any machinery or generators of any kind."

A massive storm front forced Damien to adjust course. The Friday the 13th's hull creaked as violent winds buffeted them from multiple directions. Rain lashed the viewport, briefly obscuring their view of the surface below.

"Well, this should be interesting," Damien said, engaging the ship's advanced stabilizers. "Anyone see a good place to land that isn't in the middle of a storm or surrounded by whatever's generating those power readings?"

"Scanning." Reyes said.

"Hmm, still want to hunt here? Mic no like too much rain. Also, wet climate means bugs. Mic hate damn bugs! Especially hate big bugs."

Amelia squinted into the forest through the viewport as Reyes gave Damien coordinates to land the ship. There was not a clearing large enough, but they did manage to land with part of the stern out over the water of a wide river. "I don't know. I am beginning to agree with Mic. This place looks like it might make us miserable running around out there in that weather. Can't we go someplace more....sunny?"

"We may as well explore the planet since we are already here." Ris said.

"I was afraid you were going to say that." Amelia lamented.

"Mira, you know the drill, be ready for anything." Damien commanded.

"I shall endeavor to please, captain." she said.

Damien turned back to her as an afterthought, "Any more of those suggestions that might help us level?"

"My sensors indicate the forest is alive and connected. My only suggestion is to exercise caution."

Damien sighed, "All right, not what I was expecting but solid advice." He waved for the others to follow him as he departed the ship.

The canopy above them pulsed with bioluminescent patterns that seemed to follow their movements. Each step deeper into the woods brought new waves of energy readings on their scanners.

"These power signatures are getting stronger," Reyes said.

They stepped by a couple of plants that blew out a cloud of something as they passed.

"Don't breathe the spores!" Amelia shouted, covering her mouth and nose, but it was too late. The hallucinogenic particles were already taking effect. The forest floor seemed to ripple and shift beneath their feet. "That's a quick acting hallucinogen. I am going to have to get some of that for...study."

Mic staggered, his massive frame swaying. "Trees... trees moving. No, Mic seeing things."

Through the haze, massive shapes emerged from the undergrowth. They appeared to be some kind of insectoid creatures, their chitinous bodies merged with plant matter. Bioluminescent patterns pulsed across their forms in sync with the forest's energy readings.

"Ugh, not damn bugs!" Mic slurred.

The group tried to maintain formation, but the forest itself seemed to work against them. Roots burst from the ground, creating barriers between team members. Vines pulled them in different directions while the large insectoid creatures herded them apart.

"Why do these planets always seem to be so far above the level they read as? Amelia complained.

Damien found himself separated from the others, pushed toward a clearing with Cornelius. Their blaster fire seemed ineffective against the living walls that had sprung up around them. Through gaps in the vegetation, they could see Ris and Mic being driven in another direction, while Amelia and Reyes disappeared into a third section of the forest.

The spores' effects intensified. Each crew member began seeing personalized visions designed to play on their deepest fears. Damien saw himself crashing ships, losing control, failing to protect his friends. Cornelius faced shadowy duplicates of himself, each one revealing his carefully guarded secrets.

"We need to regroup!" Ris's voice carried over their comm devices. "The forest is separating us by our combat roles - warriors, damage dealers, and support, so we can't coordinate a plan of attack. We're vulnerable divided like this!"

A massive creature blocked the path between Ris and Mic and the others, its bioluminescent patterns flaring aggressively. More animated plants converged on their position while the hallucinogenic spores continued to cloud their judgment.

"The forest sees us as invaders," Reyes transmitted through bursts of static.

"Damien, Cornelius," Amelia's voice wavered over the comm. "You two have the firepower. Try to clear a path back to the center while Reyes and I work on countering these spores. Ris, Mic - we need your defensive capabilities to hold these insectoids back once we find each other."

The forest pulsed with renewed energy as if understanding their plan. More barriers sprouted between the separated groups while the larger creatures moved to maintain the division. The living woods seemed determined to keep them apart, recognizing that their greatest advantage lay in working together.

Through the spore-induced haze, Mic and Ris found themselves cornered by three massive guardian beasts. Each creature stood twice Mic's height, their bodies a fusion of chitinous armor and living wood.

"Like old days on Centauri Six," Mic growled, hefting his weapon. "Big monsters need big smashing."

Ris ignited his power sword, the blade's energy cutting through the hallucinogenic fog. "Focus on the lead creature. I'll keep the others off your back."

The largest guardian charged, its tree-like limbs swinging with devastating force. Mic met the attack head-on, his size and strength letting him catch and redirect the blow. The creature's momentum carried it past him, leaving its flank exposed to Ris's blade.

Across the forest, Damien and Cornelius faced a different challenge. Animated vines whipped through the air while roots burst from the ground in coordinated attacks. Their blaster fire seemed to only anger the plants, causing them to grow back stronger.

"The energy patterns," Damien called out, dodging a thorny tendril. "They're channeling power through the root system. If we can disrupt the flow..."

Cornelius materialized from the shadows, his vibro-knife severing a major root node. The surrounding plants immediately wilted. "Got it. Target the connection points where the energy transfers between sections."

In another part of the forest, Amelia and Reyes struggled against waves of increasingly intense hallucinations. The spores played on their deepest fears - failed missions, lost patients, engineering disasters that cost lives.

"It's attacking our trauma responses," Amelia said, forcing herself to focus through the visions. "The chemical composition is similar to other hallucinogens I've studied. If I can synthesize a counter-agent..."

Reyes nodded, fighting his own nightmarish visions. "The forest's using our own neural patterns against us. But if we can identify the transmission frequency..." He adjusted his scanner, analyzing how the plants communicated their psychic attacks.

The three pairs maintained constant communication despite the forest's attempts to jam their signals. Mic reported successful tactics against the guardian beasts while Damien shared discoveries about the plants' energy network. Amelia transmitted chemical formulas as she developed them, helping the others resist the worst of the hallucinations.

"The root system is the key," Reyes's voice came steadily over their comms instead of his usual panic. "It's all connected - the guardian beasts, the plants, the spores. They're part of one massive organism. We may not be able to coordinate but they can."

"That's probably how they knew to separate us." Damien said.

"Then we need to find a way to coordinate our attacks again," Ris replied between sword strikes. "Is there any way we can get past their efforts to keep us apart?"

Mic slammed another guardian into a tree trunk. "Big smashing better when working together."

The forest seemed to sense their growing cooperation, intensifying its efforts to keep them separated. But with each challenge they overcame, their teamwork grew stronger.

Their wrist devices chimed periodically as new skills unlocked - combat synergies, enhanced resistance, improved coordination. The forest had forced them to adapt and grow stronger together, even while trying to keep them apart.

Through the clearing mist of spores, the separated groups found themselves being subtly herded back toward the Friday the 13th. The forest's aggressive barriers gradually shifted, creating paths that led them to converge near their landing site.

Amelia stumbled out of the vegetation first, her medical scanner still actively analyzing the dissipating chemical compounds in the air. "Was this some kind of test?"

"What?" Reyes asked. "Who would be testing us? The plants, the bugs?"

"Wait... I have proof. This whole thing was a test," she said as Reyes emerged beside her. "The forest wasn't attacking us - it was evaluating our roles, seeing how we functioned under pressure." She showed him her readings. The energy signatures were dissipating.

Ris and Mic appeared from another direction, their armor scuffed from combat with the guardians but otherwise unharmed. The giant insectoid creatures that had seemed so threatening now stood placidly among the trees, their bioluminescent patterns pulsing in gentle rhythms as if they were communicating calmness.

"I would theorize the spores weren't meant to harm us," Amelia continued. "They were reading our neural patterns, assessing our true natures."

Her wrist device chimed

Bonus Exploration Experience: Competed
Bonus Quest complete: Analyzing New Threats
Reward: Experience
Ding: Dr. Amelia Mann has reached level 21!

"Hey, not fair! Only you get bonus quest." Mic said.

Minutes later, Damien and Cornelius finally completed their circuit through the forest's challenges, joining the others near the ship. As they regrouped, a remarkable transformation began before them.

One of the larger trees began to shift and flow, its trunk reshaping itself into a vaguely humanoid form. Branches twisted into limbs while leaves formed into features. The being stepped forward with slow, deliberate movements.

"You have proven yourselves worthy," it spoke in an odd, measured cadence that seemed to emanate from the wood itself. "Your hearts are pure, your minds unclouded by malice."

"The spores were a test of character," Amelia said, recognizing the sophistication of the chemical compounds.

"Yes," the tree-being's voice had a strange reverberating cadence. "We needed to understand your true selves, your designated roles in this realm."

The forest floor trembled slightly as underground power reverberated. Through gaps in the roots, they could see complex organic fabrication systems spinning and weaving plant fibers into intricate patterns.

"The energy signatures," Reyes breathed, watching the subterranean technology work. "They're not just power sources - they're manufacturing centers."

"We craft what is needed," the tree-being confirmed. "Your separation allowed us to analyze your requirements. Now we may properly equip each according to their profession."

The fabricators moaned and sputtered as they produced specialized armor and equipment. Combat gear perfectly sized for Mic's massive frame, lightweight infiltration suits for Cornelius, reinforced flight gear for Damien, enhanced medical equipment for Amelia, and other profession-specific items emerged from the ground.

"The forest is a collective consciousness," Amelia said, examining the expertly crafted supplies. "It used the spores to read our skills and experience, then custom-designed equipment to match our specialties."

"Give it rest. You already got XP." Mic said bitterly.

The tree-being's leaves rustling with motion. "You understand correctly. We seek to aid those who prove themselves worthy through cooperation and trust. It has been our purpose for one thousand years. Some, keep us secret and some try to force us to make them armor such as what you are to receive, but we must add them to the nourishment of the forest. Your team bonds remained strong despite our attempts to divide you. This demonstrates your readiness for the gifts we offer."

Amelia examined her new medical gear, a grin spreading across her face. "Bright should see us now. He would have loved this place if he wasn't so focused on artificial power sources. Too bad he never took natural energy seriously."

The tree-being's form rippled, leaves shuddering as if caught in a sudden wind. "Thomas Bright? The one who bears the corrupted crystal? He has already walked these grounds."

Ris stepped forward eagerly, hope flickering in his eyes. "Was he found pure of heart and mind? Is there still a chance he can be redeemed?"

The forest entity recoiled, its wooden features contorting in what could only be described as fear. "We were... compelled to aid him. The crystal he wielded - its power devastated entire sections of our collective consciousness. We had no choice but to craft what he demanded."

"So you equipped him too?" Damien asked, his hand instinctively tightening on his new gear.

"Under duress," the being's voice broke in rushed segments of sound. "He cared nothing for our tests or traditions. The crystal's energy burned through our defenses, forced our fabricators to produce what he desired."

Mic growled low in his throat. "Bad man hurt forest. Mic understand why forest test us now."

After the tree-being learned of their mission to stop Bright, its entire demeanor changed. The bioluminescent patterns throughout the forest pulsed with renewed intensity. "You seek to challenge him? Then you will need far more than our standard equipment. You shall have our rarest, most preciously constructed wares. "

The underground fabricators whirred to life again, this time producing gear of extraordinary quality. Armor infused with the forest's own energy patterns, weapons enhanced by natural power sources, equipment that seemed to pulse with organic vitality.

"This is... incredible," Reyes breathed, examining the enhanced technology. "The craftsmanship is beyond anything I've seen."

"We offer our finest work," the tree-being said. "And knowledge of where you might grow stronger in order to defeat the man with the corrupted gem. There is a world, not far from here, where you can gain significant power quickly. The challenges there are numerous but manageable - perfect for reaching your full potential." He gestured to the sky, "The planet is called Antelis VII. The people there have need of your kind services, and they offer substantial rewards. You will find no Imperial presence there, no ancient ruins to attract unwanted attention. I will inform them you are coming. The people there operate by manipulating crystals. It is quite a remarkable place."

The forest entity transmitted the coordinates directly to their wrist devices, along with detailed information about Antelis VII's challenges and resources.

"Why are you helping us so much?" Amelia asked, studying the coordinates.

"Because we have seen the corruption spreading through the empire," the being replied. "The emperor is a bad man and he must be stopped."

Chapter 28: Antelis VII

Damien guided the Friday the 13th through Antelis VII's atmosphere while compensating for unusual gravitational fluctuations. Three moons hung in the violet sky, their overlapping orbits creating complex tidal effects across the planet's surface.

"These readings match what the tree-being showed us," Ris said from the sensor station. "Multiple energy hotspots, but they're different from what we saw in the forest. More... structured."

The planet below revealed itself as they descended - a landscape of crystalline formations jutting from rich purple soil. Vast plains stretched between the crystal forests, dotted with settlements that seemed to grow organically from the mineral-rich ground. The architecture blended seamlessly with the natural formations, making it difficult to distinguish where buildings ended and crystals began.

"Population centers are concentrated around the larger crystal clusters," Reyes reported, studying his displays. "They're using the formations as natural power conduits, just like the forest planet did with its trees." He whistled, "And man is there power flowing!"

Damien spotted movement in the plains - herds of six-legged domesticated creatures being tended to by some of the local population. Native birds with transparent wings soared between the crystal spires, their calls creating harmonic resonances with the minerals. The sounds of which bounced off the ship disrupting sensor readings.

"The atmospheric composition is perfect for us," Amelia said, checking her medical readings. "No toxic elements, no dangerous radiation levels. The crystal formations actually seem to purify the air."

Through gaps in the crystal forests, they could see sprawling marketplaces and training grounds. Their onboard viewscreens captured armored warriors practicing combat techniques that incorporated the natural energy flows, while craftsmen shaped crystal fragments into tools and weapons.

"Look at their tech level," Cornelius pointed to settlements depicted on his viewscreen. "Advanced enough to harness the crystal energy, but clever enough to keep it hidden from Imperial attention."

"Mic see good fighting places," the alien warrior observed. "Many challenges, many chances to grow stronger."

The ship's sensors detected regular energy pulses emanating from the largest settlement - some kind of signal or beacon. As they drew closer, the purpose became clear. Landing pads made of shaped crystal extended from the city's central spire, designed to accommodate vessels of various sizes.

"They're used to visitors at least," Damien noted, guiding them toward an appropriate landing zone. "These pads must have been built for independent traders and merchants."

"Or thieves and mercenaries." Ris continued.

"You're being negative." Damien said, "Look at this place. I doubt it's a place for smugglers and riff raff." He landed the Friday the 13th onto one of the crystalline platforms with a soft hum. Through the viewport, they could see locals approaching - humanoid figures wearing armor that incorporated crystal fragments. Their movements were practiced and confident, but not aggressive.

"Energy readings are strongest in the city center," Ris reported. "There's a focal point where the crystal formations converge. The tree-being was right - this place is perfect for learning to channel natural power sources, provided they are as friendly as he led us to believe."

The settlement sprawled out below their landing pad, its crystalline architecture creating a maze of reflective surfaces and glowing pathways.

"I'm picking up at least thirty distinct combat schools," Reyes said, scanning the training grounds. "Each one specializing in different aspects of crystal energy manipulation. The experience potential here is incredible."

The crystal formations pulsed with subtle light as the three moons shifted position, creating waves of energy that rippled through the city's power grid.

A delegation of crystal-armored warriors approached the Friday the 13th's landing ramp as the crew prepared to disembark. Their leader, a tall woman with silvery hair and armor that seemed to grow directly from her skin, stepped forward with an open palm raised in greeting.

"Welcome, friends of the Great Forest Collective. We have received a message from their chieftain through the crystal songs - know that you are welcome here. We understand you seek to grow stronger through our teachings." Her voice carried harmonic undertones that resonated with the surrounding formations. "You seek to help us as well. We welcome your service." She bowed.

Damien adjusted his new flight suit as he descended the ramp. The planet's atmosphere felt thick with potential energy, making his skin tingle. "The forest beings said we could find challenges here to help us advance."

"Indeed. I am Crystalline Master Amethys. Our people have long maintained ties with the Forest Collective through the natural energy networks that connect distant worlds." She gestured to the sprawling crystal city behind her. "All our resources are at your disposal."

Mic pushed past the others, his massive frame vibrating with excitement. "Many good fighting places! Mic see training grounds, want to start now!"

Amethys smiled at his enthusiasm. "The combat schools will welcome your warrior spirit. We have programs for all disciplines."

Amelia hung back, her medical scanner sweeping the area. "The crystal radiation levels are within safe parameters, but these energy patterns are unlike anything I've seen. We should proceed with caution until we understand how they affect our physiology."

"Your concern is noted, healer," Amethys said. "The crystals are perfectly safe - they resonate with life force itself. Many of our most skilled healers incorporate crystal energy into their medical practices. We will be glad to share that knowledge with you."

"I'd be honored," Amelia replied.

Cornelius materialized from the shadows near the landing gear, startling several of the greeting party. "The security here is impressive. Multiple layers of detection grids."

"Nothing escapes the crystals' awareness," Amethys confirmed. "They are our eyes, our power source, our connection to the natural forces that flow through all things."

Reyes was already scanning the nearest formation, his engineering expertise detecting the sophisticated energy manipulation at work. "The crystalline matrix acts as both conductor and amplifier. Fascinating!"

Ris stepped forward, his telepathy picking up the harmonious thoughts flowing through the crystal network. "Your people have achieved something remarkable here - true symbiosis with your environment. I can almost hear the thoughts or your people through the crystals."

"We can even teach you, master telepath. Our teachers will show you how to harness the energy that flows through your mind."

"Come, follow me. We have much to show you," Amethys said as she turned not waiting for them to respond. She led them from the landing pad toward the city center, explaining how the crystal formations had shaped their society. The streets pulsed with energy as they walked, responding to their presence. Local residents paused in their activities to watch the newcomers.

"Each of you will find your path here," Amethys said. "The warriors among you may train in our combat schools. Those who heal may study with our crystal healers. The technically minded can learn our methods of energy manipulation."

"I don't mean to be indelicate, Crystalline Master, but I must ask. Have you ever heard or seen the emperor, Thomas Bright, on your beautiful planet?" Ris asked.

Amethys almost seemed visibly angry. "We have heard of him here, but he has never stepped foot on our sacred ground. If he had, that would have been his last act if we could help it. He would die or we would die in the process."

"All right. That's all I needed to hear, Ris." He turned to Amethys, "when can we begin?" Damien asked, watching a group of pilots guide their ships through complex maneuvers above the city.

"Come, we shall begin presently." Amethys led them through winding crystal corridors to a vast chamber where other crystal masters had gathered. The natives' armor seemed to pulse in rhythm with the surrounding formations, creating mesmerizing patterns of light and shadow. Their silvery hair and violet eyes marked them as distinctly different from standard humanoids.

"These outsiders seek to learn our ways," Amethys announced to the assembled masters. "The Great Forest Collective vouches for their character."

The crystal masters studied the group with piercing gazes. One stepped forward. "We do not often share our techniques with offworlders. What makes you worthy?"

Damien watched as Mic straightened to his full height, but instead of his usual aggressive posture, the alien warrior knelt and placed his hand against the crystal floor. The formation pulsed in response to his touch, sending ripples of light through the chamber.

"Mic respect crystal power," he said softly. "Want to learn, not conquer."

The masters exchanged surprised looks. Amelia stepped forward next, her medical scanner carefully tucked away. "Your healing techniques could save countless lives. I would be honored to study them, not to exploit them."

One by one, the others demonstrated their own respect. Cornelius emerged from the shadows to bow deeply. Reyes resisted the urge to scan everything, instead asking permission before examining any technology. Ris kept his telepathy carefully shielded, showing he understood boundaries.

The chamber pulsed with energy as the masters conferred silently through their crystal network. Finally, the one who had questioned them nodded. "Your actions speak true. The crystals resonate with your intentions. We welcome you to our planet."

"We thank you for your hospitality." Ris said bowing deeply. He motioned with his hand behind his back for his companions to do the same. They did.

"We will assign each of you to appropriate instructors," Amethys said. "Your training begins immediately."

The masters dispersed through different corridors, each glowing path leading to specialized training areas. A towering warrior with crystal-studded armor gestured for Mic to follow him toward the combat grounds. A healer with glowing hands beckoned to Amelia.

Cornelius found himself drawn to a shadowy alcove where infiltration techniques were taught using stealth. Reyes eagerly joined a group of engineers studying energy manipulation. Ris was led to a meditation chamber where telepaths learned to channel crystal power.

Damien watched a ship soar past the chamber's windows, its pilot executing maneuvers that seemed to defy physics. His own instructor, a woman whose flight suit appeared to be made entirely of living crystal, smiled at his obvious interest.

"The crystals will teach you as much as we do," she said. "They respond to those who approach them with respect and understanding."

To demonstrate, she placed her hand on a nearby formation. The crystal pulsed with light, extending tendrils that merged with her flight suit. "We do not force the power to serve us. We work in harmony with it."

Reyes's instructor showed him how to safely tap into the crystal network's power grid.

Ris felt his telepathy expand as it resonated with the natural energy flows. Amethys watched him with amusement as he tried to understand what he was hearing in his head.

"Your forest-crafted gear will serve you well here," Amethys observed. "It too was made in harmony with natural forces. The crystals recognize this and will respond accordingly. That's what your telepathy is trying to tell you."

Ris bowed, "you are a telepath."

"I am." She gestured to all around her, "We all have our place here. You will too."

Once the crew's day of training had concluded, Amethys led them to a vast crystalline chamber deep within the city's central spire. Holographic displays flickered between the crystal formations, showing historical records of their civilization's development. The images revealed a painful truth - their peaceful society had been repeatedly victimized by outsiders seeking to exploit their natural resources.

"The Alteri remnants came first," Amethys explained, her voice tight with controlled anger. "Not the original Alteri civilization, but descendants who had forgotten their ancestors' wisdom. They saw our crystals only as power sources to be harvested."

The holograms showed massive mining operations that had scarred the landscape, leaving dead zones where the crystal formations had been stripped away. The natives had fought back to the best of their abilities, but the invaders' superior technology had given them a devastating advantage.

"We developed our own technologies to defend ourselves," she continued, leading them to a sealed chamber. Inside, sophisticated equipment merged seamlessly with crystal formations. But many of the systems appeared damaged or offline, their power crystals cracked and dim. "When you are rested, this is the service we ask from you in return."

"This looks like standard Mark VII tech," Reyes said, examining a damaged power converter. "Just enhanced with crystal integration. We could repair most of this."

Amethys nodded. "Our engineers understand the crystal aspects, but the underlying technology eludes us. We know another attack is coming - our crystal network has detected increased activity in the sector."

"More Alteri remnants?" Damien asked.

"Or others who would steal our resources," she replied. "Without our defensive systems at full capacity, we cannot protect ourselves as we once did."

Ris studied the damaged equipment. "These are basic systems for us. Power distribution, shield generators, weapons guidance - all standard technology just modified to work with crystal energy."

"We could have this running in a few days," Reyes added confidently.

Mic examined the defensive emplacements. "Good weapons. Mic help fix, make stronger."

"Your help would be invaluable," Amethys said. "In exchange, we offer full access to our training facilities and crystal enhancement techniques. Help us protect our home, and we will help you grow stronger."

"The experience gain would be substantial," Cornelius noted. "Both from the repair work and the combat training."

Amelia was already scanning the medical systems. "Their crystal healing tech is incredible. Learning to integrate it with standard medical equipment would be a huge advantage."

"Then we have an agreement?" Amethys asked, her violet eyes studying each of them in turn.

Ris glanced at his companions, seeing their eager nods. "We do. We'll help repair your defenses, and you'll teach us your techniques."

"The exchange is fair," Amethys smiled. "Your forest-crafted gear already shows how you understand working with natural power sources. Now you'll learn to merge that knowledge with more advanced technology."

"I don't know that we understand the forest tech either, I'm afraid." Ris said.

"We shall impart all we know on that subject as well, then." She smiled.

Chapter 29: Preparations

Damien adjusted the controls of the training simulator, marveling at how naturally they responded to his touch. After three weeks of intensive practice, he'd learned to channel the planet's energy through his pilot interface, making the ship feel like an extension of his body.

The simulator pod sung with crystalline precision as it activated, projecting a complex obstacle course through his neural link. Crystal formations created ever-shifting barriers he needed to navigate, their patterns impossible to predict with standard instruments. But the crystal resonance flowing through his flight suit let him sense the changes before they happened.

His wrist device chimed as he completed another perfect run

Course completed: result: flawless

Reward: 450, 000 Experience

Ding! Damien Storm increased to level 25

The crystal masters had been right about the experience gain here. Each successful integration of their techniques with his existing skills pushed him closer to the shared goal of reaching 50th level.

Taking a quick break outside of the simulator, he watched Mic in the combat arena below. The alien warrior moved with newfound grace, his massive frame flowing between crystal pillars as he sparred with three instructors simultaneously. The natural armor, whether it was Forest Collective made or Antelis VII enhanced, channeled the power of his muscles to wherever he directed it for maximum effect.

In the training arena next to Mic, Cornelius appeared and disappeared among the crystal shadows, each movement perfectly timed with the formations' energy pulses. His stealth abilities had evolved beyond simple concealment - he could now phase through solid crystal barriers by matching their resonant frequencies.

He had been told that in the medical wing, Amelia worked with crystal healers to merge their techniques with her equipment. Her curses had grown less frequent as she discovered how the natural energy amplified her healing abilities. Her latest breakthrough in trauma care had pushed her to level 27. He knew the cursing would be back, it always came back.

Reyes practically lived in the engineering labs now, absorbing everything the crystal masters could teach him about energy manipulation. His technical skills had grown exponentially as he learned to interface their technology with crystal power sources. The defensive systems were nearly restored, better than before.

Ris spent hours in the meditation chambers, learning to sense the power of the crystal energy through his telepathy. His power sword now resonated with the formations, its blade taking on a crystalline edge that could cut through nearly anything, not that it couldn't do that already. His mental abilities had expanded far beyond their original limits.

Damien's simulator pod chimed, signaling the start of another training sequence. He stepped back inside ready for the next upgraded task. This one was more challenging - atmospheric flight through crystal storms while defending against multiple attackers. He felt the crystal energy flow through his controls as he engaged the program.

After he deftly navigated the sequence, the simulator went dark. His interface signaled another level gain - 26 now. He'd mastered maneuvers that would have been impossible just a few weeks ago. He emerged from the pod to find Amethys waiting. The crystal master's silver hair seemed to glow with inner light as she nodded approval. "Your progress is remarkable. All of you have embraced our teachings faster than any previous students."

"The new enhanced gear helps," Damien said." I finally feel like I am geared up to my level.

"Indeed. The natural powers recognize each other, amplify each other." She gestured to where the others were finishing their own training sessions. "You are nearly ready for the final trials. Come, the others have gathered near. I have something very important to reveal to you all."

Damien followed Amethys through a series of descending crystal corridors, each level pulsing with stronger energy signatures. The rest of the crew trailed behind them. His crystal lined flight suit picked up unusual vibrations - something deeper than the planet's natural power flows.

"The crystals revealed this chamber during yesterday's meditation cycle," Amethys explained. "They respond to those who respect natural energy. Your presence has awakened something long dormant within our planet."

The passage opened into a vast underground cavern. Massive crystal formations created a geometric pattern across the floor, each one glowing with internal light. But what caught Damien's attention was the structure at the center - a sleek vessel of unmistakably Alteri design, partially embedded in crystal growth.

"Holy shit," he breathed, running his hand along the ship's pristine hull. Despite being sealed away for centuries, the vessel showed no signs of decay. The crystal formations had preserved it perfectly.

His wrist device pinged as it scanned the technology. The readings matched known Alteri signatures, but with modifications from the crystalline masters of old like he'd never seen before. The ship's systems appeared designed to work in harmony with natural energy sources rather than simply consuming them.

As Damien touched the vessel's control interface, a flash of memory struck him - sitting at a gaming table, rolling dice while describing a similar ship to his friends. The image felt distant, dreamlike, yet carried emotional weight he couldn't quite place. Had he designed this ship in a past life?

"The crystals say this vessel was left here by those who understood balance," Amethys said. "Not the later remnants who sought only to exploit, but the original Alteri who worked with natural forces."

Reyes was already scanning the ship's systems. "These power couplings - they're designed to channel energy without disrupting it."

The vessel's cockpit lit up as Damien approached. The controls felt familiar somehow, like something from a half-remembered dream. Another memory flickered briefly.

"The crystals have kept its systems in perfect alignment," Amethys explained. "They recognize it as kin - technology that respects natural law."

Damien settled into the pilot's seat, his flight suit resonating with the ship's controls. The vessel sprang to life.

"There's more," Amethys led them deeper into the cavern. Other pieces of Alteri technology emerged from the crystal growth - weapons designed to channel natural energy, armor that worked with the wearer's life force, medical equipment that enhanced organic healing. "Our planet has blessed you all."

Something about the discovered equipment awakened memories. Each one triggered fragments in Damien's mind - adventures shared around a table, characters brought to life through imagination, friendships forged through storytelling. The images felt important, but trying to focus on them made his head spin.

"The crystals have protected these treasures for generations," Amethys said. "Waiting for those who would use them as intended - in balance with natural power.

His wrist device chimed as it registered the technological discoveries. The experience gain was significant, but more important was how naturally the Alteri systems integrated with their crystal training. This wasn't just powerful technology - it was technology designed to work in harmony with the user's own energy.

"Take these gifts and integrate them into your gear, your ship, your lives." Amethys said. "Use them well."

* * *

Damien gazed out across the crystal spires of Antelis VII. From this vantage point atop the highest training tower, he could see the entire crystal city sprawled below. After six weeks of intensive training, it had begun to feel like home.

He pressed a couple of buttons on his wrist device and it chimed softly. He wanted to stare at his level for the fifteenth time. He was level 32 now. The progress they'd made here still amazed him. His piloting skills had transcended mere technical proficiency—he now felt the currents of space before they formed, anticipated gravitational shifts before instruments could detect them.

"Thought I'd find you up here," Ris said, emerging from the elevator. "Beautiful night."

Damien nodded without turning. "I'll miss this place."

"We all will." Ris joined him at the railing. "Did you hear the news from the crystal songs?"

"About Bright?" Damien had been trying not to think about it. "Yeah."

The crystal masters had gathered them earlier that day, their faces grave as they shared what the planet's network had detected. Emperor Bright had begun systematically laying waste to worlds where high-level training occurred, leaving devastation in his wake. The crystal songs—vibrations that traveled between worlds with similar crystal formations—carried warnings and desperate pleas for help.

"He's looking for us," Ris said quietly. "Destroying anything that might help us grow stronger."

"I thought he wanted us to catch him so he could use us to level."

"Ha, I believed that too for a while until I heard what he was doing out there. He doesn't want us to catch him. We're a full group and he's one man. He knows we have probably reached about 35th or 40th level by now and that's as high as he wants us. He just wants us within experience range."

Damien's hands tightened on the railing. "Yeah, Level 32 is nowhere near high enough to face him. He'll smoke us even *with* all these enhancements."

"True, and he's trying to make sure we don't reach 50th. All of us at that level will be able to take him down. He needs to remain high enough to defeat us.

"Amethys thinks these crystals are shielding us from his detection. That's why he hasn't found us yet."

Ris looked up at the moons. "But how many more worlds will he devastate while we hide here? I'm afraid we are going to have to face him and at least try to defeat him. All of us between 35th and 40th level might stand a chance if he hasn't also been leveling at the same rate, and I don't think he has. He's been too busy playing emperor and attacking planets so we can't level."

Damien had been asking himself the same thing all day. Should they attempt an attack? The comfort of their training paradise now felt almost selfish when measured against the destruction spreading through the core worlds. "What do the others say?"

"Mic wants to go after him now," Damien said. "Cornelius too, surprisingly."

"And you?"

Damien sighed, watching a shuttle glide silently through the night sky. "I'm torn. We need more time, more levels. But if we wait until we're ready..."

"There might not be anything left to save," Ris finished.

Below them, the crystal city pulsed with energy as it had every night since their arrival. It was peaceful here. Safe.

"I keep having these... flashes," Damien admitted. "Not just memories of before all this, but something else. Like I'm remembering things that haven't happened yet, or happened in some other version of reality."

Ris nodded slowly. "The crystals are amplifying something. I've felt it too. Sometimes when I'm deep in meditation, I can almost grasp who we really are. But it's like trying to hold water."

"Do you think we'll ever get those memories back?" Damien asked, voicing the question that had troubled him increasingly as they approached what felt like the endgame of their journey.

"I don't know," Ris said honestly. "But I'm not sure it matters anymore. These are our lives now. These abilities, these experiences—they're real to us."

Damien's wrist device displayed an incoming communication from Amelia. The message was brief: *Meeting in the central chamber. Decision time.*

"Looks like we can't avoid this any longer," Damien said, pushing away from the railing. "The others are gathering."

They took the elevator down in silence, each lost in thought. The central chamber glowed with enhanced light as they entered. Amelia, Reyes, Cornelius, and Mic were already there, along with Amethys and several crystalline masters.

"The crystal songs bring more warnings," Amethys said without hesitation. "Three more training worlds have fallen to the emperor's forces. He grows more desperate in his search for you."

"Or his distain for us." Ris said.

"How many dead?" Mic asked, his voice uncharacteristically soft.

"Thousands," one of the masters replied. "Perhaps tens of thousands."

Amelia cursed under her breath, her medical scanner clutched tightly in her hand. "We can't just sit here while he slaughters people looking for us."

"But we're not ready," Reyes argued. "He's level sixty at least. We're barely past thirty."

Damien felt all eyes turn to him. As the pilot, his assessment of their chances mattered. As he looked around at his companions—his friends—he realized how much they'd all changed during their time here. Not just in levels or abilities, but in how they saw themselves and each other.

"If we stay," he said slowly, "we might eventually reach level 50, but by then, how many more will die? The crystals shield us here, but they can't protect everyone else. We can't be that selfish can we? He has us over a barrel. We have to at least attempt to use everything that we've learned, every piece of equipment we've uncovered, every weapon we've enhanced to try and defeat him."

* * *

Damien eased into the pilot's seat of the newly upgraded Friday the 13th, The combined Alteri and crystal systems answered his touch as if alive, each component perfectly tuned to operate in synchronicity. They felt like they were engaging *before* his fingertips touched them they were so sensitive.

Beyond the viewscreen, the crystalline masters gathered for their departure. Amethys stood central among them. The image of her dutifully waiting for them to depart constricted his heart - these individuals had evolved into more than mentors during their time here.

"The crystal network will hold you in its memory," Amethys's message flowed through their communication array. "If you ever seek refuge again, the formations will direct you back to us."

Damien initiated the main systems, observing energy course through crystal-embedded pathways. The vessel's original technology had been utterly transformed, fused with both forest-craft and crystal innovations. Even Mira's synthetic intelligence now vibrated with the elemental power. Reyes had seen to that.

"Engineering shows all green," Reyes reported from his console. "Crystal energy integration performing at peak efficiency."

"Defensive systems and armaments harmonized," Cornelius confirmed. "The crystal matrices are boosting our protective capabilities as expected."

Mic manned the tactical station, his hulking form decorated with shimmering new plating. "New weapons excellent. Mic prepared to defend vessel."

Ris positioned himself at the sensor array. "Ascend," he instructed quietly.

Damien activated the thrusters. The craft responded with remarkable elegance, ascending through the violet-hued atmosphere without the slightest vibration.

The settlements diminished below, their towers gleaming with farewell beacons and messages wishing them safe passage, and expressing hopes for their eventual return. His throat knotted as he contemplated how profoundly this world had transformed them all.

As they soared higher, the vessel's systems resonated with energy, every element functioning in flawless harmony with the others.

The purple atmosphere grew thinner around them, celestial bodies becoming visible through the viewscreen. Damien charted their trajectory toward the central systems, aware that somewhere in space, Bright was carving a destructive path through civilizations searching for them, and that they were likely heading toward their demise.

They escaped Antelis VII's gravitational influence, the planet's violet radiance fading behind. Damien cast a final glance at the world that had protected and empowered them. The crystalline masters' ultimate contribution - their ship converted into something capable of truly challenging Imperial forces.

"Route established to the core worlds," Damien announced, his grip steady on the controls. "Prepared to activate hyperdrive."

"Proceed when ready," Ris directed.

Damien triggered the hyperdrive, and Antelis VII disappeared in a brilliant flash as they commenced their journey toward whatever fate awaited them in the core worlds.

Chapter 30: Memories

Damien's hands glided over the instruments as the Friday the 13th soared through hyperspace. It took little effort to keep the powerful ship steady and on course.

"Several vessels exiting hyperspace ahead," Ris reported from the sensor console. "Imperial patrol ships, half a dozen. They are scanning the area."

"If they detect us, they will try to drop us out of hyperspace." Damien said.

"They can do that?" Reyes asked.

"Yep, they sure can." Ris replied. "In fact, brace yourselves."

Damien responded to the alarm that a hyperspace disruption wave was incoming by gently guiding them out of hyperspace. If they hoped to damage his ship by forcing it out of hyperspace abruptly, they were about to be disappointed. The patrols almost immediately materialized around them, their artillery already powering up. The primary ship broadcast an order for immediate capitulation.

"Bright's scouting units," Cornelius noted from tactical. "Subspace chatter confirms they were searching for any trace of us in the commercial routes."

"Seems they succeeded." Damien smirked. Those ships might have been worrisome before the 13th got its upgrades." He chuckled, " but now it's time to demonstrate what we acquired on Antelis VII."

The patrols initiated attack, energy streams cutting across the void. But the Friday's newly enhanced barriers absorbed the blasts effortlessly. The shield network actually became more powerful as it redirected the incoming assault.

"Mic prepare weapons!" The energy they just gave us ready to be thrown in face! He locked onto the nearest patrol vessel.

"Engineering confirms all systems are at peak performance," Reyes announced. "Crystal energy grid is boosting our capacity by threefold."

Damien maneuvered them into a corkscrew, the vessel responding as if it were an extension of his own form. Their recent practice allowed him to anticipate the patrols' attack sequences before they executed them. He navigated between their formations, creating ideal firing opportunities.

"Target secured," Mic declared confidently. "Mic destroy enemy vessels!"

The 13th's improved weaponry struck with remarkable impact. Energy streams cut through the lead patrol's defenses as if they were nonexistent. The ship detonated in a spectacular burst as its engine core destabilized.

Two more patrols attempted to outflank them, but Damien had already anticipated this. The vessel twirled elegantly between their assaults, crystal barriers flashing as they captured and repurposed the energy. Mic's counterattack disabled both crafts with pinpoint effectiveness.

"Their coordination is collapsing," Ris informed, tracking the conflict through both instruments and his enhanced mental abilities. "They've never encountered technology like our crystal enhancements."

The remaining patrols tried to withdraw, but Damien kept them contained. The 13th's weaponry found their targets with lethal precision. Within moments, the entire Imperial reconnaissance force had been transformed into floating wreckage.

"That felt quite satisfying," Damien remarked, conducting a swift systems evaluation. The vessel hadn't even been taxed. "Everyone unharmed?"

"No injuries," Reyes verified. "Barriers are actually more robust now after redirecting their attacks."

"The Antelis VII specialists definitely knew their craft," Cornelius remarked. "This vessel is remarkable."

Damien experienced a wave of accomplishment as he observed the aftermath. Their time on Antelis VII had converted them from mere survivors into a legitimate combat unit. The patrols hadn't been able to challenge their combined capabilities.

"Mic appreciates new weaponry greatly," the alien warrior commented with pleasure. "Destroy Imperial vessels effectively."

"The crystal energy signatures remain balanced," Ris announced. "We could challenge an entire armada with these systems."

"Yeah, sure, let's maintain perspective," Damien cautioned, though he had to concede the victory was gratifying. "A victory like this does make it feel like we might have a chance when we go up against Bright." He charted a fresh course through hyperspace, carefully avoiding additional potential Imperial patrol routes.

"I bet those patrols will have transmitted our coordinates," Reyes noted, examining the navigation displays. "If they did, Bright will realize we're approaching the inner systems now."

"Excellent, I hope so." Ris positioned himself behind Damien's seat, examining the galactic maps. "Maybe he will set up a rendezvous point closer to us and farther away from the more populated worlds."

"You do understand he's likely gained additional power while we were training?" Damien glanced toward his companion. "His capabilities could be vastly expanded."

Ris scoffed, "Oh, you can bank on that. He would seek out all the advantages he could get beyond just leveling, which reminds me. Did everyone get their stim order in to Mira? If we're going to have any hope of success, we are going to need those stims."

"I did." Amelia said.

"I think we all did." Reyes said.

"Good, keep them at the ready."

Mic want to know what level Bright made. We may have chance now."

"The wretched tyrant's probably reached level 70 by now," Amelia contributed from her medical post. "Perhaps higher."

"Which is why we require a strategy," Ris stated, fumbling with his new power sword hilt. "We can't simply rush into the inner systems expecting favorable circumstances. We're going to need to be smart about this attack."

"Mic suggest finding emperor's vulnerability. Strike powerfully, strike swiftly."

"The Laucnar is his strength and his potential source of weakness," Reyes explained. "The crystal specialists helped me comprehend its mechanisms. It's not merely corrupting him anymore - it's altering him fundamentally. He may be weakened if we can separate him from it."

"Easier said than done." Ris said.

Damien recalled the archives they'd discovered, the cautions regarding synthetic consciousness merging with organic minds. "You believe his transformation and dependance on the Laucnar is creating vulnerability?"

"The gem's influence is expanding faster than his control," Reyes elaborated. "Each level he gains distances him further from humanity. The crystal specialists indicated natural energy counteracts artificial power of that nature."

"Which explains why our new crystal technology might effectively harm him," Cornelius added. "The patrols' weapons barely affected our barriers, but the crystal matrix didn't simply block their assaults - it completely disrupted their energy configurations."

Damien contemplated this while adjusting their route. The 13's upgraded systems responded immediately to his commands. "Interesting, we need a plan to wrestle it away from him."

"We can't even get close to him." Ris said.

"But we do possess the advantage of unpredictability," Reyes stated. "Bright's hunting us, but he's unaware of our crystal improvements. He's expecting the same vessel that narrowly escaped his Death Moon."

"So?" Ris said.

"The 13th's signature is entirely altered now," Reyes confirmed. "The crystal matrix conceals our energy patterns. Imperial sensors will struggle to track us."

Damien examined data from their recent confrontation. The patrols' weapons had been captured and redirected by their barriers, the crystal technology actually strengthening from the attacks. But Bright's abilities would be considerably more formidable.

"We'll need flawless coordination," he said. "Everyone's new capabilities working cohesively. The crystal specialists trained us to channel natural energy as a unified force."

"Mic prepared to defeat emperor," the alien warrior declared. "Crystal power strengthens Mic."

"It transcends mere strength," Ris cautioned. "The crystal energy must circulate through all of us, operating in harmony. That's what the specialists endeavored to teach us."

Damien manipulated the controls as a sudden wave of unease spread across the bridge. Ris had frozen at his station, his hands clutching the console.

"He's penetrating my thoughts," Ris said through gritted teeth. "Bright - he's communicating directly to me."

Damien maintained the vessel's course while observing his friend struggle with the telepathic contact. The crystal fragments in Ris's equipment pulsed irregularly as he resisted the intrusion.

"What's his message?" Damien inquired, noticing how the ship's crystal matrix seemed to vibrate with Ris's discomfort.

"He wants a meeting. Cryon V." Ris's voice was tense. "Claims it's time to conclude this conflict definitively."

"Cryon V?" Damien accessed the navigation charts. "That's in the abandoned sector - uninhabited, devoid of natural life. Merely a dark mass orbiting a fading star."

"Ideal location for a decisive confrontation," Cornelius remarked from his position. "No bystanders risked in the exchange."

"There is that." Reyes said. "No one will be collateral damage."

Damien established the course while Ris continued communing with their former ally.

"He's transformed all right," Ris stated after extended silence. "The Laucnar - it's beyond controlling him now. He's evolved into something else entirely. I barely recognize his thought patterns."

"The crystal specialists warned this might occur," Damien said, "The more power he accumulates, the further he deviates from his original identity."

"He continuously speaks of concluding the game, of final triumphs and absolute power." Ris shook his head. "It's as if he's lost connection with reality completely. He doesn't appear to understand this isn't simply a simulation created by the Jaddus Collective anymore."

"He is losing his humanity to the Laucnar," Damien realized. "It just like in many of the stories we've read over our lifetimes. Corruption of someone good by the influence of something evil. It's classic."

"Or perhaps he chooses not to stay connected to reality," Cornelius proposed. "Remember his preference for villainous roles in our sessions? Now he embodies the ultimate malevolent emperor in reality. He might actually find it...fun!"

A memory resurfaced when Cornelius suggested Bright's preference for paying villains in their games. The vision had them around the table again, playing games. Bright directing the fun while they played out scenarios. He had to shake himself out of the vision to refocus on what he was doing.

The Friday the 13th hurled through space taking its crew to their meeting with destiny. After about another hour of hyperspace, Damien's blood ran cold as his adrenaline spiked, Cryon V appeared in their instruments - a black orb against the cosmic backdrop, circling a red giant star in its final phase. No evidence of life, no energy signatures except for a single massive reading at the coordinates Bright had provided.

"That's him," Ris confirmed, monitoring the sensors. "The Laucnar's influence has grown immeasurably. The crystal matrix can scarcely process the readings."

Damien guided them into orbit, the vessel's flight systems straining slightly against the dead world's oppressive atmosphere. Even the crystal technology seemed subdued here, as if the planet's very essence suppressed natural energy.

"This location feels wrong," Damien observed, noting how the crystal fragments in his flight suit pulsed weakly. "As if it actively resists life itself."

"That's why he chose this place," Reyes said. "This place is a soul-sucking void."

"A dying star orbited by a lifeless world," Ris remarked grimly. "The perfect arena for whatever Bright has orchestrated."

Chapter 31: Final Showdown

Damien powered down the Friday the 13th's systems as they landed on Cryon V's barren surface. The usually vibrant crystal technology pulsed weakly in the oppressive atmosphere, like it was struggling to maintain its energy. He double-checked his enhanced flight suit's seals - the planet's thin atmosphere was barely breathable.

"Everyone ready?" he asked, standing from the pilot's chair. The others nodded grimly, double checking their weapons and armor.

As they were preparing to open the hatch, Ris gasped and leaned against a console. "The data core - it's activating!"

Damien felt it too - a surge of energy. Images flooded his mind: a gaming table surrounded by friends, character sheets scattered across its surface, dice rolling across felt. Snacks of cheese puffs, tortilla chips, and bowls of salsa lying about. But these weren't just fragments anymore. The memories crashed over him in vivid detail.

He remembered his real name, his life before the Jaddus Collective had brought them here. The others seemed similarly affected, their expressions shifting as their original memories returned.

Their wrist devices chimed simultaneously:

Final Quest Available: The Emperor's Fall
Warning: Enemy level 75 - Extreme Danger
Accept quest? Y/N

"75th level!" Damien checked his own interface even though he had looked at it dozens of times already - still only 32. "Even with the crystal enhancements, we're completely outmatched."

"That's nothing new," Ris said. "We all knew what we were walking into. None of us suspected beyond hoping that he would still be 60th."

Through the viewport, they could see Bright waiting on the planet's surface. The Laucnar's energy writhed around him like living lightning, its blue-green glow a stark contrast to the dead world's darkness. His form seemed to shift and flow, barely maintaining humanoid shape.

"Our crystal armor is the only thing giving us half a chance," Ris said. "Without it, he could destroy us with one shot."

Their devices chimed again as they accepted the quest. The crystal fragments in their gear pulsed stronger, reacting to their renewed sense of purpose. But something else tugged at

Damien's mind - understanding of what completing this quest would mean.

"If we win, we can go home," he said quietly. "Back to our real lives, our original memories fully restored."

"Do we want to?" Cornelius asked what they were all thinking. "These powers, this ship, this life we've built - it's more real to me now than anything I remember from before."

Damien looked around at his crew - his friends, both in their previous life and this one. The weight of their restored memories pulled equally strong, reminding them of who they'd been. "I don't think it's a coincidence the data core opened and this quest was given. We have a choice now."

"We don't have to decide yet," Ris said, checking his power sword's crystal matrix. "First we have to survive this fight."

"No, I mean we can choose to leave and go home now before the fight." Damien said.

Ris shook his head, "That's not an option for me."

"Not me either." Mic said.

"We might as well face this." Cornelius said. "We will always live to regret it if we cower and run."

"Fuck! I guess we're doing this." Amelia added.

Damien nodded, drawing his blaster. Whatever choice they made would have to wait until after they faced their former friend. "I knew the cussing would return."

"It always fucking does." She replied.

The landing ramp lowered with a hiss of hydraulics. Bright's twisted form waited below, the Laucnar's artificial power felt like a perversion after experiencing the natural power of Antelis VII. Their wrist devices showed his level in purple text - so far beyond them it seemed impossible to challenge him.

Damien watched Bright's twisted form as they approached across Cryon V's barren surface. He briefly scoped out the area and identified several natural rock formations that he could use for cover. He diverted his gaze back to Bright. The Laucnar's energy writhed around their former friend like living lightning, making it difficult to even look directly at him.

"Thomas," Ris called out. "We don't have to do this. You must have your lost memories back now too. It's not too late."

For a moment, something flickered in Bright's distorted features - a flash of recognition, of the person he'd once been. "Ris? I... I remember you. The gaming table, the stories we created..."

"Yes, Thomas, The data core held your memories too."

But the moment passed. The Laucnar's power surged, and Bright's form twisted further. "No! I am beyond such childish things now. I have transcended your limited existence!"

The attacks came without warning. A wave of blue-green energy swept across the dead ground, so powerful it shattered the rock beneath their feet. Only their level appropriate armor saved them from instant annihilation.

Damien fired his blaster, but the shots dissipated harmlessly against Bright's power. Mic charged forward, his massive frame protected by his crystal armor, but Bright casually swatted him aside with a gesture. The alien warrior crashed into a rock formation fifty meters away.

Ris's power sword flared with energy as he engaged Bright directly. The two clashed in a storm of natural and artificial power. But even with his enhanced abilities, Ris was hopelessly outmatched. A blast from the Laucnar sent him flying backward, his armor cracking from the impact.

"Is this all you've learned?" Bright's voice boomed across the battlefield. "Your crystal techniques are interesting but ultimately nothing compared to true power! You are all still pathetically, laughably low level. None of you are above 35th level. You're not even to the level I was the last time we met." he laughed maniacally.

Another wave of energy knocked them all off their feet. Damien's flight suit barely absorbed the attack. Through the natural resonance of the crystal fragments in his gear, he could feel the horrible wrongness of the Laucnar's power - artificial consciousness twisted into something monstrous. He crawled behind one of the rock formations for cover while he aimed his blaster.

"Captain Storm!." Mira's voice came through his comm. "You gave me permission to make suggestions when I saw opportunities., remember?"

"Kind of busy right now, Mira!" Damien rolled away from another energy blast as it struck the rock formation he was hiding behind.

"The crystal matrix in your equipment - it can be tuned to match the Laucnar's resonant frequency." The android's voice was urgent. "Like shattering a wine glass with the correct pitch.

If you can achieve harmonic resonance while Bright is channeling its power..."

"Mira, remind me to give you a huge kiss when I get back on board!"

"I'd rather not, sir, I am no longer programmed to give that sort of pleasure."

Damien began manipulating his suit's crystalline matrix. The crystal masters had taught them about natural frequencies, about how energy patterns could be disrupted by matching and amplifying their vibrations.

"It doesn't matter how powerful he is," Mira continued. "The Laucnar itself is crystalline and can be shattered if you hit exactly the right frequency. But it has to be while he's actively using it."

Damien watched as Bright casually swatted aside another of Mic's attacks. Their former friend was toying with them, demonstrating his overwhelming superiority. The Laucnar pulsed in his grip, its power flowing through his transformed body.

"Everyone!" Damien called through the comm. "Focus your crystal energy on my signal. Match the frequency I'm about to broadcast!"

The crystal fragments in their gear hummed as they prepared to channel their power together. Bright laughed, misunderstanding their actions as another futile attack.

"You still don't comprehend what you face," he raised the Laucnar, artificial energy building to devastating levels. "Enough of this. Let me show you true power!"

Damien activated his wrist device's broadcast function, linking it to the crystal matrix in his flight suit. "Everyone get behind me!" he shouted. "This is going to get messy!"

The others scrambled for cover as he adjusted the frequency, searching for the exact pitch that would match the Laucnar's resonance. He had to be quick so he made an educated guess about the right frequency level. Bright continued gathering power, blue-green energy swirling around him in a terrifying display.

A high-pitched whine filled the air as Damien tried to find the right frequency. The crystal fragments in his gear vibrated in perfect harmony. Bright's twisted features suddenly showed recognition of what they were attempting. Damien made a couple of adjustments. The pitch increased just enough to match. He suddenly had it - the correct resonance frequency.

"No!" Bright tried to redirect the Laucnar's power, but it was too late. The gem's crystalline structure began to resonate with their combined energy.

The sound reached an impossible pitch. Damien's flight suit barely protected him from the sonic assault. His teeth even hurt. Through squinted eyes, he watched cracks appear in the Laucnar's surface.

The gem shattered with a deafening crack. Raw artificial energy exploded outward, engulfing Bright completely. Their former friend's scream cut off as his transformed body disintegrated under the power he'd tried to control.

The blast wave knocked them all off their feet. Even with their superior armor, the impact was devastating. Damien felt ribs crack as he slammed into the ground. Through blurred vision, he saw the others similarly wounded.

"Medical emergency protocols engaged," Mira's voice came through their comms. "Initiating triage procedures."

The android emerged from the Friday the 13th, moving with mechanical efficiency toward Amelia first as was the protocol. The medical officer was barely conscious.

"Hold still," Mira administered emergency treatment. "Your healing abilities will be needed for the others."

Once stabilized, Amelia staggered to her feet and made her way to Mic. The alien warrior's massive frame had absorbed significant damage, but his field medic skills would be crucial for treating the rest of the crew.

"Fucking hell," Amelia muttered as she worked. "That was some blast."

Damien watched through pain-clouded eyes as they treated each other's wounds. The technology in their gear slowly began to reactivate, helping accelerate their recovery. Where Bright had stood, nothing remained - not even ashes.

"He's gone," Ris said softly once they'd all been treated. "Our friend is really gone."

"He was gone long before today," Cornelius replied. "The Laucnar took him from us months ago."

Damien looked at his wrist device - their levels had jumped significantly from the encounter, but he felt hollow about it. They'd lost one of their own, someone who'd brought them together in the first place.

"So what now?" Reyes asked as they gathered near the ship. "Do we try to go home? Can we even go home?"

"We still don't know why the Jaddus Collective brought us here," Damien said. "Or if anything they told us was true. Was the visitor center attack real? Are they even who they claimed to be?"

"Mic say we keep going." The alien warrior checked his newly healed injuries. "Find truth about why we here."

"He's right," Ris said. "We need answers. And we've only scratched the surface of what we can become in this world."

Amelia checked her wrist device, "Shit, killing a purple 75th level boss mob jumped me to fucking 42nd level!"

"You really should find another cuss word, Amelia." Cornelius said. They all looked at each other before bursting out into laughter.

After they had expelled all their nervous energy and adrenaline by laughing it off at Cornelius' joke, they stood in silence for a moment, remembering their friend and mourning what he'd become. The crystal technology pulsed gently through their gear, a reminder of how far they'd come and how much further they could go.

* * *

Dr. Thomas Bright opened his eyes. As they focused on his surroundings, he realized he knew the place. He was lying on the polished floor of Satellite 2 above the first planet and the visitor's center. His head throbbed as he pushed himself up. The curved window showing the planet beyond, the high-tech control panels, the sterile white walls - it was exactly as he remembered from his first arrival. He was here for just moments before it was determined his starting point would be on the Harne mining planet.

But something felt different. The overwhelming power of the Laucnar no longer coursed through him. His body felt weak, limited, human again. He touched his face, finding the disfiguring scars gone. His wrist device chimed softly as it initialized:

Tutorial mode engaged
Welcome to Space Lords of Strata
Character level: 1
All abilities reset

Bright laughed, the sound echoing oddly in the empty control room. Of course - they'd destroyed the Laucnar, but death wasn't permanent in this world. The game mechanics had simply respawned him at the starting point.

He checked his equipment - basic clothing, a standard blaster, minimal supplies. All his emperor's riches, his cosmic powers, his technological marvels - gone in an instant. The crystal resonance that had shattered his precious gem had reset everything.

But his memories remained intact. He remembered it all - the mining facility, finding the Laucnar, his rise to power, his final confrontation with his former friends. Their crystal-enhanced technology had been clever, he had to admit. Using natural frequencies to disrupt artificial power - he should have seen that coming.

His wrist device displayed his status:

Basic combat training available

Initial quests unlocked

Warning: Character progression required

"Back to level 1," he mused, examining the basic blaster. "How appropriately humbling."

Satellite 2's computer system activated, its feminine voice filling the room: "Welcome, Dr. Thomas Bright. Please proceed with initial tutorial."

He ignored it, already familiar with the process. The others thought they'd won, thought they'd ended his reign of terror. But they'd forgotten the most basic rule of gaming - death was just a temporary setback.

The Laucnar was gone, yes. But there were other artifacts of power out there. Other paths to greatness. And this time, he had the advantage of knowing exactly how the game worked.

His device chimed again:

New character path available

Warning: Previous abilities and equipment lost

Begin new progression? Y/N

Bright smiled as he pressed Y. The others had their crystal technology, their natural energy manipulation. But artificial power wasn't the only route to supremacy. Perhaps it was time to explore a different path, one they wouldn't expect from their former gamemaster.

The computer's voice interrupted his thoughts: "Tutorial bypassed. Previous experience detected. Please proceed to equipment selection."

"That's new, they must have implemented a patch to allow for starting gear." He moved to the supply lockers, examining the basic gear available to new characters. It was almost amusing - going from commanding an empire to scrounging for starter equipment. But he'd risen to power once before. He could do it again.

His device registered his first quest acceptance:

Basic Training initiated

Current objective: Reach level 2

Warning: Previous quest lines invalidated

The doors slid open, revealing the path to his new beginning. Bright checked his minimal equipment one final time before stepping through. The others would never expect him to start over. They'd assume he was gone for good, destroyed along with the Laucnar. To his knowledge, none of them had ever died in the game before and therefore they were unaware they would respawn.

Their assumption would be their undoing. Because this time, he wouldn't make the same mistakes. This time, he'd build his power differently, more carefully. And when they finally realized he'd returned, it would be too late.

The computer's final message followed him out:

New character progression commenced
Welcome back, Dr. Thomas Bright
Shall we play again?

About the author

Beckett hails from Texas but he never felt he fit in to the Texas crowd. He has always been different and that's all right with him. He loves Science Fiction, Fantasy, and Horror. Sometimes he likes all three at once. He writes to be free, so he writes freely. Fantasy means you fantasize about things real and unreal, so if you can dream up things like demons, aliens, vampires, wizards, and more you can fit them into any story.

A tabletop roleplayer since the 1980s and a gamer for just about as long, Beckett has played Everquest, WoW, LOTRO, Star Wars the Old Republic, all the Diablos, and Baldur's Gate 3 among others for years.

www.ingramcontent.com/pod-product-compliance
Lightning Source LLC
LaVergne TN
LVHW041657060526
838201LV00043B/466